WHERE

WILD

PEACHES

GROW

WHERE WILD PEACHES GROW

A Novel

CADE BENTLEY

LAKE UNION
PUBLISHING

Text copyright © 2022 by Shondra C. Longino
All rights reserved.

No part of this book may be reproduced, or stored in a retrieval system, or transmitted in any form or by any means, electronic, mechanical, photocopying, recording, or otherwise, without express written permission of the publisher.

Published by Lake Union Publishing, Seattle

www.apub.com

Amazon, the Amazon logo, and Lake Union Publishing are trademarks of Amazon.com, Inc., or its affiliates.

ISBN-13: 9781542031219
ISBN-10: 1542031214

Cover design by Leah Jacobs-Gordon

Printed in the United States of America

To my mother, Leslie Vandiver, who still inspires me.

CHAPTER ONE

*We are forced to take a great deal of Care to weed them out,
otherwise they make our Land a Wilderness of Peach-Trees.*

—*John Lawson, 1709*

Natchez, Mississippi

It was those damn peaches.

At least that was what had been whispered about. Neighbors stood watching from front porches and spoke in hushed tones over leathery, evergreen boxwood hedges from their driveways. None too shamed to send their good riddance to Carmella and her ill-fated baking escapades.

Carmella Burkes directed the movers. Hands outstretched, flabby arms jiggling, her lips cherry red. Sweat covered her pasty, tawny-powdered face. The two men scrambled to hoist her belongings from the small once-white cottage into the fourteen-foot U-Haul backed up into the yard. Hastily packed cardboard boxes and stuffed black plastic bags spilled out the door onto the awning-covered portico and were piled under the red crape myrtle tree. All owed to swift retribution for her picking those peaches and baking them into a pie.

Peaches from the tree at the house she'd rented from Jasper Davenport on North Rankin Street weren't for picking.

Everybody knew that.

But Julia Curtis, driving down Cemetery Road, past kudzu-covered trees and age-old granite headstones peeking through the wrought iron fences of the Natchez City Cemetery, knew better. She knew the real reason her father was dead. It wasn't because of Carmella. It was because of her sister.

It was half past ten the morning after the death of the only parent she had left when Julia drove past the Devil's Punchbowl on her way to her grandmother's house. Windows down. Radio off. The last vestiges of summer smells of sweet water lilies and duckweed, the mustiness of damp dirt, and the thin, distant chirping of yellow-bellied warblers swirled through the car. She kept her eyes straight ahead. She'd conditioned herself long ago not to even glance toward the canyon-turned-kudzu-covered-sinkhole. Not even when she sat with Mamaw on her rickety porch, with its collection of differently styled and colored chairs, just a couple hundred yards across the road from it, sipping on a chilled glass of sweet tea.

That place had caused them enough trouble.

She pulled her truck into the crumbling concrete driveway of her grandmother's 1850s home, with its odd-angled additions made from mismatched oak and chinaberry wood. Her daddy used to say it was cobbled together with a nail and a prayer.

The house sat in the middle of a yard that was mostly dirt with spurts of green that were more weeds than grass. In the front was a weeping willow, its branches sweeping the ground and swaying with the breeze that struck the clapper of the copper windchimes hanging from the porch rafters. Out back, in a yard that stretched out to the horizon, was a cluster of fragrant lilacs, two magnolia trees, and a hundred-year-old oak tree. And like every piece of land owned by the Davenport family, there was a patch of peach trees growing wild.

Her grandmother was already waiting on the porch, as was her nosey neighbor, Miss Gus.

Opal waved to hurry Julia on and to keep her out of Gus' snare as soon as she pulled up. They had to go make the funeral arrangements.

"When is Peaches coming?" had been the first thing Raymond Donaldson had asked when he had walked through her door the day before to take her father's body to the funeral home.

Mr. Donaldson did transport and other odd jobs for the funeral home that would take care of Jasper's remains, like driving the cars filled with families to and from the services and setting up the floral arrangements. Someone Julia had known for years, Raymond Donaldson had recently been stopping by her office and purposely, it seemed, running into her as she went about town, although he'd never done more than make small talk.

That day, though, he had something specific he wanted to chat about.

Julia was sure he'd already heard about what Carmella had done. She should have known it wouldn't take long for people to start talking about her sister because of it. And those were the thoughts that took over. Filling up her mind with things that now needed to be done to lay her father to rest and what other consequences it would bring. Like her sister. Julia couldn't even take the time to grieve.

"I don't know," Julia had said. She wanted to add she didn't care, but that would have just been rude.

He looked up from his work, covering her father with a sheet. Nodding to his assistant, who had waited, hands folded, to bring the black gurney over and help lift the body when told.

"Peaches not coming?" He looked at her, skepticism showing in his eyes.

Everyone still referred to Julia's younger sister, Nona, by her child-hood nickname, even though people around Natchez hadn't seen her in ages. Not since she'd left. In the middle of the night. More years ago than Julia cared to remember.

She, like their mother, had abandoned the family.

Julia liked to think of her mother as dead. She was as good as dead. Long gone. Never heard from. Never talked about. Not even by the people she used to know. And that had helped Julia's thoughts of her fade.

But Julia didn't have that luxury with Nona. Everyone remembered her and always wanted to know what she was doing up there in Chicago. A quick internet search would have told them all they wanted to know.

What Julia wanted? To forget all about Nona, just as she'd done her mother. Nona had carelessly and unforgivingly turned everything upside down. And when she had, everything had fallen on Julia.

Peaches.

They were on everybody's mind, all the time. On all the land her family owned (except Julia's house, she'd refused to put one on her property). Everywhere they didn't belong, invading her life. Everywhere *but* in the Devil's Punchbowl, and that had made it nearly impossible for Julia to erase Nona.

"I don't know," Julia had said, crossing one arm across her torso, the other hand rising to rest on her forehead. She, as of late, had looked forward to "bumping" into Raymond. She liked the attention he'd given her, something she hadn't had from a man in a long time. Something she hadn't ever stopped wanting, but something she hadn't been able to find. Her conversations with Raymond seemed to round out her life. Make it complete. Less tenuous. More normal. And the way he smiled at her made her feel pretty. Wanted. Desirable. And not so alone.

And it kept her mind off of things, like what if things had gone differently with her and Marcus, but she knew that was water under the bridge.

But she wasn't intent on today's topic of discussion. "She's so important up there, you know. She might not be able to get away."

"Not even for her daddy's home-going service?" He raised an eyebrow.

"Life ain't always like we want it to be."

"Ain't that the truth," he said. "Much as your father loved those peach trees, they ended up killing him." He shook his head. "Everybody knew his first rule was not to go picking from 'em."

"She was new around here." Julia shrugged. "Didn't know no better."

He stopped what he was doing and stood straight up. "Now, you can't tell me that Mr. Davenport here"—he nodded to her father's body—"didn't tell her about them peaches."

She glanced at the outline of her father's body stuffed in the opaque black bag, ready to be wheeled out. Last thing on his mind: an absent daughter. But Julia wasn't surprised—Nona was what he'd always thought about. From the day she'd left and to what had upset him the day he died.

Julia looked at Raymond. Wasn't no fooling him. Everyone who knew her father knew those peaches were all he had left of Nona. Nona had protected those trees from the time she first heard the story about them. And after she left, so had their father.

"First thing I thought," Raymond said, unlocking the wheels with a click of his foot, not waiting for her to answer, "when I heard, was who makes *pie* with peaches?"

Evidently Carmella Burkes did.

Julia took in a breath so as to keep back an inappropriate chuckle that was bubbling inside her chest. She remembered thinking the same thing. Everybody she knew would have made a cobbler.

"Thank you, Mr. Donaldson," Julia said as he pushed the gurney out the front door. She thought this was a time to be formal. There was third man at the bottom of her steps who had ridden over with him but not come in. She didn't want to sound familiar with Raymond in front of his coworkers.

"Mr. Donaldson?" he said, and chuckled. "That's what you calling me now?" He locked the wheels and walked over to her and took her hand. "I'm sorry for your loss, Julia, and I want you to know you can call me if you need anything." He gave her a warm smile and gently squeezed her hand. "And I do mean *anything*."

Julia pushed the thoughts of yesterday, of Raymond Donaldson's last words, out of her mind and what popped in were more images of her father's last day. Images of Carmella scurrying across Oak Street when Julia had driven home that day. She had seen Carmella on her way home from showing a house. A covered pie dish in Carmella's hands. Only the soles of her black Mary Jane shoes touching the sidewalk, her steps quick as if the heat from the asphalt was scorching them. And it hadn't been long after Julia had gotten home that her father had come in.

Jasper Davenport had moved in with his daughter Julia and her son after his stroke. He'd kept a little place in Vidalia, a short jaunt across the Natchez-Vidalia Bridge. One room and a kitchenette, just big enough for him but not a place to recuperate.

There'd been plenty of room for him in her big colonial revival house on historic Linton Avenue. Opal had grumbled about it, said she could take care of her child while he was on the mend. But the large parlor-like room with the abundance of windows and natural light converted into a downstairs bedroom for him so he wouldn't have to climb any steps was decidedly the right choice. He'd been recuperating just fine—use of his left arm coming back and eating good—he'd in fact been out on his daily constitution when he'd seen Carmella.

"Calm down, Daddy. You're going to give yourself another stroke," Julia had said when he had exploded through the front door. His hooked cane punctuating each word, flooding the air with spittle as his anger bellowed out. White foam bubbling at the side of his mouth. He'd found out that Carmella had used the fruit from the "forbidden" tree to make peach pie. "Why you let'n that get you all stirred up?"

She'd ushered him into his room and sat him on the side of the metal hospital bed she'd rented for him while he grumbled on about how ungrateful "that woman" was.

"You just sit still," his daughter told him. "I'll get you some water from the kitchen. That'll help you get your wits about you."

"Water ain't gonna help me none."

"Neither is all that yelling."

He'd calmed down somewhat, but only after Julia let him sit in the recliner she'd gotten from Webb's Furniture on Franklin Street instead of on the bed. And after she promised she'd fetch a cup of coffee, not water, from the kitchen. She grabbed hold of the handle on the chair and propped his feet up before she left.

"Never mind the ninety-degree weather he'd just come in from," she mumbled as she poured hot water from the pot she'd heated on the stove into his favorite mug. The heat typical for a September day in Natchez, it didn't in no way match the heat coming from his temper on display. That concerned Julia because the rest of him still needed a lot of healing.

She handed him his mug and rubbed her hand over his head of soft gray hair. Moist beads of sweat still lingered.

"I'm fine." He waved her hand away.

She clicked on the oscillating fan on her way out, pulling the pocket doors closed as she backed out of the room and heard him grumble, "That woman has got to leave my house," his voice raised enough to hear through the door. "I'm going down to the courthouse and evict her as soon as I finish this cup of coffee."

He never did finish that cup. She had found it turned over on the table, still-warm liquid dripping onto the floor. Him slumped in his chair. His anger raising his blood pressure, causing another cardiovascular accident.

Or so they were called.

Julia brought her mind back into the present as Mamaw gripped the handle over the door. The tires of Julia's truck bumped over the unleveled apron into the parking lot in the back of Robert D. Mackel & Sons Funeral Home. It had been who Mamaw had directed her to call to pick up the body when Julia had telephoned with the news. The whole ride over, they'd both been quiet. Julia tangled up in the thoughts of the last moments of her father. A father she'd grown close to in the years after her mother and sister had left. The first and maybe only man she knew she could count on.

"They've taken care of all my boys," Mamaw had said about the funeral home. "Did a good job on all of them. No need to change now."

Opal Davenport had outlived all four of her children.

Julia held one of the double glass doors open for her grandmother. The cold breeze from the air-conditioning filling the foyer of the funeral home wrapped around her as she stood waiting for Mamaw.

Five foot tall, her body bent forward with age, Opal Davenport had a look of determination on her face as she ambled in. She held on to the doorframe to help keep her balance, the dark skin of her hands wrinkled, her fingers curled. She wiped the sweat from her face with a handkerchief, her head covered with her wig she kept for funerals. Someplace she went more than to doctor appointments as of late.

Miss Ann May, funeral director, stood patiently and waited for them to make it to the doorway of her office. She was the granddaughter of the founder and nearly the same age as Julia. Both had attended Natchez High School at the same time.

They sat and talked about the day for the service—the Saturday after next—the number of cars needed—two—who'd write the obituary—Mamaw—and what color they wanted on the spray that came with the package they picked out—white.

Miss Ann gave a nod. "Let's pick out a casket."

The two followed her down a hallway of closed doors filled with the sweet aromatic fragrance of roses and lilies to a room at the very end. Motion-sensor lights popping on when Miss May pushed in on the double doors. Mamaw didn't hesitate. It took Julia at least a moment of pause before she crossed the threshold. Putting her father away was a lot to take in.

Mamaw ran her hand across the top of a bronze casket and placed her hand on the cool satin pillow, giving it a squeeze. "This is the one I like."

"That one's a little more than what we discussed," Ann said.

"Put him in this one," Mamaw said. Her lips firm. Breathing heavy through her nostrils, she looked at Julia and gave a nod.

Julia stepped up. "We'll pay whatever it costs."

Mamaw gave a grim smile. "That's it, then."

Ann gave Julia a hug before she left and whispered in her ear, "I'm so sorry about your dad. We'll take good care of him."

"Thank you," Julia said, and grasped Ann's hands inside of hers. She couldn't break down now. She had to see about her grandmother.

Julia kept an eye on Opal as she drove her back home.

"You need anything before I take you back in? Need to stop anywhere?"

"No. I got everything I need at home."

"You okay then?" Julia asked.

"I'm fine," Mamaw said, and pulled her pocketbook closer to her chest.

"You sure?"

"What? You think I'd lie?"

"No, ma'am. I don't think you'd lie."

"Well then. I said I was fine."

Julia hadn't seen Opal shed a tear for her son. She thought maybe when a person got to Mamaw's age, eighty-seven, death doesn't bother a person as much anymore, because they've seen so many go. Even when it's their own child.

Julia had heard her grandmother say a time or two she didn't have any tears left to cry.

Maybe it was something as simple as that.

Julia had plenty, though. Many nights she'd find tears rolling down her face that were unexplainable. And she couldn't imagine not being overwrought with pain and uncontrollable tears if something happened to her son.

Julia hadn't cried over the death of Jasper Davenport either, but that was for an entirely different reason.

CHAPTER TWO

Chicago, Illinois

Sometime in its history, the Devil's Punchbowl had been a cave carved out by the badgering waters of the restless Mississippi, until its roof fell in, devoured by the tide. It left behind a misshapen bowl two hundred feet down with juts, like fingers, spiked upward from its sandy floor. Overgrown with undergrowth and piled high with tall tales and small mischief. It was ripe for storytelling.

"Storytelling is how history was created." Dr. Nona Davenport, professor of African American Studies, punctuated the end of her lecture with her usual maxim. "But our stories have often been supplanted with deliberate misinformation. Revisionism. Done to tell a different story. A better story. It has, for us, stagnated civic discourse and made our thread in America's social fabric a patchwork, all through storytelling. Incorrect storytelling."

A retiring glance at her audience—students, some freshmen but according to her class roster, mostly sophomores—before lowering her eyes back to the sheets of paper with her notes on the lectern in front of her. A first day of a new semester in her popular, often-taught Black History: Rewritten and Undocumented class still made her insides flutter and her mouth dry. New-class jitters she called them, but it wasn't only on first days she was out of sorts. That had become her norm.

Lingering after class but not reaching out, Dr. Davenport licked her lips and took a sip from the bottled water she kept under the podium, waiting in case a student approached with a question or wanting to make an impression, but today she was anxious to go. Eli was coming home. She moved with measured ease, stuffing her notes into a folder and pushing them into her messenger bag.

The large auditorium located on the first floor of a stone building named for a graduate who'd gained some prominence more than a century ago had easy access to the adjacent parking lot. Keeping an eye on the clock on the wall, she heard the echo of the big door slam as the last student vacated the room. She slung the messenger bag over her shoulder, used her key card to unlock the exit, and eased out the back door.

Smacked with the sun of the late-summer day, she didn't pick up her step until her feet hit the concrete. She heard her cell phone ring deep inside her bag, but she didn't take the time to fish it out. Shoulders relaxed, she clicked the lock on her black Kia and eased into the front seat. She had forty-five minutes to get through the late-afternoon traffic and make it to the airport before Eli's plane landed.

The man in her life. He'd entered unexpectedly and without any prior thought on Nona's part. Of needing a relationship. An other half.

She hadn't even wanted to go to the mixer that night.

It was a year ago on a day much like the one she'd just emerged into. Warm. Breezy. The sun hanging low in the sky. But, unlike this day, she wasn't eager to be anywhere other than home.

She'd just made tenure, and as a rite of passage, the mixer was expected by those who didn't know that Nona wasn't one to mingle. To Nona it felt like Hell Night for initiation into a sorority. Not that she'd ever been in one, but she could just imagine. Torture.

A prism of hazy colors refracted from the strand of bistro lights strung across the outdoor space. Muffled laughter, the sweet smell of mixed drinks. Nursing her own cocktail—a drink of orange and cranberry juices with a splash of water—Nona plastered on a smile and planted her backside on one of the bar-height chairs. She nodded whenever someone passed where she'd parked herself, munching on a celery stick that came with the buffalo wings she'd ordered when she noticed him. Eli.

His nicely trimmed black beard. His smooth brown skin. Eyes that seemed to see right into her soul. The smile just for her.

She placed the stick of celery down, wiped the corner of her mouth with a paper napkin to make sure none of the blue-cheese dressing lingered, and wondered, not wanting to run a finger over them, if she had anything in her teeth.

They had talked the rest of the night. Something she hadn't done with anyone since she'd left home. Since it had ended with Marcus. Since the beginning of the change in her. A change brought on by being a country girl in a big city. Of nursing a broken heart longer than she thought was possible. Of Nona missing her father. And Julia. All those things seemed to be put at bay, at least for the night, and Nona had been happy she'd come.

It didn't go unnoticed and was mentioned more than once in the coming days among her colleagues. Dr. Davenport had become part of a conversation. A change from her usual reticent demeanor and stand-offish behavior. Quiet. Shy. And although no one said it to her, for the first time since they'd known her, Dr. Davenport had stopped looking uncomfortable.

Waiting curbside, car idling, she tapped the Phone button on her dashboard. She hit History on the phone screen and saw the missed call. A number with a 601 area code.

Natchez.

Mamaw.

She glanced at the glass door where Eli would be coming through. Nona knew if she called Mamaw back, it'd be hard to get her off the phone.

"I just got one thing to tell you," Opal would say, and that one thing would turn into twenty. All gossip. All about people Nona didn't know. Didn't remember. People she didn't care to remember. Or care what they'd done or didn't do or who they did it to.

"Just one more thing," when Nona would tell her she was driving. And before Nona could answer, *"You can't talk and drive?"*

Nona knew how the conversation would go.

"Mamaw," Nona would explain. *"There's someone in the car. I can't talk right now."*

She knew they'd be all the way to Eli's apartment before she'd be able to get her off the phone.

"Oh, are they more important than talking to your grandmother?"

Nona pressed the button on the screen and returned to the radio panel.

She'd call her grandmother back later.

She smelled him as soon as he opened the car door. That familiar scent. Woodsy. Fresh. It always made her smile.

Eli Bryce slid into the passenger side. Shifting in the buttery beige leather seats, he turned to kiss her. Just a peck. He knew how she felt about such things in public. She hadn't ever told him, but those things reminded her of Marcus. When they were together, they hadn't cared who knew about how they felt about each other. They'd been young and in love. There was no place for things like that in the life she lived now.

"Do you want to drive?" she asked. He usually did, but she didn't want to assume he'd want to, especially since he'd gotten into the seat next to her. Sometimes he enjoyed when she drove.

"You drive," he said.

The airport driveway had become busy while she waited. A car parked almost parallel with hers. A car in front. She was nervous. Found it hard to think. He did that to her. She'd come to rely on him. To help her get through. To help her be more sure of herself and the things going on around her.

"So how did it go?" she asked, trying to maneuver around the cars, her head turned away from him.

"I think I may have it in the bag." He sounded sure. But he usually was sure about himself, even when he'd run into obstacles. He always tried to get her to be the same way.

"You got the job?" She put on the brakes and turned to him, right in the middle of traffic.

"Hey, be careful!" he said, and reached out for the wheel, as if he could take over driving from where he sat. He pointed out the window with the other hand. "Watch where you're going."

The job meant a move. To New York. For *him*.

What would become of her after he left?

What would become of *them*?

She knew firsthand how distance could tear a relationship apart. She'd experienced that before.

A journalist with a Pulitzer under his belt, Eli Bryce was a media darling, and he was more than ready to take his bite out of the Big Apple. It was where he was meant to be. Where he should be.

"You got the job." She repeated. This time it wasn't a question, because she knew she shouldn't have ever questioned he would.

"I'm not so sure we should talk about it while you're driving." A slight frown crossed his forehead, and he nodded at her. He picked up on the sadness in her voice. "We'll finish this conversation when we get to my place."

His place was a loft. Wide. Spacious. Lots of windows. Lots of dark décor. He had a chef's kitchen and pipes running across the ceiling. A walk-in closet that was larger than her tiny bungalow.

She liked her place best, although being with him anywhere was better than not being with him at all. She wouldn't want to relinquish the awareness of herself to live among the modern motif that was his space. Hers was better for the life she'd allowed herself to envision with him, although she knew it wouldn't be one she'd get to decide.

Her place. Classic brick. Trim painted white. Inside and out. A front door made from oak and painted peach. Inside—books. Bookshelves in corners and tall from floor to ceiling along walls. Books on tables and shelves and stacked in corners. It was what she'd immersed herself in before she met him.

But it seemed to her, after he came into her life, that she'd also found comfort in the window seat in the dining room. There was a cushion with pale-pink stripes, and throw pillows—some apple-green, some snow-white. Some with lace and fringes. Some with polka dots. And the memory of the familiarity of the two of them together whenever they sat there. Or when she sat in the reading nook in an upstairs corner. In a place where they'd sit in the two upholstered chairs they'd found as they strolled at a flea market in Rosemont one lazy fall afternoon. And the history her downstairs living space told, with its plate rails and radiators. Creaking floors, pocket doors, and built-ins around the brick masonry fireplace.

Like a history she hoped to make with Eli.

The history that she *thought* she'd like to share with Eli.

Some days she had a nagging somewhere deep inside that it wasn't the presence of Eli that she hoped would define her history, even with all the feelings she had for him, but that her history wouldn't count if it didn't involve family. She'd quoted it in nearly every book she'd envisioned herself writing. The ones she'd wanted to write. But in the few articles she had managed to publish, those needed for tenure, she'd introduced the idea of how history always involved human beings. Human interaction.

And she had that with Eli. An interaction. One that had filled over the hole in her heart like the kudzu had covered up the sunken canyon of the Devil's Punchbowl.

She had had that history before. Memories of it tucked away in the small recesses of her mind. Far enough in that it rarely could get out, but her mind was stuffed with memories. Her childhood. Her family. Her interactions with others. Before she had locked herself in a shell. A casing that held tight who she used to be, surrounded by all the things that made her who she was today.

Only when she opened herself up, letting the memories seep into her consciousness, the pain bubbled up and hurt started all over again. So she stopped remembering about her life before. Her family. Her lost love. It made her a different person. But it made her able to get through each day and come out at the end of it unscathed.

But if you'd asked her later in life, after she'd been satisfied her history had correctly been set—carved out like that cave in Natchez but strong enough to stand the tide—she would tell you that she knew all along the importance of remembering. That she knew her future couldn't exist if she hadn't kept it tethered to her past.

It had been why she held on to little things. Like how she'd kept a copy of the title search done when she bought the house. All the families who had lived in her house. All the history of it. All from the time it was first built.

History was important to her.

"You okay?" Eli asked.

"I'm good," Nona said, thinking this wasn't the best time to talk about what the possibility of his new job would mean for their relationship. He had to know she didn't want to go. To be anywhere else. To live anywhere else. How were they going to make that work?

Plus, she didn't want to argue or cry or whatever emotion that conversation would stir up. Not now. She hadn't seen him in three days. She just wanted to enjoy being with him now.

"How about a little music?" he said, reaching for the dial on the radio. "I don't know why you listen to these talk radio stations. You know, music feeds your soul."

At the same time Eli reached to change the station, the phone rang on the car's dashboard.

"Natchez," Eli said.

Mamaw. *Again.* Nona thought.

Not taking a chance on him answering the phone, even though his hand was only reaching for the radio tuner, Nona brought her hand up to move his. "No," she said. "I'll call them back." But in her haste, her hand hit the button on her steering wheel, and the connection went through.

Shit.

She'd have to talk to Mamaw now. That conversation would probably take up the entire car ride with Eli.

Shit.

"Hi, Mamaw," Nona said, putting a smile in her voice.

"It's not Mamaw, Peaches. It's me. Julia."

Peaches . . .

Nona held her breath and closed her eyes. She hadn't heard anyone call her that in years. She glanced over at Eli, out the corner of her eye, nervous about him hearing about her other life. A life she tried hard to hide. The one where she'd abandoned her family. Let pain and pride keep her away from them. He wouldn't ever do a thing like that.

"Peaches?" He mouthed the name when he caught her eye, amusement on his face.

"Julia," was all Nona could say, and barely so.

"Peaches, you there? I've been trying to call you."

"I'm here," Nona said. Not bothering to question why she used her long-forgotten nickname. She tried to keep her eyes on the road, realizing just then if Julia was calling, something must be wrong. "Is Mamaw okay?" Her mouth went dry with the words.

"She's fine." Nona could hear Julia sharply drawing in a breath. "Thanks for asking about me. Your only sister." Disdain in her voice. "Haven't talked to you in twenty years."

Eli touched Nona's leg. She let her eyes meet his and heard him repeat—in a whisper, an inflection in his voice—"Twenty years?"

"Julia. It hasn't been twenty years." An exaggeration Nona felt compelled to quell. "More like fifteen." She hunched her shoulders. "Or something."

Now she was irritated. She grunted, put on a blinker, and changed into the passing lane. The faster she went, maybe the faster this conversation would be over. "I just thought if you were calling . . ." She became still. "I just thought something might have happened to Mamaw."

"No. Like I said, Mamaw's right as rain."

"Good."

"It's your *father*."

Their words overlapped, spoken at the same time.

"What?" Nona asked. She felt her heart drop. "What's wrong with Daddy?"

"We're orphans now, Nona. Daddy died this morning. He had another stroke." Julia had always been so dramatic, but these words had shaken Nona.

"Died?" Nona's voice went faint. And shaky. The word sticking in her throat. She swallowed hard and swiped a hand across an eyebrow. She felt Eli's hand on her arm. But then she didn't. All at once, she couldn't feel anything. Or see anything. Not clearly. The space around her had bunched up and squeezed out all the light. The world outside of her closing in around her. Enveloping her. A hazy darkness that had been like she'd fallen toward a black hole. Dark. And narrow. And wrong.

She thought maybe she should pull over. Not have to concentrate on driving. Concentrate on doing anything. At least until she could see again. She flicked the blinker on, looking over her shoulder to see when to switch lanes, but there was too much traffic.

Breathe.

That was the next thought that came to her. Because now, in the middle of the highway, she realized she couldn't catch her breath.

Maybe her heart had stopped beating. She drew in a breath through her nose and blew it out through her mouth. She placed one hand on her chest and did it again. In. Out. Balminess washed over her entire body, and panic kneaded up across her forehead.

"Are you okay?" Eli shifted in his seat to face her. She looked at him. She didn't have the words to answer. Because she wasn't sure if she was. And as she wondered what she could say, she found herself wondering why she felt like she did. Hadn't she already buried her father? Along with her thoughts and feelings for all the people she'd left behind. It had been the only way she'd found to make it through all those years without the painful prick of her past.

She put her hand back on the steering wheel. Put more pressure on the gas with her foot. And felt the light of the sun swirl back into her view.

"Nona," her sister's voice came over the car speakers. "We planned the funeral for next Saturday. To give you time to come home. To pay your last respects."

Respectful had not been something she'd been to her father.

She hadn't ever bothered to call him after she'd left. Be it twenty or fifteen—or however many years she'd been gone. She hadn't called him or even asked Opal how he was whenever they talked. The last time she'd shown him any respect, or had any conversation with him, was when he'd come up to Chicago, not long after she'd left. She had refused to talk to him because she knew what she had to say to him would not be nice.

Not even after he traveled all that way and tried to persuade her to come back with him. Not even after he said how he missed her. How he loved her and how his heart ached that his little girl had left home. But her anger had made her heart hard, and she hadn't given one thought to his words.

Now it was her heart that ached.

And she wondered why she'd never thought about this day would come. Or stopped to realize how much it would hurt when it did.

CHAPTER THREE

Nearly Thirty Years Ago

A melting pot that bubbled up inimitable cultures and cuisine, Louisiana was a land of swamps, music, and raucous festivals. A state with a completely different set of laws than in any of the other forty-nine. And with a city, Vidalia, not even quite a mile and a half across the Mississippi from Natchez, it was a great hiding place if you happened to run into some trouble.

Trouble like the kind Jasper Davenport found himself in right before his daughter, Nona, turned six.

Johnny Miller was black as tar and just as slick. He was a cheater and a gambler. "And them two things together," Opal Davenport often told her son on more than one of his Sunday evening visits, "can get you into a whole heap of trouble."

"And," she said as she set a plate of food in front of him on one particular Sunday, "now you're responsible for more than yo'self. You got a wife and two little girls." She sat down in the kitchen chair next to him, the plea evident in her eyes. "Please don't go get tangled up in no mess you can't get out of."

Jasper didn't see it as mess. His mama didn't know what she was talking about. Johnny Miller had the golden touch. He knew how to make money. Big money. Be it cards, numbers, or dogs, whatever game he played, he always won. And while Jasper did keep down a job and had earned respect in his neighborhood as a family man, a little extra income wasn't gonna hurt none, especially since he was trying to buy a house for Cat and the girls.

Cat Montgomery was beautiful, and he told everybody, whether they asked or not, that he had loved her from the first time he saw her. Even though that day she'd been walking out of the school yard with Willie Hawthorne. He'd followed them, ducking behind trees or bending down to tie his shoe when one of them looked back his way, ending up outside her house.

Jasper just couldn't keep his eyes off her or stop his heart from doing somersaults when he thought about him being the one standing there on her front stoop.

Cat was light-skinned with hazel eyes and big ol' dimples cut into her cheeks. They made Jasper melt every time he saw them. She was soft-spoken, and the way she stretched her words out made everybody listen extra hard to see what else she was about to say.

They'd met in high school, and she had big dreams and no plans. But after he'd taken her from Willie, all those little hearts and lipstick stains she'd left on the notes that she stuffed inside his locker made him want to try to figure it out. And just when he thought it might not be possible to give her all the things she wanted, that maybe he wasn't the marrying type and he should bail, along came Julia.

She was the mirror image of her mother. Good hair. Light eyes. And a smile that lit up her father's heart. She was sassy, bossy, and smart—old folks used to say that she was getting out of the way for the next one. And though he'd considered doing it to Cat, he knew there was no way he could give up on his bubbly baby girl. So, he kept trying to please them both. Johnny Miller was the one who could make a way for him to do that.

It wasn't long after Johnny Miller became a permanent fixture in the Davenport household that little Nona came along. People said she looked like Jasper spit her out, wasn't no denying her, they'd say. Not that he would have, because even though she did look just like him, he knew Cat would never go out on him.

Dark skin. A little bitty thing with big eyes that were full of wonder and a mass of coarse black hair that stayed as tangled as a tumbleweed. Nona did things her own way. Bold. Intrepid. From the time she could walk, she took chances and would often act before she'd think. Always ready to jump in with both feet. She'd climb kudzu-covered trees and hang from the vines or get lost for hours in their ground cover among its thick storage roots on her journey to visit Middle Earth. She'd wade out into the Mississippi in her yellow galoshes and with her homemade stick pole to fish for whales and search its shores for caves that surely touted hidden pirates' treasure.

She believed in the goodness of everybody, her own immortality, and the inherent honesty of every person she came across.

Julia often had to be her anchor. But she never minded. Nona, the baby of the family, was her baby, too.

And for the most part, they were a happy family. Most of the time.

Nona always said she didn't remember much about the night her father left to hide out in Vidalia, especially since she didn't realize at the time that it was a bad thing. What she did remember was the rain.

It was fast and hard and pelted against the windowpane, jolting her upright out of her sleep. And when the lightning crackled, and the thunder boomed and rolled precariously close to the window by her bed, she jumped out and over to her sister's bed. But she wasn't there. Scared, she left the room to search, knowing Julia would protect her from the reverberations of the downpour.

But Julia remembered exactly what happened. It wasn't the rain that had woken her. It was the sounds of her parents arguing.

Her mother scolding. Her father pleading.

The *I told you so*'s.

The *I know you did.*

None of those realizations changed what came next.

"Shh!" Julia hushed her little sister when she came, rubbing her eyes and whimpering because she was scared. She put her arm around little Nona and pulled her in close to comfort her and keep her quiet. She didn't want her eavesdropping discovered and be sent off back to bed. Julia wanted to know what the commotion was about.

Their father was drenched in water, his face wet. Julia didn't know if it was the rain or tears that ran down his face.

Her mother stood in her pink chenille bathrobe with clenched fists, body tight, and when she wasn't yelling to her husband through clenched teeth, she held her trembling lips tight. Julia could hear her spent breath rattling through her nose as she hissed out each angry breath.

Julia knew that look. It was the same one Nona had whenever she came into the house with muddy boots upon return from one of her adventures and was forced to stop in her tracks. Being yelled at about staying out so long and no one knowing where she'd been. Or when she was sent to bed without any supper after apologizing to Miss Polly for picking the flowers she'd just planted on her husband's grave at the city cemetery. Nona explained she just wanted them to be a centerpiece on the evening's dinner table.

Strong-willed and determined. Defiant. She bucked expectations, even though she was too young to know what others wanted of her. She did know they rarely comported with what she had in mind. It wasn't easy to deter Nona from her course. And she didn't cry. Fists balled. Breathing heavy. Tears never emerged.

And now her mama was trying to be as strong as Nona.

Johnny Miller had *roped*—their mama's word—their father into some illegal enterprise, and the police were after them both.

Her daddy wasn't sure if the police knew about him, *yet*, so he said. But as soon as they did find out he'd been with Johnny, they'd be on him like white on rice. He told their mama he didn't want to go to jail, which is where he was sure to end up if they caught him. So he had to leave Natchez. At least for a little while.

And one thing the sisters did agree on about that night: they never saw the suitcase that was at their father's feet. Not once did they notice it the entire time they stood, peeking around the doorframe, until he said he had to go. And then it became the largest thing in the room.

"Julia," Nona said, yanking on the sleeve of her sister's pajamas.

"Shh!" Julia said again.

"Where is Daddy going?"

"Didn't I tell you to shush?" Julia gave Nona's arm a tug to quiet her. "Do you want them to hear us?" She leaned in close to her sister. "Then we'll never know where he's going."

"Probably on an adventure." Shushing by anyone never got Nona to actually do it. "Is he taking us with him?" Her eyes gleamed, the gravity of the situation never entering her mind.

"The only place you're going is to bed, just like you always have to do when you don't listen."

Julia took her sister by the hand and led her back into the room they shared. She put Nona in her bed and then climbed in with her, gently patting her until Nona fell asleep.

At some point, Julia heard the front door to the house open and close, the rain letting up, and her mother crying.

She eased out of the bed, making sure not to wake Nona, and listened at her parents' bedroom door. She only heard one side of the phone conversation, but it told her everything.

"Johnny was up to one of his schemes . . . Of course, Jasper followed in behind him, doesn't he always? . . . No, Mama P., we don't need you to come over, we'll be okay."

Her mama was talking to Mamaw. Maybe she could make her daddy do right. But Julia wasn't so sure. She was always fussing at him, and he was always apologizing, telling her he'd do better. But it was easy for Julia to see that he didn't always keep to that. Sometimes, when she was with him, they'd leave out of Mamaw's house, hop back into the car, and drive off to go and do just the thing he'd told his mama he wouldn't do. He'd wink at Julia as he jerked the car into gear and make her promise she wouldn't tell. "Because if you don't, I'll buy you an orange soda." Her favorite. And when she was with her daddy, she drank a lot of those.

"I don't know when he's coming back," her mama answered into the phone. "He told me he's gonna stay in Vidalia until all this blows over . . . I guess . . . No, ma'am . . . He said he's gonna send us some money . . . No, ma'am, I don't have no idea how he plans to get any money . . . Yeah. I wish he'd just stop hanging out with Johnny, too."

After her father left, Julia tried to comfort her mother by being more helpful around the house, keeping an eye on Nona—keeping her clean, fed, and out of trouble—especially when Cat decided to go to work a few hours at the dry cleaners on St. Catherine Street. And never mentioning her father, because that always made her mother cry. It turned out that Cat Davenport wasn't as rehearsed as Nona when it came to holding her tears at bay.

Nona, on the other hand, saw nothing amiss. She contended that her father was gone on an adventure and encouraged her mother, so she wouldn't be sad, that maybe she should take one, too. She explained to her mother, in great detail, how much fun all her own exploits had been. And to prove her point, she picked up great adventure picture books on her weekly class trip to the school's library to share with her mother.

It didn't take long for Cat to take Nona's proposition to heart.

CHAPTER FOUR

Chicago, Illinois
Present Day

"Peaches?"

Eli hadn't said much on most of the drive home from O'Hare International Airport after she hung up with her sister.

He watched as she swiped the iPass at the all-electronic toll collection and headed south on I-190 West past Rosemont and merged onto I-90 near West Bryn Mawr Avenue. She drove over the three-lane concrete road, out of DuPage County, weaving around the cars, switching from lane to lane, for the five miles or so into Cook County. Traffic was unusually light for the more than fifteen miles into downtown Chicago where he lived. She was quiet and reacted nothing like she knew Eli thought she should. He thought of her as fragile. Nona knew that and leaned into it. And perhaps he even thought that Nona would cry.

She didn't.

She stiffened up after the news came. She clenched the steering wheel, and blinked her eyelids tight enough that he thought they might stick together. He thought that she must be fighting back the tears because he knew her. Quiet. Reserved. But not strong enough to stop the tears from flowing at the death of a father she hadn't seen in years.

She had to have love for him. She had to have regret for the pro-longed absence. Eli tried not to stare, but he watched and waited for that familiar response to all that he had just discovered happen. And when it didn't by the time she exited onto Armitage Avenue, her silence was making him anxious.

He ran a hand over his pants pocket. Then gave it a pat. The black velvet box he'd put there to pull out and present to her once they'd gotten back to his house felt warm against his leg. Ready to be taken out. Or, it might just be the heat from his nerves. Nervous, he realized, because he was feeling the grief he thought she should.

She hadn't ever spoken about her father, or sister, for that matter. Not in the year they'd been dating. But she was the quiet sort.

She didn't like to venture out in conversation or undertaking. She was happy with books, whether reading or writing them. He liked that about her. That he could be Nona's rock and be an anchor as he pushed her to venture out.

But she was being stronger than he'd ever known her to be.

And for whatever reason, it made him love her more. And the hurt he felt for her father's death and the sister's estrangement cut even deeper.

So, when she put on the blinker to turn onto West Illinois Street, he felt like he needed to say something, and "Peaches?" was what had come out.

She looked over at him for a long moment before turning her eyes back to the road.

He expected she wasn't going to answer at first. But before she reached his place—the redbrick, 1900s converted warehouse that was the Lofts at River East—she said, "It's what people called me back home."

And then she chuckled. Not one filled with merriment or any mea-sure of mirth, but one filled with irony.

"But Julia has never called me Peaches. She hates that name." Nona took in a breath. "And me."

"What did you do to her?"

"I've always wondered that, too."

~

Natchez, Mississippi

"Oh my word, Julia Ann Curtis! I have been looking all over for you." Her accent thick, vowels drawn out, she came through the door of the Davenport rental property on Rankin Street. "Who thought you'd be here? At the scene of the crime!"

Sanganette Gautier-Preston. White. Prim. She incorrectly, by most accounts, considered her size twelve, five-foot-four-inch frame to be petite and her thinking progressive. An aficionado of designer heels and designer purses, she was always overdressed in the classroom full of sixth graders at Harris-Harper Elementary School where she taught. Her hair was blonde and curly, her eyes blue and heavily mascaraed, and her nose straight, delicate, and usually in the air.

"This is not a crime scene, Sanganette." Julia came walking out of the kitchen. A dark-blue pantsuit and sensible heels were more her style for work.

"Whatever do you mean? What happened in this very place is what struck your father down." Her voice softened. "I've come to bring my condolences . . ." Then, Sanganette scrunched her nose in disdain as she turned to survey the room. "She was a disgusting woman. She couldn't have been from around these parts. She would've known better."

"She wasn't."

"That is obvious." She flicked a hand down her skirt like she was brushing away a gnat. "So now what are you going to do with this place? I mean after you clean it." Her face lit up. "Oh! I've got an idea. I've got this low-income African American little boy in my class, and I think his mama is having trouble with paying for the place they've been staying. Maybe you could let them stay here."

"It is clean. And do you mean let them stay here for free?" Julia's voice echoed through the empty space.

"Yes. Charity. We have to help those less fortunate. Teach them what's best for them if they don't know themselves."

"I'm going to sell it."

"Sell what?" Sanganette drew out the words, shock covering her face.

"*Every*-thing." Julia pursed her lips and gave a curt nod. She had decided it as soon as she had walked through the door that morning. "This house. Whatever my daddy owned. I'm going to do a title search and put up For Sale signs."

"Maybe it's *you* who needs to be shown some charity. Sit down." Sanganette placed one hand on Julia's back and grabbed her arm with the other. She tried to lead her to the lone chair that sat in the middle of the dining room. "You need a cup of water? J'eat yet?"

"I'm not hungry." Julia shook her head. "And I'm doing fine." She wiggled away from Sanganette's grasp. She didn't have the patience for others right now. But she knew there was no getting rid of Sanganette. "I'm just not going to deal with these rental properties Daddy had. Bad tenants. People trying to take advantage of you. I don't have the tolerance for it." She gave a knowing nod to Sanganette but did not let on that it might be too painful to keep up the day-to-day things that had been a part of him.

"So, you just gonna sell it all?"

"I am."

"What about Peaches?"

"What about her?"

"I mean"—Sanganette waved a hand around the room, her face perplexed—"doesn't she have a say-so?"

"No," Julia said, and walked toward the front door.

Sanganette sucked her tongue, a crease formed across her forehead, and she emitted a groan. "How could she not?" She followed Julia. "Are you telling me your sister isn't coming back for the funeral? How you plan on doing all of this without her?"

"What does her being here have anything to do with anything? Daddy left everything to me."

"He did?"

"Don't sound so surprised. I was the only one here. The only one who stayed with him. Took care of him. Why would he leave anything to anyone else?"

"What about your Mamaw?"

"She's too old to handle all the land he had, and he knew it."

"Have you seen his will?"

"Don't need to." Julia opened the screen door and stood back to let Sanganette out. "I already know what it says." She locked the door behind them, and the two stood on the front porch.

"Betcha not looking forward to seeing her, huh?"

Julia stared out into the distance at nothing in particular and didn't say a word. Sanganette could probably tell she didn't want to talk about her sister, but for her, curiosity always took precedence over discretion.

"Well, I'll tell you," Sanganette continued. "It was the first thing that Ruby said when he heard your daddy died. 'When will Peaches get here?'" She attempted to imitate his voice. "He thinks they're still friends after all these years apart."

"She never did anything to Ruby."

"I know." Sanganette hesitated, but it was evident she wanted to say something else. "But I just don't want my baby brother getting hurt again. You remembered how he cried when she left. Or how he acted when he found out she was with . . . Oh!" She shut her mouth tight like she was holding something inside of it.

"Go ahead. Spit it out."

"What?" Sanganette made the word into two syllables. Her voice up an octave, her tone turned like she didn't have the faintest idea what Julia was alluding to.

"Marcus." Julia raised an eyebrow. "You know that's who you wanna talk about. All this talk about Ruby is just a ruse."

"It is not." She acted insulted. "He *was* upset. And you know it." She pursed her lips to speak and blew out a breath. "I wasn't going to say anything about . . . you know."

"Mm-hmm. Right."

"I wasn't. But since you brought him up." She stepped in closer and lowered her voice, as if she was keeping others from hearing what she had to say. "She don't know about the two of you."

"I know she don't know." Julia blew out her own exasperated breath. "How could she know?"

"Right," Sanganette readily agreed. "But when she finds out, then what?"

"Then nothing. I don't feel no remorse. No guilt. What's done is done. Plus, she left him and never came back. Never called. I was good for him. To him." Julia raked her teeth over her bottom lip. "He was good for me."

"I ain't gonna argue with that, but to marry your sister's fiancé, be it right or wrong, is gonna cause some friction."

"What's done. Is. Done."

"You right 'bout that."

"Plus, Nona is the reason we had to grow up without a mother. Putting all those ideas in our mama's head. She was already vulnerable seeing her husband leave."

"Peaches was six. She didn't know no better."

"She might've been six, but she was the devil."

"Is that why you married Marcus? To get back at Peaches?"

"No." Julia shut her eyes momentarily. "I married him because he was there for me."

"And you loved him." It came out more like a question.

Julia looked at Sanganette. "And I loved him. Still do. Even though we're not married anymore." She blew out a breath. "He was good to me. For me. He was good to my son. Our son. How can you help but to love a man like Marcus."

"All of this is drawing up a whole lot of history."

"Whatcha mean?"

"I can't say I can remember you mentioning your mama one time since she left."

"That's because, to me, she died a long time ago. No need talking about the dead."

"You've never heard from her?"

"What!" Julia started down the stone slab steps, agitated. "Don't be silly. She left and never looked back. Never called us. Never came back to see about us. Not even one birthday card. As far as I know, she really is dead."

"Julia." Sanganette's voice was soft. Comforting.

"Matter of fact," Julia said, and cut an eye at Sanganette, "I hope she is dead."

Sanganette followed Julia and went down the steps.

"I know it hurt you when she left, and you probably never dealt with that."

"Are you my therapist now?" Julia asked.

"No. Your friend. I've been your friend ever since then. Remember?"

"How could I have time to grieve over a mother who left when I had a sister and a father to take care of? Somebody had to do it until she came back."

"That was the problem. You thought she was coming back, and you never came to grips with the fact she wasn't."

"She said she was coming back. She told the both of us she wasn't leaving us. She was going to get a place and come back and get us. I trusted her to do that."

"And she let you down."

"I can't talk about this now." Julia's breaths were short and quick. Her heart picked up its pace. "My father is dead. The only parent I had left. I don't want to talk about things that happened decades ago. Stirring up all those bad times. Those hard times. I suffered enough because of them."

"C'mere, girl. Give me some sugar." Sanganette held out her arms, and Julia stepped into them, letting the touch of her friend ease the tension the talk had caused her. Sanganette kissed Julia on the cheek and gave her friend a tight hug. "It's gonna all be okay. I promise. Now," she stepped back but held on to Julia's hands. "I got to carry Preston's Mama to the doctor, but if you need me, I'm only a phone call away, you hear?"

Tears brimming in the corner of her eyes, Julia nodded ever so slightly so they wouldn't fall down her face.

"Bless your heart." Sanganette put a finger under Julia's chin and gently nudged it up. "It's all gonna be okay. It really is." She headed down the walkway to her car, which was parked across the street, but stopped at the tree lawn. "We're still the same size, right? Size twelve?"

Julia nodded.

"Well"—a proud look crossed her face—"I still got that black dress I wore to Big Daddy's funeral. I'll never wear that thing again. So, if you need it, just let me know. I'll take it to the cleaners, and it'll be as good as new."

With that, she nodded and smiled at Julia, who hadn't moved from where she'd stood on the walkway in front of the house, then turned and walked across the street, got into her shiny white Beamer, and drove away.

CHAPTER FIVE

Natchez had a behemoth history to be such a small place. And in its nooks and crannies and around not-so-discreet corners stood reminders of its patent past.

And in its unwieldly tale Nona had gotten tangled up. Looking back, she supposed she could have chosen to do things differently from what she'd done. She just wasn't sure, though, she could ever muster enough courage, if she could go back, to redo things. Or even fix them now.

And she didn't want to have to return to find out.

Eli was safe. With him she didn't worry about things. She went along, not giving a second thought about what to do or how it should be done. He made the choices, and she didn't have to think whether everything would be alright, he'd make sure they were. That was one of the qualities she liked about him. He knew what she liked.

He'd pick the things they'd do. Where they'd go. What they'd have to eat. She didn't have to offer her opinion. He had one for the both of them.

She'd made a lot of bad choices on her own, many she was just grasping. And she didn't want to do that anymore. Like not talking to her father for all those years. Not taking the time to find out what happened to Marcus when he'd left her stranded at that bus station.

And why her sister, who she had trusted, told her father what she had planned.

She had put that all behind her until her sister called. Calling, she thought, frustrated, when Eli was there in the car. That was what she got for not calling the number back when it first appeared on her phone.

She hadn't said a word on the drive back after the phone call. Not because she hadn't had anything to say—she'd been bursting at the seams. Filling up and brewing over with thoughts and words about her father. About her feelings. About home in Natchez. But Eli was distracted with something else and appeared not to have the attention to expend on her. He'd begun to tap his leg with his hand once she pulled off the freeway. Slowly at first, but the closer they'd gotten to his place, the more the cadence picked up. His long, slim fingers agitated, seemingly directing the beat of her heart.

Nona couldn't ever remember a time when Eli had been angry with her, and that made her unsure of what his actions meant now that he knew some of the things she'd done. But she didn't want to face that inquisition now.

They hadn't ever talked much about her family, she had only ever mentioned Opal. Saying she was her grandmother who lived in Mississippi but nothing much more. He spoke often of his. They had plans to fly out to California for her to meet them over the holidays.

Eli was raised in a two-parent home. An only child, he believed in the hierarchy of family. Everyone had their roles. Nona had spoken to his parents over the phone only a few times, customary, she thought, for couples just starting out. But during those times, she hadn't felt adequate. She'd come from a broken home. She didn't want to carve a path into their good graces or be scrutinized by them. The only family she cared to talk about with him, though, was the one the two of them would make together.

If that time ever came.

Because then she wouldn't have to think about the family she'd lost.

She hoped their time would come. To be a family. But she had hung on that kind of hope before, and it had broken her. After she'd left Natchez, she had changed. And by the time she was able to put herself back together, she wasn't the same.

Where she'd once been curious, now she was reserved. Where she'd been eager, she was now thoughtful. And where she had once loved with boldness and wholeheartedness, she now gave her heart with forbearance. Because that was the only way she could keep her emotions from overflowing and consuming her.

And now she was going to have to wade back through those muddy waters. Face all the questions of why she hadn't ever returned. The reasons why she left. And see the people who were responsible.

There was no way she couldn't go. Anger. Distance. Upheavals. This was about being there for family.

And more important, she knew it was time to go home.

And at some point, she was going to have to explain it all to Eli. How she used to be. She knew that would cause a rift between them, an even bigger one than the one that would come with his new job. How she hadn't always been as fragile as she was now. And what would he think of her then? Disappointment? Disbelief? Disdain . . .

Feeling vulnerable, she didn't go into his place with him, one of the few times she hadn't done as he had asked. Maybe the only time.

"Sometimes people need to grieve in their own way," he'd said, the car door open but him not moving from his seat. "But do I need to worry about you? Don't I need to keep you here with me?"

"Nope," Nona said, and shook her head. "I just need to get back to my place."

Nona drove through downtown, stopping at lights, waiting for pedestrians to cross, turning corners by rote. Down Wacker Drive and along West Randolph Street. Past tall buildings. Under the bridges and overpasses until it changed to neighborhoods of single-family houses and brick apartment buildings.

And by the time she pulled up to her house, she realized with all the churning her mind had done, she hadn't rested on the thought of her father being dead.

But without thinking about it, what she had planned had everything to do with him.

She was going into the house to figure out what to do next. She had to make reservations, only she didn't know when she should go. Should she go only for the funeral, showing up the morning of? Or should she try to spend time with what family she had left?

Mamaw.

It would be good to see her grandmother.

She'd have to pack a bag. What all would she need? She had to call Dr. Davis, her department head, to have someone take over her classes. And she had decided to drive to Gary, Indiana, to deliver the news about her father in person, and then it made sense to fly from there to Natchez. To home.

So that was what she did over the next few days. She handled it methodically, crossing things off her list as she prepared to go. The decision to go and stay for a visit turned out to come easy. It just felt right. Somewhere inside her, a tugging—longing—for family seemed to overtake everything else. It had been harder, she found, trying to decide what clothes to pick and what to wear to say goodbye to her father.

And say hello again to all the people still there.

Nona called Opal and found out all the particulars. It had been a Thursday when Julia called with the news. The funeral wasn't going to be until the following Saturday, a full week away.

"You know black folks wait for everyone to come from out of town to have a funeral," her grandmother had said when Nona asked why it was so far away.

Discussion of the services ensued, songs Nona remembered from her childhood, but the names of the designated singers not even familiar. Who'd sent flowers already, frustrating Opal, "because them flowers will be as dead as Jasper by the time we have his service." And how she planned on writing the obituary herself and on making a red velvet cake for her granddaughter in celebration of her coming home. "Even if it is for such a sad occasion, I'll still be overjoyed to see you."

Cake and death notices all in the same breath.

Still, with all her grandmother's words, Nona felt an anticipation that sent tingles down her fingertips and up her spine. A flutter in her stomach and the knot that had grown in her throat was making it so tight that she had to open her mouth to breathe. At first, Nona wasn't sure if it was a portent of something good or bad.

Five days after Nona got the news about her father, she drove to Gary. She parked in front of the house, and while she sat there, she called Eli and told him her plans. He said he wanted to go with her, scolding that she should have let him know what she was doing in time for him to take the time off.

It was too late for that.

Then his conversation vacillated to wanting to be the one to take her to the airport. He questioned, several times in several different ways, why he hadn't been the one she'd picked to do that.

For the first time since she'd come to rely on him, she found she didn't want to share her reason. But that didn't deter Eli. He needed to know the airlines she was taking and if she'd gotten a good deal. He asked had she packed everything she needed. And did she know that TSA didn't allow but so many ounces of any liquids she planned to take with her.

She didn't have an answer to any of that. Or perhaps she didn't want to explain herself to him. And that made her feel bad. She'd never felt that way before. It made her start to second-guess the decisions she'd made, including telling him what she was planning in the first place.

After hanging up the phone, she left everything in the car and went up to the door and rang the bell. The house was small but familiar, the smell of burned sage wafting around its corners. When Nona was there, it made her feel like she wasn't as lost. She didn't question so much the decisions she made or all the things she thought about wanting to do.

"Hi, sweetie. C'mon in."

Nona smiled, happy to see her even under the circumstances. "Hi." She gave her a hug—a tight squeeze. "Thanks for agreeing to take me to the airport."

"Oh, sweetie, I'm just glad you thought to ask me."

Cat went by the last name Hawthorne nowadays but still had a glimmer in her eyes, a youthful shape, and a pretty face. Like Nona, she'd lost that Mississippi accent, but she still exuded Southern grace.

"What time does your plane leave?"

"I'm going to leave first thing in the morning. I was hoping I can stay here tonight."

"Of course you can." She led her down the hallway to the spare room. "And while you get your bag, I'll fix you something to eat, and then we can talk. Okay?"

Melded into the warmth of small glowing candles surrounding her in the small dining room, Nona hadn't talked much during the meager meal of leftover rice, a runny egg, and toast to sop it up. She didn't finish half of the can of Coke.

"I'm going to try and get some sleep," was all she said once she'd finished.

Nona sat in the dark on the side of the bed and practically held her breath until she didn't hear any noise coming from the kitchen. Dishes washed and put away. Lights no longer showed under her door. The door to the other bedroom closed.

Once it was quiet, she cracked open the window and smelled the rain that had started up, drumming against the windowpane. She slipped into the cotton eyelet gown and crawled into bed.

She slept through the night, awaking long before the slight tap on her door and a voice asking if she needed anything before they left.

And just in case that "anything" meant saying something about her father, she said no.

"You call me." Cat rubbed Nona's arm as she put one foot out the car door. They had pulled up to the curb in the departure area of the airport. "You know, if you need me or anything."

"Okay, Mama," Nona said. "I will."

CHAPTER SIX

Natchez, Mississippi

Julia finally cried. Standing on that walkway in front of the house on North Rankin Street. All alone as dusk set in around her. The tears came. They came so hard, they racked her body—making her shoulders quiver and her chest heave. And for a long while, she didn't know what those tears were about. The last five days had been a nightmare.

But she was sure those sobs weren't for her father.

She couldn't give anything for him. Not yet. Not because she was glad he was gone. She wasn't. If anyone had asked her as she poured that cup of coffee the morning he came in, livid about the peach pie, she would have told them that everything, including him, would be fine. Even though the doctor had said he had a long way to go to be out of the woods, she could see the clearing, and to her, it looked bright and shiny. No reason to think her father wasn't going to be around an hour later, or for that matter, years later.

And it wasn't because she didn't love him, because she did. He'd been her first best friend. After her mother left, he'd slid right into her job—combing the girls' hair, teaching them how to shave their legs, picking up feminine products for them when the time came, and chasing boys off the porch when they visited. It had been the three of them, together, and they'd been happy.

It was just that she'd been mad at him. Had been for a long time. And she had to assure herself that selling off all his property had nothing to do with her anger with him. He had called it his recompense for nearly losing everything. Blessing bestowed for his past failings.

But later that night, as she lay in her bed unable to sleep, her eyes fixed on the ceiling medallion, she thought about how long she'd stood on that walkway. She realized that her father wasn't the only one she was mad at. She was mad at her sister and mother. And what's more, she realized they had been the reason for her tears.

Death brings up all kinds of thoughts. Of things long forgotten. Good memories. But also those strands of bad ones weaved in.

They'd left her, was where her thoughts had floated to. Left her there in Natchez when she needed them. She had needed to lean on them when her boyfriend, Bisset Brown, had sat on her for what seemed like hours. Not letting her up, not even when she'd said she'd do just what he asked. Or the time he'd locked her out of the house and she'd sat half the night on the porch steps, in a thin gown, not knowing who to call and too embarrassed to ask for help anyway.

She had needed to celebrate with them on her wedding day. On the day her son, Jayden, was born.

She had needed them—her mother, her sister—for encouragement. For protection. For help. Because families were supposed to be together. That was just how it was.

And Julia knew if they'd been there, she wouldn't have gotten into a relationship with Bisset Brown in the first place. A white man. A looker and a charmer. She would have been smarter about what love meant and who you should love.

And she definitely wouldn't have married Marcus, because he would have been Nona's husband.

Julia blamed them both for all the wrong choices she'd made. For leaving her and giving her no say-so about it.

Her father couldn't come back. She wasn't upset with him for that. He didn't intentionally leave. But her mother and sister had.

Julia got up early the next morning. She had yet to hear from Nona. She hadn't even heard confirmation of whether her sister would show up. Not sure, like everyone else in town seemed to be. But if she did come, she was going to need a place to stay. Julia had plenty of room to accommodate her. And where else would her sister go?

She shuffled off to the kitchen after dressing. Throwing on an old pair of jeans and an emerald-green T-shirt she'd picked up in Las Vegas. It reminded her of *The Wizard of Oz* slot machine where she'd won four hundred and fifty dollars on the last day of her trip. Sponsored by the local board of realtors, where she'd been a member for twelve years, it was the first time she'd done something like that for herself. Ever.

It was right before her father had taken sick.

Right before Jayden became an aloof teenager, now always just out of reach.

She warmed her hands on the side of the mug brimming with steaming black tea and blew into the top of it.

It wasn't a cold morning. The birds had started singing, and the rays of sun shone through the windows of the house not long after she'd given up on trying to sleep. No chill from a draft in her century-old house. It was her insides that needed warming.

The house was quiet and empty without her father, even though Jayden was upstairs, still asleep in his room. Jasper Davenport believed in breakfast. "Best way to start the day," he'd say.

By this time, if it had been one of those days where she'd indulge him, she would have been cooking bacon in her aluminum skillet, spreading butter on bread to toast in the oven because that was the way he liked it. "Don't put my bread in that toaster. I don't like all those lines through it." As if that made it less desirable. And he'd fight her over scrambled eggs with cheese.

"Cholesterol for breakfast," she'd announce when she sat the plate in front of him. "Not good for a man who just had a stroke."

"The day they tell me I can't eat no more bacon and eggs will be the day I'm ready to die."

"They already told you that," Julia would say, the same conversation they'd have each time she cooked it for him.

"Yep. And I ain't dead yet." He'd spread some mixed jelly on his toast. He'd have her pick up little containers of it from Eat at Joe's, one of his favorite diners. "Shows they don't know what they were talking about."

Most days her daddy got oatmeal. And most days Julia had to throw more than half the bowl of it away. She'd bought sugar packets to keep him from taking scoopfuls from the sugar dish. He didn't like those either.

She sat her mug on the table, pushed herself up from the kitchen chair, got the oatmeal out of the cabinet, and pitched it into the trash. Another memory that threatened tears. She wished she'd made some oven toast to go with her tea.

Julia needed to get back to packing up her father's room. The make-shift bedroom didn't have much left in it. The medical supply company had picked up the hospital bed, portable potty, and the walker. He hadn't liked using any of them. A friend of his had picked up a cane from Jamaica, intricately carved and painted in yellow and green, and was, so her father decided, the only help he needed. Julia had agreed with the physical therapist that he needed more support. He proved them both wrong.

Julia pulled out a box from the corner. Nearly hidden when the bed had been in place, it had been the only box her father had brought from his apartment when he moved in with her. What she'd found on her first attempt to clean out his apartment in Vidalia had stopped Julia cold.

A picture of Nona.

It was exactly how Julia remembered her. Even the dress Nona was wearing was one Julia had given to her for her first date with Marcus. She'd been all grins.

Julia smiled at the memory. She'd had a difficult time taking that picture, she hadn't been able to get her sister to stop twirling.

That memory from that photo hadn't been so hard to take. Though the second picture was.

It was of her mother. Cat Montgomery. That was what Julia had taken to calling her. By her full name. She wasn't "Mom" anymore. And she wasn't Mrs. Davenport, Jasper's wife. And in spite of what she'd said to Sanganette on the sidewalk in front of that house on North Rankin, Julia didn't wish her dead.

She hoped Cat Montgomery was still alive. Julia knew she'd never get past what the woman had done—leaving her girls—to follow some man up north. But she wanted to see her. Needed to see her.

Most times, it wasn't to talk to her, although she had questions galore, but to look at her again. To watch her like she used to do when she was little. Peeking around the doorway to the kitchen as her mother hummed a tune, doing this and that—cooking, washing dishes.

Her mother always made her a part of what she did. Made Julia feel as if she was Cat's good friend. Her confidante. The one she shared her secrets with. Giggled with. Cat would burst through the door from shopping and tell Julia all the things she'd seen and done on the way while the two of them would put up or try on whatever Cat had brought home. She'd let Julia be her helper in the kitchen, taste the food, and ask what else she should add. Julia had been the one to help her put her earrings on and to fasten her necklace when Cat and Jasper were going out. Cat had always made Julia feel an attachment to her that Julia thought couldn't ever be broken.

But somehow it had been.

Julia understood her mother's explanation to her of why they had to go. Jasper had hurt her. And Julia understood that Cat wasn't leaving them for good. Just for a little while. Cat was coming back. Back to get her and Nona. And it wasn't because Cat didn't love them that she was leaving in the first place. She loved them to the moon and back. It was just sometimes mommies and daddies staying together didn't work out.

But Cat hadn't come back. Even though she had promised she would. Julia had often heard her father say how much he missed her. And it made her wonder why he hadn't ever gone to bring her back.

And soon feelings of missing Cat turned into feelings of anger with Cat. And Julia decided she'd just be happy with the parent who had decided to stay. Julia convinced herself that she didn't need her mother. No longer loved her. And the memory of her faded away, just as all the days, months, and years that Cat had been gone.

And even Jasper, after a while, had stopped speaking about Cat. Julia assumed her father had written off the woman, just as she had. Until she found that box with a picture of her in it.

That picture wasn't as familiar. Julia didn't have any memory associated with it. It just brought back glimpses of her. A snapshot of Cat Montgomery pushing her hair back in place as she stood in front of the bathroom mirror. Or sitting Peaches on her lap and reading to her or bending over to tie her shoelaces that never seemed to stay tied.

Only her sister wasn't Peaches back then. She was Nona. So that made all the memories Julia had of her seem distorted.

And other times, Julia wanted more than just to look at Cat Montgomery. She wanted her to come back to give an explanation that was fully plausible. Completely forgivable.

But Julia didn't think there were any words that could do that.

Jasper Davenport had directed Julia to throw away everything in his apartment, save the one box, when he had come to live with her after his first stroke.

Julia hadn't ever understood why Jasper had decided to move back to Vidalia instead of living in one of his houses in Natchez. He'd gone there to hide out when she and Peaches were kids, but then lived in Natchez while Julia and Nona had grown up. It wasn't until after Julia was out on her own that he'd gone back. And it wasn't until she'd gone to see if there was anything else to keep, contrary to his wishes, that she'd learned why. She'd found the secret he'd been keeping.

It seemed her father was always chasing after things and people who didn't want him.

"Did you cook?"

Jayden had appeared in the doorway. Finally up, he could help her take the last of the things out to the trash. He was fully dressed, unusual for the fourteen-year-old so early in the morning. Long and lanky, like his father, he stood, scratching his head. Up, it seemed, but not fully awake.

"What about a 'good morning'?"

"Good morning. Did you cook breakfast?"

"How about a 'let me help you with PaPa's things'?"

He stood in the doorway and looked at her. This time not repeating the words she'd offered.

"I need you to take these things out to the garbage," Julia said.

"Why are you throwing his things away?"

"What do you want me to do with them?"

"Keep them. For memories. Keepsakes," Jayden said.

Julia was sure he could read the face she was making. The one that said she had no interest in those things. And if he knew their history, the stories behind those things, especially the pictures—about how those people had abandoned her and Jasper, he wouldn't have asked that question. But he pressed on because they meant different things to him.

"You at least keeping the pictures, right?"

"What pictures?"

"The ones in there." He nodded toward the box on the floor. The one Julia had sealed up, with the pictures inside. The one she'd given a swift kick to. She felt like kicking it again.

"If you already went through the trash, you could have just taken it outside."

"It's not trash, and I didn't go through the box. PaPa showed them to me."

"Them?"

"Yeah. Aunt Peaches and Grandma." Julia took in a breath and held it for a moment.

There wasn't any reason for him not to know about his family. About his heritage. But once one lie is told, it is easy to pile more on top. Julia always felt he was too young to know anyway. She was raised being taught that kids just shouldn't be in grown folks' business. But now, as he grew, she didn't want Jayden to know how she'd kept so many things from him.

"I may as well tell you now," Julia said. "I'm selling all his property, too."

"His houses?" Jayden looked angrier with those words than sad about the loss.

"Well," Julia said. "Maybe I could keep one for you." She smiled at him as if the compromise would make him less upset.

"I can't believe you're selling them."

"And why would I keep them?"

"I'm going to get some orange juice," he said, and started to leave.

"Hey," Julia called after him. "Don't walk away from me when I'm talking to you."

"I thought you were finished," Jayden said, reappearing in the doorway.

"I'm not."

He turned his head and stared at a wall, not offering a response.

"I need you to help me finish straightening up in here."

"My dad is coming to pick me up."

"When?" She glanced down at her watch. "You didn't tell me he was coming." She ran a hand over her hair and gave a tug on her sweatshirt and tried to smooth it out.

Maybe she should go and change clothes.

"I told you, Mom. He wants me to help him down at the bar. Get it ready for PaPa's repast." He waited for her to confirm she knew. "Today and tomorrow," he added.

"I need you to help me here," Julia said, looking down at the boxes, exasperated. "I have to get my father—your grandfather's—affairs in order. One reason you stayed off from school."

"I stayed home because I was sad about my grandfather dying."

"People are going to be stopping by here, too," Julia continued. "We're the ones who had a death in the family, you know."

"I know." He raised his eyebrows. "That's why I'm going to help Dad. PaPa was family to him, too."

"Hello?"

The screen door opened. That time it didn't make any noise when it shut, unlike Julia's heart. It was beating in her ears, and she hoped it didn't show in her chest. He made her feel like that sometimes. An unending love wrapped up in guilt and gratitude, pain and remorse.

Marcus Curtis. Right on cue.

Appearing in the doorway, he said his greeting again. "Hi." He gave a small smile. "Door was open." He pointed a thumb back toward it.

Julia ran a hand over her hair again. If she'd known he was coming . . .

51

"I came to pick up Jayden," he said. "He's going to help me down at the bar."

She wouldn't have thought if he turned up at her door it was for anyone else but Jayden. It had been a long time since he'd shown up for her.

Standing next to their son, Marcus tugged gently on his bottom lip with his teeth, his one hand balled into a fist and held by his other hand resting in front of him. It was easy to see they didn't match. The definition of Marcus' muscles—the bulge with the flex of his arm, strong pecs filling out his shirt. In his youth, some touted him as the most good-looking man in Natchez. Marcus' skin was smooth and dark. A little gray clung to the beard he sported.

Jayden was lighter than Julia. A dust of black hair worked its way over his top lip, a faint shadow on his cheeks. But as much as they didn't resemble each other, Jayden had adopted a lot of Marcus' ways—concern for Julia's father being one of them, in spite of all that had happened that night twenty years ago.

Through the years, Marcus, even after her father had gotten sick, had come to spend time with Jasper. Bring him food. Sit and talk. Now hosting the repast.

"I didn't know he was going with you today. I thought he'd help around here. Get it ready for company."

"Company?" Marcus was interested in that. He swung around and allowed his eyes to sweep the rest of the house that was visible from where he stood. Then up the steps, like that company might be coming his way. If he knew Nona was coming, it wasn't because Julia had told him. They never discussed her sister.

"I don't even know if she's coming," Julia said, reading his mind. Never saying her name. But those unspoken words wouldn't hide how he still felt about Nona. "Haven't heard from her since the day I told her Daddy died."

There wasn't any change in his expression with that news. He asked Jayden if he was ready to go. Marcus would get her son that breakfast he'd been asking her about. For all that had happened, he was a good father.

Jayden promised to take the trash out when he got back and glanced again at the box, then at his mother, as if bidding her to reconsider getting rid of the contents inside.

After Julia heard the screen shut behind them, she rooted herself at the front door and watched them until they were out of sight.

CHAPTER SEVEN

It was all make-believe.

The Turning Angel. An inescapable canyon. Peach trees growing wild in Natchez.

The love of a man.

That had been her history. All made up. And for all this time, she'd tried to forget it.

In town, a breeze washed through the car she'd rented at the airport, carrying the scent of cut grass, the pungent odor of carriage horses, and the smoky aroma of meat grilling out back of a barbeque joint somewhere blocks away, making her mouth water. It nagged at her memories. Distant. Still not quite familiar. She could have easily been somewhere else.

It had been the touch to her father's hair, the tuft of soft gray lying on that satin pillow, and after leaving the funeral home, the swat of muddy waters hitting her nostrils after she turned onto Cemetery Road. A waft of the fragrance of apricot coming from the sweet olive trees rushing in. Those were the things that told her she was home.

And she was happy for that. Happy about that. More so than she would have imagined. And she didn't mind that one bit.

Nona had stepped off that plane and decided she needed to find a place to stay, because surely she couldn't stay with anyone in this place.

Not now. Because if this happiness she felt was followed with regret and that was to show, then the people who had betrayed her would take it as her having forgiven them. For her being weak.

Although that was how she felt.

And even before she visited her grandmother, the only person she thought she still cared about, she went to see her father.

She knew if she saw Jasper all laid out, there would be no doubt about the things that were real.

She stood close to the casket. Afraid to touch him. She stepped back and took in a breath. The fragrant musk of the flowers—pink carnations and red roses and white lilies—made her lightheaded. She felt as if her feet were sinking into the thick pile of the sapphire carpet with taffy-colored flowers strung together with black vines.

The bronze casket caught the stray rays that came through the rectangular windows set high up on the walls.

He looked old. And she couldn't place his hands. Too frail to be the ones of her father. The creases and folds were off, and there was so many more. The thin skin that covered them was worn, his nails dark and thick.

She didn't think back to the last day she'd seen him. The day she'd been defiant, standing her ground, telling him she wasn't coming back to Natchez. It was the day he'd pulled her up from that canyon that came to mind.

He had come back from Vidalia. It had been more than three weeks after their mother had left the sisters with their grandmother. He'd come out of nowhere. Unexpected. Leaning over the edge of Devil's Punchbowl after she'd fallen in. Calm, he smiled down at her.

"Daddy." She'd called to him like she expected him to be there. "I hurt my arm."

"I'm coming down to get you," he'd said. "You gonna be alright."

Standing next to his casket, Nona could almost hear the rustling of the kudzu engulfing and obscuring the canyon where she lay all tangled up. Those were the hands she remembered. Smooth and strong. Tightly gripping the heavy vines as he made his way down to her.

"Sanganette said slaves got trapped down here." Nona herself had now become a prisoner of that canyon. Sprawled in the blanket of the glossy leaves where she'd landed when her hands slipped and she'd lost hold of the rubbery vines. They'd invaded the space and spread from one side of it to the other. She had twisted and shifted her body to make her unmovable arm not hurt as much.

"Did she now?" he'd asked.

"And she said there's peach trees down here. I just came to see 'em."

"Looks like that wasn't such a good idea." He spoke between heavy breaths. Sweat beading on his forehead. The hot afternoon sun beaming down. His hands and feet searching for strong vines to wrap around.

"They're wild. Nobody planted them. And nobody can eat them."

"Do tell. Wild peach trees?" His words implied she was telling a tall tale. "Seems to me," he said, "nobody eats 'em 'cause can't nobody get to 'em."

"And you know what made them grow?" Nona was still explaining her fascination with them.

"What?" he'd asked.

She remembered that then he took a rest. Keeping his eye on her. Never losing that smile. His chest heaving, his descent proving to be a lot harder than hers.

"The blood from the slaves dying down here." She didn't know if it was the talking or seeing her daddy, but her arm didn't seem to hurt as bad. So she kept talking. "Union soldiers wouldn't let them out of here. It was like thousands and thousands of them that died. That's why you can't eat none of the peaches."

"Not that I've ever seen any peaches." He grunted out the words. "And tell me, Nona, what do you know about Union soldiers?" He was nearly to her. She could see the dirty soles of his shoes. A tiny hole in one.

"I know that they must not have been very nice."

He never bothered to explain any differently to her. Not about Union soldiers or about the lack of peach trees. He went along with her then, and later with her obsession. Perhaps then his only concern was about saving her.

Later, during those times when Nona looked back over her life and choices—some forced, others easy—she'd often thought she should have been appreciative of that.

"How we gonna get back up?" Nona had asked once he made his way down to her.

"I sent Ruby off for help." He clung to those vines near her and held on tight. "Couldn't leave you down here all by yourself until somebody comes, now, could I?"

She hadn't been all by herself. Ruby had been there. He was always there. He'd helped her devise the plan to see the trees and had stood guard when she clung to a vine to take her first steps over the edge. And it was his scream that married with hers when she took that tumble.

"How'd you know I was down here?" She knew Ruby hadn't had time to tell anyone, let alone enough time for her father to get there from Louisiana. "I didn't cry, and even if I had, you couldn't have heard me all the way in Vidalia."

"I just knew," he said. "I knew something was wrong and I needed to get here, back to Natchez, to see about my girls."

"Are you going back?"

"I'm never leaving you again," he'd said, and smiled.

Nona pulled her hand away from his head of gray hair and ran it over the satiny blanket that lined the casket, then left the funeral home.

She couldn't say how long the two of them had stayed down in that canyon before someone came to pull them out. Her daddy hanging on vines as close as he could get to her. The thick growth underneath nestled her in a shiny, leafy hammock. But once the two of them were pulled out, feet planted back on solid ground, her father had picked her up. His shirt wet with sweat and perfumed from the purple kudzu blossoms, he'd held her close to his chest. She'd wrapped that one uninjured arm around his neck and placed her hand on a tuft of then-not-so-gray hair as he carried her to the waiting ambulance.

She'd gotten lots of doodles and autographs on that cast. One hand on the wheel, she unconsciously rubbed the arm where it had been all those years ago, all that history flooding back nearly overtaking her with emotion.

She'd come down this same road on her way to her grandmother's house from the hospital. Up on her knees, she watched out the back car window for the umpteenth time to see if that angel inside the cemetery actually did turn and watch the cars as they passed by. It was that day, after spending three days away, that she found the first peach tree that her father had planted at the back end of her grandmother's yard. And probably the only one for miles and miles.

"Now you don't have to go jumping into canyons to find a peach tree," he had said. The pride in his words showed in the grin on his face and the swell in his chest.

A tree she guarded, sitting under it for hours at a time. Kicking off her crusade, she made sure no one ate any of its fruit and vowed never to do so herself. Her first brush with history, she was determined to protect its legacy. A decision that stuck with her for a long while and one that gave her a nickname that had lasted even longer.

~

"Peaches!"

Sitting on her front porch was Augusta McClure. Grin as wide as a mile. Arms waving fast enough to make a breeze. Mamaw's neighbor. She knew and shared everything that went on up and down the road. She was high yellow and long-winded, as Nona's grandmother used to say. Opal never was too keen on light-skinned people. Except she liked

Julia, even though she took her complexion from their mother, Cat. A woman Opal definitely didn't like. But that was another story.

Climbing out of the car and walking to stand in front of it, it seemed to Nona that the woman had been sitting in that same chair the last time she'd seen her. More than twenty years ago.

"How you, Miss Gus?" Nona said, rooted to a spot in the driveway. "I don't go by Peaches anymore."

She flapped a dismissive wave. "You'll always be Peaches to me. Sitting out back. Guarding that tree." She beckoned for Nona. "C'mere, let me take a closer look at ya."

"I gotta go in. Mamaw's waiting for me."

It wasn't exactly true. Nona had said she was coming in time for the funeral. But she hadn't ever given an exact time. Her grandmother had no idea when she'd arrive. She hadn't wanted any fuss or to give her grandmother any time to "prepare a little room" for her to stay. Or time for any family, Julia included if she was so inclined, to show up, wanting to see her.

Besides her grandmother, there wasn't anyone else Nona cared to see or to spend any more time with than the time it took to bury her father.

On the plane ride down, though, she realized she wished she had spent more time with him. She realized how much she'd missed him. How much she loved him. How good a father he'd been.

And with each of those thoughts, she felt a gush of hurt from the hole she'd thought she'd covered up long ago. It made her whole body tense. Her throat dry and her fingertips cold.

"C'mon over here," Gus called. Nona hadn't moved from the car door after she shut it. "I'da known you anywhere." Gus rocked back in her chair and folded her arms. "Chile, you ain't changed a bit."

"Nona."

She heard someone calling her name.

Nona's grandmother had come out of the house. She was holding the screen door open with one hand, a wooden cooking spoon in the other. Bent over with age and not as many teeth in that smile, but it was the one Nona remembered. Warm and welcoming. The same smile her father had had.

"Miss Opal," Gus said loud enough for her voice to carry to the porch next door. "She was just coming over to see me. I ain't seen Peaches in a month of Sundays."

"Neither have I," Nona's grandmother said. "And she came to bury her father. Spend time with her family. Not listen to you and your gossip."

"Go on, now. I just wanted to say hi," Gus said. "And I'm just like family."

"Not close enough." Opal waved a hand at her neighbor. "She's coming in here with me."

"Peaches," Gus called over. "I'm sorry to hear about your daddy." Gus pressed her praying hands together. "You've got my condolences."

"She don't go by Peaches no more," Opal said. "Which shows you ain't as close as you think you are."

Nona made a beeline toward her Mamaw, happy to see her and happy not to have to chew the fat with Gus. She'd spoken to her grandmother often over the years, but there was nothing like her smell. Her touch. Looking into her eyes.

"She still sittin' on that porch, waitin' for that husband of hers to come back," her grandmother muttered.

Nona stepped onto the tottering porch floorboards, careful not to put her foot into the gaps between them. "I thought she was the one who sent him packing."

"That's just the story she tells," her grandmother said, keeping her words low. "And you know there ain't always a lot of truth in the stories that fall out of some folks' mouths." She leaned her weight against the wooden screen door and held out both her arms. "Come here, baby. Give me some sugar."

Nona put her arms around her grandmother and held on to her warmth. "Hi, Mamaw."

"I sure have missed seeing you." Her grandmother pulled her in tight.

"I've missed seeing you, too."

Her grandmother pulled away. Tears fell out her eyes, missing her sullen cheeks. "My address ain't changed none. You knew right where to find me."

Nona didn't know what to say. There wasn't any excuse for being absent. Sorry now for having done it. Look what that had gotten her with her father.

Although for a long time, she hadn't thought that she loved him. Or cared what happened to him. All she had cared about was what he'd done to her.

But her grandmother hadn't played into any of the reasons she'd left. Or why Nona felt abandoned and betrayed by the others left behind the night she'd run away to Chicago. She'd been convinced, a conviction she had carried around with her for twenty years, that they all had acted selfishly. Her father. Julia. Marcus.

And that hurt, too, was familiar.

The loss of family can do peculiar things to people. Especially when all were lost at once. For Nona, it had turned her inside out. But she'd been always too convinced of their betrayal to ever think of returning. There was nothing left in Natchez for her anyway.

"Why didn't you bring your suitcase in?" her grandmother asked, letting the door shut behind them.

"I'm not staying."

Nona walked behind her grandmother and felt as if she'd been transported back in time. Warm memories flooded her brain. Nona had sent her grandmother money from time to time. In amounts, considered by some, a tidy little sum. Her grandmother evidently hadn't spent it on her house. Nothing much was different.

The monochromatic room hadn't changed except for a pop of color, with the new turquoise colored recliner replacing the beige one that had been there when she'd left. The same lamp with the fringe around the bottom of the shade sat on the scraped-up end table. The same lumpy couch with a slipcover over it. The crystal bowl that sat on the edge of the coffee table stocked with candy that wasn't for eating, her grandmother often warned, it was only for guests. Nona had often complained that they never ate any of it either.

With Nona's words, her grandmother stopped. Nona nearly bumped into her. "What do you mean, you're not staying? In Natchez?"

"No. Here. I didn't want to put you out."

"Put me out where?"

Opal knew exactly what she'd meant. And Nona knew the things that needed to be done for her to stay weren't anything much.

"I didn't want you making a fuss." Nona said the words anyway.

The twin beds in the back room where she and Julia used to sleep were probably made up with fresh linens—the sheets a different color from the pillowcases but all clean and, knowing her grandmother, ironed with sharp creases down the middle. Nona imagined a soft calico quilt, probably picked up at one of her grandmother's shopping trips to the thrift store, folded and laid across the bottom of the bed. All just waiting for Nona. And the smell coming from the kitchen meant food was already cooking.

"Something smells good," Nona said, hoping to change the subject.

"It's your dinner," her grandmother said. "The one you're eating before turning in for the night. In the bedroom down that hallway right there." She pointed with the spoon.

"Mamaw—"

Nona knew she couldn't survive shrouded in all the old memories of what her grandmother was offering. She was here to bury her father and not to dredge up all the past entanglements and betrayals.

"Don't want to hear it," her grandmother said. She held up her hand the same way she had when Nona was little, when she'd come in with torn clothes and try to explain her cuts and bruises. "You can't leave until after Monday anyway."

"Why?"

"I'll tell you while I finish cooking." She waved that spoon to get Nona moving. "In the kitchen. And we got company in there. I don't want no sass talkin' in front of 'em."

"Company?"

"Yep. Didn't think you could come back home after all these years and not expect people to show up to see you, now did you?"

"No one knew *when* I was coming."

"He knew you *were* coming, though. Been here every day since word got out."

"Who? Who's in there?"

"Go on in there and see." Her grandmother pointed the wooden spoon toward the kitchen. "He'll be happy to know it won't just be the two of us for supper tonight."

CHAPTER EIGHT

Slavery, the very source of our existence, is the greatest bless-
ing both for Master & Slave that could have been bestowed
upon us.

—*Stephen Dodson Ramseur, Confederate General*

Julia watched as Sanganette sashayed down the hallway, heels clack-
ing on the shiny linoleum floor, her pantyhose swishing as her thighs
brushed against each other. Julia had come to meet her for lunch and to
pick up the dress Sanganette had had dry cleaned. The one she'd worn
to her own father's funeral. The one she was insisting Julia wear to hers.

"I've been waiting for you." Julia looked down at her watch. "You
don't have long for lunch." Julia held up the brown paper bag filled with
food from Great Wok. Chicken lo mein for Sanganette. Spicy curry
shrimp for Julia.

"We're fine." She waved a dismissive hand, then as an after-
thought, she gave Julia a smile as she walked through the doorway of
her classroom.

"Where've you been?"

"The principal's office," Sanganette said.

"You've been bad?" Julia chuckled.

"No. He has." With a flick of her wrist, she flung the book she had in her hand across her desk. "He wants me to use *that*." She pointed a finger at the textbook that had landed askew. "I can't teach from that."

"Wha . . . why?" Julia could barely get her words out. "What's wrong with the book?"

"Everything." Sanganette bucked her eyes and pursed her lips. "It makes me ill-equipped to teach our children."

"Ill-equipped?" Julia repeated her words in the form of a question.

Sanganette had been teaching impressionable, as she liked to refer to them, sixth graders for the past sixteen years. She loved her job and was sure, as she often asserted, that her students loved her as well. Because she was a good teacher. An effective teacher.

Julia hadn't ever seen her in action, but she knew her tactics. When it came to the Confederate history of Mississippi, Sanganette taught what she believed, whether it was contrary to the truth or not.

"Up until now, I've always been able to get any curriculum material I wanted. I needed."

"What changed?" Julia asked, although she could have probably guessed.

"William Bishop, M. Ed., showed up." Sanganette plopped down at her desk with the words.

Julia sat opposite from her in one of the chairs sized for one of Sanganette's students. "The new principal. You've told me about him."

"Calls himself a progressive educator." Sanganette narrowed her eyes. "Harris-Harper Elementary will, I'm sure, rue the day it hired him. With his hands-on philosophy. Encouraging the"—Sanganette made air quotes—"utilization of community resources and projects based on service-learning."

"What does that mean?"

"It means he's stupid." Sanganette slowly, with the tip of her finger, pushed the textbook off the side of her desk. It landed with a thud. "Do you know he called a meeting because he said he wanted 'valuable input' from everyone on what textbooks we use."

"And that's bad?"

"Staying-after-school-for-a-month bad."

Sanganette's philosophy was that not many people, other than her, understood what needed to be taught to the impressionable minds of Natchez's future citizens. Other teachers, she had often lamented to Julia, were not as adamant about instructing in the correct history of the South and the war between the states. Sanganette wanted her students to leave her class and be able to state facts. Her favorite saying: "She didn't just educate the power of their minds but of their heart and hands."

Julia knew that Sanganette's facts were like that sunken canyon on the Mississippi—they'd never hold water.

What the principal wanted, Julia thought, wasn't what Sanganette advocated. But Julia knew what Sanganette's concern was. And Sanganette would work her way around to telling her.

Meanwhile, Julia opened the brown bag and sat out the cartons filled with their lunch. She'd had this conversation many times with Sanganette. The idea that slaves were happy in their discontent. Trying to reconstruct a past that wouldn't shed a bad light on her forefathers. But it wasn't just that the "light" was bad. What had happened had happened. It was evident just in Sanganette's assumptions and the privilege she asserted each time she thought she could change history through a book filled with erroneous facts.

Julia hadn't ever tried to change Sanganette's belief. The facts about much of black peoples' history lost. Lied about. Excused. Families torn apart. An imperfect record that left them untraceable. But Julia knew that was what Nona was trying to do. As best she could fill in the gaps that had been made. Ever evident in the article Nona had written about the Devil's Punchbowl, and Julia was settled with letting her sister teach the teacher the truth.

"I'm not against field trips," Sanganette said, pulling the carton of lo mein over to her. "I like it. All for it." She opened up the container and took a whiff. "Living local history should be embraced by every child who sits in the classroom." She pushed the black plastic fork into it and pulled out slivers of chicken and steaming noodles. "But the history of the South is presently, and literally, falling down around us." She stuffed the food into her mouth. "Mmm, that's good." She held up a napkin to her mouth. "I mean, just look. Historical monuments being spray-painted and toppled. The centuries-old battlefield flag being ripped from flagpoles." Chewing and swallowing between words, she dug back down into the container "And all these protests springing up everywhere is just disheartening."

Julia had been eating as well. Listening to the diatribe she'd heard from Sanganette a hundred times. As her friend, Sanganette expected compassion and commiseration from Julia, because Sanganette felt she was right. It was nothing they'd ever agree on. It was not something that Julia felt Sanganette would ever see the truth of either. At least not from any words that Julia could offer. "So what does that have to do with the book?" Julia glanced at the floor, and nodded her head toward it.

"Those goddamn textbooks, ordered by the district, only put into words all the actions these history haters are taking."

Julia almost choked on her forkful of rice. "History haters?" She chuckled. How Sanganette could be so passionate about things that were so wrong.

"It's not funny." Sanganette wiped her mouth and dug into the bag for soy sauce. Sprinkled it into the carton she'd already started to devour. "That bunch of sacrilegious, Southern-history *haters* are inspiring all this foolishness, and, to my dismay, unabashedly urge it."

"We've had this discussion before. And I don't know that—"

"Don't tell me you agree with Peaches." Sanganette interrupted her.

"What does Peaches have to do with this?"

"You know good and well she is pushing every time she opens her mouth to have the contributions to these great United States by the Confederacy be completely erased from our history." Sanganette looked at the book on the floor. "Just like that one does.

"The books we had," Sanganette continued, "were just fine." She closed her eyes and took in a breath to calm herself. "It helped my students to develop knowledge of their American heritage. It taught them to recognize and put in historical context the important persons of the past."

Julia had stopped listening. She had long ago told Sanganette her views, ones that matched the truth and not Sanganette's version of it. But it was hard, as Opal had often said, to teach an old dog new tricks. The lies of the South had ben embedded in its landscape, its culture, and the textbooks Sanganette sought to teach from. Others were taking up the mantle to right the wrongs, teach what was right. Others like Nona.

Julia's mind went to thoughts of her sister.

Julia hadn't heard from Nona. Still wasn't sure she was coming. Regardless if she'd let it into her conscious thoughts, she had hoped her sister would. It was why she had called her. Why she'd called back after Nona didn't answer the first time. And Sanganette was right. If Nona was here, leastways what Julia could tell from what she'd discovered Nona was doing up north, she wouldn't be happy with Sanganette's rant or her wishes to educate the children of Natchez in what she considered Southern pride.

Julia had read the article, the only one she could find by her sister, that said teaching students a romanticized version of our history wasn't teaching our country's true history and was detrimental to the growth and education of our nation's children. And Nona had noted in the article that she knew about that firsthand.

Born and bred in Natchez, as were the past ten generations of Gautiers, Sanganette's very existence was steeped in the past. People were kicking up a ruckus to change it, and Julia knew her friend would feel that she, too, would have to kick up a ruckus to keep it.

Her daddy, Randolph Gautier, God rest his soul, was a descendant of the French colonizers establishing the first permanent settlement. The very foundation of what was to become the twentieth state of the union. The claim staked and encompassed in France's Louisiana during the 1700s. Their stronghold in the region was over long before the rise of the Confederacy, where his family's legacy shined. A direct ancestor, a colonel in the Confederate States of America, had won a battle in Vicksburg, even though the war was eventually lost there.

Sanganette couldn't say for sure she had been seated on her daddy's knee the first time she'd learned of her family's lineage. But she could recite every word of it, and it was just as endearing to and ingrained in her as if she had been. And that was how she had developed her love for the antebellum period and become a Civil War aficionado. It was in her blood and in her heart.

Julia knew that, but what she loved about the work Nona was doing was that it was to right the wrongs that mentality had caused. It was to teach history as it was documented. As it had been told through the words of those who experienced it. Not of those who felt bad for what they had done. It was Sanganette's story that had led Nona to choose her passion, form her beliefs of what needed to be taught. Disseminated. It was a bad and incorrect thing—Sanganette's views—but something good had come out of it. A change that stretched further than Sanganette's sixth-grade classroom.

Unfortunately, the pedigrees Randolph Gautier boasted of, even with the help of a modern-day genealogy service Sanganette had engaged, couldn't be proven definitively.

Sanganette, however, had no reason to doubt what she'd been told. And she lived and taught by it.

Randolph had been brought up by a cousin of his mother's. Leaving him there with the promise she'd return shortly. It took more than fifteen years for that to happen.

But it was in his cousin's care, around a dinner table that most nights was just about bare, that Sanganette's father learned about his past.

The grand tales of his great or great-great and sometimes even more greats than young Randolph could count, of how the fathers before him were instrumental in raising up Natchez. Business-savvy inhabitants, they were part of paving the path to the industrialization of the Deep South. The center of the slave trade, Natchez produced so much cotton Mississippi became the richest state in the entire country.

But what captured Sanganette's attention were his renditions of how their ancestors had fought and died in the war for their state's rights, their independence. It made her drink up everything she could learn about it and share it with everyone she could.

"Don't get it wrong," Sanganette often recalled her father saying. "Our French forefathers failed miserably in establishing their hold on the land, but they were great thinkers and had an adept hand at the handling of business affairs."

"Like you, Daddy?" Sanganette would ask.

"Yes, dear, just like your daddy." He'd brush a hand over her blonde ringlets. "They cleared the land of those pesky Natchez Indians and made way for this here land to become civilized."

"Pesky?"

"Stubborn. I tell you, girl, they were a stubborn lot." She'd giggled as he shook his head and squinted his eyes, baring his teeth. "Had no foresight. Couldn't see what this country was going to become and what it was going to take to make the South great. Now, the blacks back then, they knew their place and were happy. Wanted to be a part of the enterprise."

And what did he know of blacks? Julia had asked of Sanganette other times she'd relayed the story. Never given an answer that made sense or showed Sanganette's intent, Julia had given up asking.

Sanganette had just picked up his discourse, trying to make the South less racist. Less cruel. More forgiving. All the things it wasn't.

And he had informed his young child often of the state of affairs in the "good ole days."

And Sanganette found, it was true, the South had been great. Once upon a time. Her father's stories, inspiring her to study its shared part of this country's great history and what had been a motivating factor in her wanting to teach others. Sanganette saw no reason not to make sure that those times were not forgotten, and the truth be told.

"So what's your plan?" Julia asked. She knew the sea against what Sanganette believed in was steadily rising against her.

"I'll buy the books."

"Yourself?"

"I've got the money to do it. And I think it's important."

While her teacher's salary wasn't anything to brag about, she had an inheritance. Not from her father with his storied past, but from her mother. "That Damn Yankee," as her father referred to Margaret "Peggy" Beard, hailed from New York City and from a family of old money. But even with Randolph's illustrious legacy, he'd come from a poor family and marrying well, even if his bride wasn't a Southern belle, had been his only way into the society he sought.

But, to his chagrin, when That Damn Yankee died, she'd left him penniless and had left the bulk of her money to Sanganette and her brother, Ruben, in a trust fund.

Both Sanganette and Julia were only ten years old at the time.

Julia knew it had been that kinship, an absent mother, that had been the bond for their friendship. The two had often shared how now they each struggled sometimes with their mother's face and voice at times becoming elusive. And Sanganette would often say that all she had left was what had been left to her—a piece of artwork or two and money. Lots of money.

Julia felt her mother had left her with nothing.

Peggy Beard Gautier's money was always present. Present for everyone to see. She loved to spend it, and Julia, although never asking how much had been left to her, imagined it was more money than she herself would ever have in her lifetime. But Sanganette didn't mind at all sharing it. With anyone, and especially with her father when he was alive. She had made sure he was well taken care of until the day he left his earthly body.

Added to her Southern birthright funded by Northern bank accounts, Sanganette liked to brag that upon graduation from Ole Miss, where she'd been a cheerleader, a sorority sister of Gamma Epsilon Delta, and valedictorian of her class, she had married well. Albert Beauregard Preston, a defensive linebacker during college, was now a hedge fund manager with political aspirations. At the moment, the two lived in a grand and elegant home she'd built from the ground up, one reminiscent of the antebellum revival architectural style. And Sanganette had always envisioned, whether her home address was the governor's mansion in Jackson or the White House, she'd still teach, regardless.

And regardless of any budgetary decisions or constraints, Sanganette made clear to Julia, in between mouthfuls of chicken lo mein, she was going to make sure her sixth graders would preserve and uphold the glory days of the land where they lived. And no, it wasn't only meant to venerate the memory others were trying to obliterate, but, she proclaimed, licking the last remnants of her lunch from her fork, it was to set the record straight.

CHAPTER NINE

Ruben Gautier looked like he was in his forties. That was Nona's first thought when she saw him sitting in her grandmother's kitchen chair.

Which he practically was. Nearly forty. Middle-aged. Just as she was. But he was the first person Nona had known as a child that she'd seen all grown up. Her parents and grandmother had always seemed old, and except for her father's hands in that casket and his gray hair, none of them seemed to have changed much.

It had taken a minute for her to recognize who he was. And seeing him surprised her, and so did the smile that appeared out of nowhere, without much consideration, and landed on her face.

Ruben stood when she entered the room, and a certain expectation rushed in under her skin and gave her heart the splurge of extra beats. Awkward but pleasing. Not sure how to act, but her reaction was sure. She was happy to see him.

And of course, he'd been there to wait for her. He always had. Nona saw that his eyes were filled with the same anticipation.

"Peaches," he said hesitantly, as if he were afraid it couldn't really be her. Her name floated out on his breath. His eyes warm and welcoming.

"She don't go by Peaches no more, Ruben," Nona's grandmother said. She'd gone over to the stove and turned the flame up under the cast-iron skillet. "She uses a grown-up name, just like you do. I done told you that."

"It's okay," Nona found herself saying, and then, "Ruben." She spoke his name, trying it out for the first time. She'd never called him that. "I don't mind."

"And you call me Ruby," he said. "Please." He didn't try to hide his smile. "Always call me Ruby."

And there they were. Back to grinning at each other. The way they used to.

It took Nona back. Back to a time when everything didn't seem to weigh heavy on her. To a time when she wasn't afraid. Where everything was open for her exploration. And everything in the world didn't seem to be against her.

It had been Ruby who always showed up. Every day. Knocking on her grandmother's screen door. Asking for Nona to come out to play. Ready for whatever she had conjured up—what adventure they'd be on for the day.

He was there the day Cat had dropped Julia and Nona off, headed north with the promise she'd be back to get them. Curious about the new girls moving in down the street that his neighbor, Opal Davenport, had told him were coming.

"Somebody to play with," she'd said. And so he stood at the end of Mrs. Davenport's driveway, waiting for them to come.

He was there when they drove up and had watched Nona's every move from the time she got out of the car.

Nona remembered how he hadn't backed down when she'd called over to him and asked, "What you staring at?"

And how, not saying a word, he had grinned at her. His two front teeth missing. Dark hair hanging in his eyes, arms and legs tan, his wide blue eyes not hiding his amusement with her. So Nona walked to the edge of the driveway, not two feet away from where he stood, and stared right back.

Always on her side, he'd been the only one who'd asked whether it was okay to call her Peaches once people started calling her that, because if she hadn't liked that name, he'd told her, he wouldn't either.

Back then, she didn't care what people called her, or what they said. Back then, she wasn't as fragile. All the things that made her like she was now—reserved, reticent, often irresolute—hadn't taken root. And if you asked anyone who knew her back then, they'd tell you that not one of those things had ever been a part of her.

The chicken sizzled as Nona's grandmother laid pieces into the hot grease. Adjusting the knob on her white gas stove.

"Monday there's going to be a reading of the will," Opal said.

"Whose will?" Nona asked and took a seat. Ruby followed suit. "Daddy had a will?"

"Yes, your father had a will. Why wouldn't he have one?"

Nona shrugged. "I don't know. I wouldn't have thought he had anything to leave."

"You thought like Lit," her grandmother said.

Nona braced herself. She knew what was coming next.

"Thought he had farted and he had shit."

Her grandmother's way of telling Nona that her way of thinking was faulty.

"He got a will," Opal said, "and you got to be here while his lawyer reads it."

Nona blew out a breath. She'd have to change her flight back home.

"So, you alright?" Ruby's hands were folded on the table in front of him. Nona had taken the chair to the right of him. "Really sorry to hear about your father. I know this is a lot to take in."

"Thank you," she said. She traced the outline of the yellow squares on the tablecloth with her finger. "I don't think I thought about it happening."

Nona gave a glance toward her grandmother, wondering if her "thought" about her father dying was going to garner her another round with Lit. But Opal was busy with her chicken.

"We all die," he said. "It was just your father's time."

"Not when I hadn't talked to him in forever."

"Twenty years."

"So I've heard," she said, remembering how Julia had corrected her. "Time flies . . ."

Ruby didn't finish the saying, and she could attest to the fact that time hadn't passed because of her having fun.

By the time Nona's grandmother had speared the chicken with her large two-pronged fork, put it on one of her "good" Thanksgiving platters, and placed it in the middle of the table, old easiness and familiarities had effortlessly crept into the conversation.

Among greasy fingers and a pile of used napkins, Nona learned that more stores on East Franklin closed than she could remember were there. Same with all the people who had died, although she did remember Dr. Walters, who had set her arm all those years ago and, ironically, died from complications of a broken hip. There were tourists coming in, people moving north. Her grandmother, placing herself in competition with her neighbor, dipped into the gossip mill. She ran down who had married whom and how many babies they'd had. Ruby offered, quite enthusiastically, that he had yet to participate in any of those life rituals. She smiled at his admission, and not that it needed to be said, didn't offer that she, too, hadn't. She'd found he somehow had kept up with her.

What it sounded like to Nona was that nothing much had changed. But that didn't bother her.

Ruby told how he had become a lawyer. Working as a defense attorney and in civil rights. The latter he attributed to Nona. But Nona protested. She'd gotten her degree, sure, but she hadn't even become a professor of Black Studies, written any published papers or any significant work (there was a manuscript of a book, though, safely tucked into a locked desk drawer in her home) by the time he'd gone to law school, and she said so.

"I turned to civil rights practice after I read some of your papers." He turned and smiled at her, but it didn't ease her confusion. She wasn't even ever sure of herself. How could someone map out their life based on what she'd done?

But she didn't say anything about that time. Those were the years of her metamorphosis. The loneliness. The anger. The realization. A rippled effect that slashed through Nona and magnified the divide in her psyche. Coupled with the sadness of what she'd left behind, it had led her to being unsettled and unsure. And paranoid. With every stare and whispered conversation, she'd been sure that folks around knew how she'd let a lie told to her by Ruby's sister, Sanganette, circulate inside her, bubble into her decisions and beliefs.

And no one mentioned how her father, who she'd never be able to reconcile with now, went all the way to Chicago to beg her to come back home.

And though none of that was spoken about—her learning the truth had been the catalyst for all those things—they swirled around the small, cozy kitchen.

The undertones of those things bounced around their conversation as they finished up their meal and scooped up another bowl of banana pudding with stiff browned peaks of meringue. First in the way they reminisced about her broken arm. And how easily she learned to ride a two-wheeler once Ruby took over her instruction from her father. And then, years later, how for weeks Ruby would go out of his way to walk by the bus station after she left for Chicago to look for her, in case, somehow, she'd decided to come back home. It made her feel good to know that he had missed his friend.

It had gotten late. Her grandmother had turned in for the night after Ruby had said good night. The flickering light of the passing cars said that it was dark and that she'd stayed at her grandmother's later than she'd intended. Their conversation around the kitchen table with its yellow-and-white plaid tablecloth and purple flowers, more stem than petals, still swirled around in her mind.

She stepped out onto the porch to clear her head.

It irritated Nona that she liked how she felt in her grandmother's house. Comfortable. At home. Like there hadn't been a two-decade gap since the last time she'd been here.

The night air felt different in Natchez. It was clearer. Less cluttered with the sounds of the big city. Chicago was always busy.

The mild breeze off the Mississippi River. Cooler. Calmer. The cast of the silvery full moon and the sway of the drooping branches and elongated leaves of her grandmother's willow as the air moved through them made Nona think of Marcus. How they used to walk to the house after the movies or a late supper at the diner on nights like this. How they'd hang on the porch until her father made her come in. That same breeze would come through the open window of her bedroom right before she'd hear him call her name.

She wondered what had become of him . . .

Nona folded her arms across her torso as a warm breeze floated through the air. It was the same kind of night it had been the last time she was in Natchez. The night she left home for good.

Julia had been the one who told their father that Nona was planning to elope with Marcus. She had to be. Julia had been the only one she'd confided in.

Julia had wanted to know what Nona was up to when she caught her going out the back door as she was coming in from a night with her friends.

"I know if I'm coming in, it's too late for you to be going out," Julia had said.

Nona had already hidden her luggage in the bushes. Preparing to go. It wouldn't be time to meet Marcus for another two hours, but she had checked on that hidden suitcase and the bus ticket she had tucked away in her purse a hundred times.

"Just going out to get some air."

"With Marcus?"

"No." Nona shook her head like meeting Marcus was an absurd thought. "Not with Marcus."

Julia's teasing smile made Nona uncomfortable. "It's after curfew, whether you've got an old boyfriend or not."

"He's not old," Nona had said.

"Older than you. He's grown."

"So am I."

"Not even in your dreams."

Nona's frustration with her sister's words was obvious in her flared nostrils and the drumming of her fingers on the frame of the open back door. Julia wasn't her mother. Nona hated that she tried to act like it.

"If you are sneaking out," Julia continued, "you'd better be careful."

"Marcus'll take care of me."

"I know he will. You got a good man." Julia tilted her head, nodding her approval. "I'm just telling you to be careful. You don't want Daddy trying to stop you from seeing him."

"He can't do that." Nona put her back to the screen door, moving closer to her escape route.

"Yes, he can. And he will."

"Not after tonight."

"And what is that supposed to mean?"

And maybe it was the nervousness. The anticipation. The sheer happiness that Nona was feeling. Or maybe, deep down, it was just that it was her sister. Julia. The same Julia who used to help her put her hair in ponytails at just the right height and find the left boot of her favorite yellow galoshes that always seemed to get lost. And the same Julia who got her adventure books from the library and stayed in bed to read with her when she was sick with the measles. After all, Julia at one time had been her closest confidante and ally. It was only after their mother had left them with their grandmother that their relationship had become thin and tenuous.

Whatever the reason, the words had just tumbled out. Fast and jumbled and with elated eagerness. Nona told her sister that she was going to elope with Marcus. Yes. The man who was older than she was, maybe too old per her father. And yes. The one she was old enough, no matter her age, to know that it was really love that she felt. The grown-up, last-forever kind.

They were off to Chicago to tie the knot. And then, hand in hand, they were going to walk down Michigan Avenue, go to the Navy Pier and ride the Ferris wheel, and take a boat tour down the Chicago River. And then, once they returned to Natchez, they were going to spend the rest of their lives together and make lots of babies.

The two of them had made those plans on a starry night, lying out in a grassy meadow. It hadn't been long after they met. At a dance in school. He a senior, she a freshman. They had seemed to fit together like hand in glove. Everything came easy and natural with them. He made her laugh. She made him want to be more. Better.

"At what?" she had asked.

"Everything," had been his answer.

Before him she had wanted to expand her adventures—go away to college. Sail down the Mississippi. Go whale watching. See the world.

But not after. Nothing seemed more fulfilling than being with him.

The unexplainable feeling that only comes when the love is true.

The exuberant confession came to a hasty halt when Sanganette came knocking at that back screen door with the sweater Julia had left in her car. After Sanganette came in, Nona, standing at her back, had made the gesture of a key locking tight her lips. Julia nodded and said out loud, with Sanganette as witness, even though she had no idea what she was a witness to, that she promised not to *ever* tell a soul. Even though she knew that it wouldn't be long before everyone found out.

Nona sat on the front stoop, pulled her legs up close to her chest, and wrapped her arms around her knees. She closed her eyes and tried to get rid of those thoughts. Determined to replace them with thoughts of Eli.

Her first thought, though, was that she didn't have a memory of Eli and her on a night like this. Hanging out. Walking. Holding hands. Maybe it was because Chicago nights were often cold. The breeze floating off Lake Michigan brisk. Or maybe that just hadn't been their kind of relationship.

Wasn't their kind.

Ah . . . Nona wondered why she had thought of it in the past tense.

Nona tried to picture what he was doing. Sitting on the edge of the couch, a glass of beer and the remote close by on the coffee table. His attention caught by sports on that sixty-inch screen television that still seemed dwarfed in his nearly three-thousand-square-foot loft. Or maybe he was sitting behind his desk, working on a story. His mind occupied. His time so often constrained.

He had called her already to see how the flight went, just as she was going into the funeral home. She'd told him she'd call him later.

She hadn't done that yet.

And if asked why, she wouldn't have been able to come up with an answer.

She stood up with a grunt and ambled into the house, holding on to the screen as she let it shut, leaving the front door open. Walking gingerly across the floor. She didn't want to stir her grandmother.

Nona walked into the kitchen and turned off the light. The only one still on in the house. Her grandmother had turned in for the night not long after Ruby had left, fully expecting Nona to stay in her and Julia's old bedroom.

Nona felt her way through the dark to the living room couch. She stepped out of her brown slacks and tawny-orange summer sweater and laid them across the coffee table. Her fingers led her to the throw her grandmother kept folded and draped across the back of the couch. The same one, now frayed and limp, that had been there twenty years before. Lying on the sofa, Nona wrapped herself in the softly crocheted cover, sniffing in the scents of twenty years of the smell of home. Long-buried memories.

She fell asleep to a warm wind that blew across the river and through the door, bringing with it the chirping song of shiny black crickets and the trill of the pint-sized screech owl nestled camouflaged in the bend of a nearby tree.

~

Morning came with a waft of bacon from the kitchen. And through the front door, still open, came the rising heat of the sun from the start of a Mississippi day.

Nona threw off the light blanket and sat up. She didn't move or make a sound, wanting to just take in being there. On Mamaw's couch. In Mamaw's house. Waiting for her father to walk through the door to get her.

"Morning," her grandmother called out. "I'm making breakfast and that red velvet cake I promised you."

Nona smiled. Her grandmother didn't miss anything. Even with her being on the other side of a wall and Nona trying to be quiet, she knew she was awake and starting to stir.

"Morning," Nona called back.

"You gonna need something out of that suitcase you don't wanna bring in here to put on after you get washed up for breakfast."

Nona pulled in a breath through her nose and stretched.

"I locked the screen door." Her grandmother spoke over the sounds of the kitchen and through the old plaster walls. "Leavin' it open all night. Times ain't like they used to be. Make sure you lock it after you come back in."

She stood up, reaching down to grab the clothes she'd worn the day before to slip them on to go outside. They weren't there.

"I washed your clothes."

Nona waited. She knew her grandmother would tell her the next move.

"I got a sundress you can put on to run out to the car." Nona padded off toward her grandmother's room. "I put it on the bed in your room." She made a U-turn.

How had she not heard her grandmother? Nona had slept right through Opal busying herself over her head.

Fussing around with my clothes, she thought. *Fiddling around in the kitchen. Making bre . . .*

Nona opened the door to the small room and stopped in midthought.

Nothing had changed. She shouldn't have been surprised. Nothing in the house had. But the two girls hadn't used that room in more than twenty-five years. Shouldn't it be a sewing room now? Or overrun with keepsakes, odds and ends?

She didn't want to be flooded with memories again and kept her mind on the task at hand. Last night had been enough. She went to the bed and found the sundress spread across it, one she recognized she'd sent to her grandmother as a present. The tags still attached. She found a pair of scissors in the nightstand.

The yellow flowered dress looked freshly ironed, probably because her grandmother hadn't ever taken it out of the box she'd sent it in. Seemed like that would have been a good time to remove all the labels.

Next to the dress was a toothbrush, towel, and washcloth. Nona saw no need to get her luggage out of the car. This would do, she thought, as she draped the dress over her arm and picked up the items for the bathroom. She knew she'd be stuck if she did bring that bag in the house. Her grandmother would probably unpack it herself and put Nona's things away in a drawer.

Nona decided she would wear the sundress to the hotel—a hotel she had yet to make a reservation in—and return it to her grandmother before she left. Which, she had found out at dinner the night before, would be a day or two longer than she had planned because of the will her father had left.

Nona had purposely come the day before the wake and had made plans to leave the Sunday after the funeral. As usual, when her plans changed after her grandmother's announcement, Nona didn't complain about it. Didn't question why she had to be there when the will was read. Nona was sure there was nothing in it for her.

She hadn't been compelled out of a sense of duty or capitulation but from a sense of family and, she had to admit, love. It was what her father wanted her to do, and she wanted to give him that.

She went into the bathroom, washed up, and brushed her teeth. She'd just slipped the dress over her head when she heard a knock on the front screen door.

"Hey, come on in." She heard her grandmother open the squeaky door.

Nona had wondered if it was Ruby, back already. She wasn't sure how she felt about that. She did take another look in the mirror, though. Ran her fingers over her eyebrows, fiddled with her hair, and even opened the medicine cabinet to see if there was some kind of moisturizer inside she could smooth over her face so she didn't look ashy.

There was an exchange of words that Nona couldn't quite decipher. But when she heard her grandmother say, "And don't call her Peaches," she knew it couldn't be Ruby.

"Hi, Aunt Nona." A teenager with a mop of dark curls and the emergence of adolescence evident in his gangly limbs and the peach fuzz on his face stood facing her as she came around the corner into the living room. Her grandmother stood by, a proud smile on her face.

"Aunt Nona?" Nona answered back and looked at her grandmother.

"That's Julia's son," her grandmother said.

"Julia's son?" Nona's heart flipped. "Oh my."

"His name is Jayden." Her smile got wider. "Go on," her grandmother said. "Give your auntie a hug. This your family."

Nona held open her arms. "Yes, Jayden. Come give your auntie a hug."

The boy obliged, his eyes—ones that looked just like Julia's—lighting up.

"I can see your mother in you," Nona said, releasing her embrace. "I didn't know." She looked at her grandmother, stumbling over her words. "I didn't know Julia had a son."

"You would if you had come home," her grandmother said. "And if you ever wanted to talk *about* Julia."

"How old are you?" Nona asked, not giving any response to her grandmother's remark.

"Fourteen."

"He come by here to see you," her grandmother said. "Ain't that sweet?"

"It is." She took him by his hand and swung it. "And I'm so happy you did." Nona looked past him. "Did you come by yourself? Did your mother come with you?"

Nona wasn't sure how she felt about seeing Julia. Last time she'd seen her, it had been right before Julia had betrayed her. Telling their father she was running off to marry Marcus. It was because of her that she wasn't able to be with the man she loved.

But that was twenty years ago. And now Nona loved Eli. And, as her grandmother would say, Julia was family.

Nona had learned what not seeing family for that long could do. It had taken her father away from her before she'd had time to reconcile. It had given her a nephew she didn't know.

"No. My mother's not here," Jayden said, answering his aunt's question. "My father brought me by. You wanna meet him? He's right outside."

CHAPTER TEN

The oldest city in the state, Natchez was located on a high bluff over-looking the Mississippi, lending itself to magnificent views of the river. A colorful past. Its landscape dotted with antebellum homes, remnants of slave quarters, and Indian burial mounds left over from the architects of its past rulers—Native Americans, the French, English, Spanish. And if any of those dwellings were to be put on the market, Julia Curtis could probably sell them.

Filled with history and atmosphere, Natchez during slavery was one of the richest cities, housing half the millionaires in the nation. And even now it had more homes on the National Register of Historic Places per square mile than anywhere else in the country. And, in spite of the citizenry inside its borders since its inception in 1716 never exceeding thirty thousand, Julia had amassed for herself a small fortune selling its real estate.

Well, in the sense that she was *fortunate* having the life she had. And she had learned most of what she knew from her father.

She flipped the business card she'd found in Jasper's apartment when he'd first moved in with her back and forth through her fingers, contemplating. Not that she *would* call the name on the card, of course she would, but she wondered *how* she would approach him.

Alex Marchetti was the property manager for Jasper's property, and Julia needed to tell him she would be taking over everything. All her father's real estate. She would need a list of the properties and for him to get them ready to sell—send notices to any tenants with move-out dates and make sure the properties were cleaned, painted. Because she would need listing photos.

She had initially worried what it would take to get Nona to sign whatever interest she had in the property over to her and had prepared herself for that conversation. But with it looking like Nona wasn't coming to say goodbye to their father, Julia felt her sister probably wouldn't put up much of a fight. She'd be able to do just as she pleased.

"Hello, Mr. Marchetti." Julia would have preferred to call him from her office phone, but like Jayden, she'd taken bereavement days. It would have been awkward to go back to the office just to make a phone call. "This is Julia Curtis, Jasper Davenport's daughter."

He told Julia to call him Alex and went on to apprise Julia that he already knew who she was. Jasper, Alex told her, spoke of her often. And with that, Julia smiled.

"Mr. Davenport talks about both his daughters," Alex said, which caught Julia off guard. Her smile dissipated, and the calm-but-in-charge demeanor she'd settled on portraying fell by the wayside. No more small talk—she moved on to the point of her call. That didn't go as she had planned either.

"Mr. Davenport," Alex said—she could hear the confusion in his voice—"had a pour-over will and a trust. No disrespect, Ms. Curtis, but I don't believe anything can be done with his properties until they go through probate."

A will.

Julia said goodbye and pressed End on the call. She sat the phone down on the table.

It appeared to Julia that it wasn't Nona she'd have to deal with concerning Jasper's properties, but Jasper himself. She had no idea he had written a will. Something else to pile on.

She'd been the one there for him. Was there a chance that he was going to show his appreciation by splitting up her inheritance with the people who hadn't been there for him? Who hadn't shown him how much they cared for him? Julia didn't so much *want* it, as she thought she *deserved* it. It would be unfair for it to turn out any other way.

The morning already wasn't going well.

It was the second day in a row that Jayden, picked up by his father, had left her at home to ready the house by herself, and the sixth day she'd been home from work. She thought she'd get much more done than she had.

She placed her open palms on the kitchen table where she had sat to make her first-thing-in-the-morning phone call and pushed herself up.

"May as well get the mail."

She soon regretted that decision.

It hadn't been the only sympathy card in the mailbox. The one she got that day. Sealed up in a goldenrod-colored envelope. Chicken scratch for letters. Postmarked El Paso, Texas. No. Because of her job, her mailbox had been overstuffed with cards, many from former clients, every day since the death notice had appeared in the *Natchez Democrat*.

She'd made a ritual of sitting at the kitchen table and opening them right away. And today was no different. She returned to the chair she'd just occupied and rifled through the letters. She fooled herself into thinking that she'd check the cards of condolences first, wanting to be sure to respond promptly to each one. But Julia knew, if she was honest with herself, she wished there would be one from Cat Montgomery. The estranged wife sending her well-wishes to the people she once called family.

But Julia had no idea how her mother would know her father had gone on to glory. She doubted whether she had kept up with the family.

Or that she'd cared that her husband (was he still her husband? Julia wasn't sure) had died, or that she cared about Julia and Nona. It was easy to lose track of folks when you had every intention of staying in touch, but it was harder when you planned it. Julia wondered how hard it had been for her mother to stay away from them.

Julia wished, though, that the sender of the card she held in her shaking hands *had* forgotten about her.

Usually, she would've been at work and wouldn't have even seen the mail until the end of the day.

Julia tried to keep up with technology. Her job mandated it. She used social media to promote her business, posting pictures of properties up for sale and the ones she'd sold. And although there'd been a time when she wrote out a contract using the top of her car as a table, all the paperwork now was electronic. And just like with her job, she had made her personal life paperless, too. Bank statements, credit card bills, even her mortgage payments and utilities were taken care of on an app. Which gave Julia more time to work—at first to keep her mind off the pitfalls in her life, and food in the mouth and shoes for her ever-growing child.

When Jayden was younger, he'd trekked along with her. With all his cuteness, he'd helped her form bonds with people in her office, prompting them to offer her special treatment and recognition. She became well liked and well respected. The office, though, wasn't where she excelled.

Sure, she had been instrumental in creating the Magnolia Landmark Realty scholarship and getting the office to sponsor the local peewee baseball team, which coworkers soon discovered was the team her son played for. But it was the selling of houses where she did her best work.

The top sales agent in her real estate office for nearly all of the twelve years she'd worked there—most sales volume and gross sales for the year nine years running—she'd taken more continuing education classes every year than needed. Certainly more than any other real estate agent she knew, making her an expert. An expertise she'd parlayed into a side job as an appraiser, which helped her to get a license as a broker.

Julia loved what she did and considered herself a good agent. The best agent. It had made her, as a single parent, able to give Jayden all the Xboxes and PlayStations he wanted. A stable home. A good school. And most important, it had provided her with valuable self-growth. She now prided herself on being a good listener, being known for honest dealings with her clients, and for staying relevant. She believed people cared about her.

Her days were long—often showing a property by flashlight. By being out and about, she'd developed strong ties to the community, even, like her father, purchasing income property around her neighborhood, although she'd sold off most of it to start a college fund for Jayden. Every year she sent holiday cards and calendars to people she'd sold houses to over the years, keeping in touch. Being a good neighbor. A pillar of society.

And being busy helped her to keep at bay those bits of anger that she had sometimes. Anger at her sister. Her mother. The way she'd let them drag her down and almost lose who she really was.

But she hadn't always been in a good place. And that stupid card reminded her of it.

People had been dropping off more food—spaghetti, a spiral-sliced ham, casseroles, and deviled eggs—than she and Jayden could ever eat. Even if people did drop by. She had decided to give the food to Marcus to serve at the repast. But now she shoved all of it aside. Setting the card down on the kitchen table, she plopped down in the chair and stared at it.

Bisset Brown, sending his sympathies, saying he might try to come back to Natchez for the funeral, and asking about her son.

Their son.

It made her sick to her stomach that she'd given Jayden such a legacy, and even sicker that she'd once thought she loved that man. She'd gotten over him, but not the hate she felt for him or for the things he'd done to her.

Back in those days, when she was weak. When she first met Bisset, it was obvious that Marcus was still heartbroken over Nona leaving.

And it was just as obvious Julia was still irritated by it.

Marcus used his heartache to make a plan. He vowed more times than Julia could count to go after Nona. And had only been stopped when Jasper Davenport had quelled Marcus' pining by saying he'd go up to Chicago and bring her back.

Julia used her heartache to justify the hole she dug for herself. For taking a drink or two and for talking cross to anyone who fell in her path.

Marcus had taken a job down at the Starlight Lounge. Sweeping and mopping floors after they closed at 2:00 a.m. Carting crates of whiskey and bottled beer to the bar from the delivery trucks and back storeroom. Julia would go sometimes, late at night, and sit at the bar. She, too, wanted to talk about Nona. Because, although she kept it hidden, she missed her sister. And while Marcus stocked and emptied trash, that was just what they did.

A dark, dank, sweet-smelling place, Starlight's lights were low and its air smoky. It lent itself well to sad stories and drunken tears.

That was how she had met Bisset.

He was tall and slight. His voice low. His demeanor serene and self-contained.

It was the calm that she needed.

And he cared about *her*.

So she thought.

Vowing that he would never leave her.

And she believed him.

"Something about that boy," her grandmother had said the first time Julia had brought Bisset around. She'd shook her head. "I can't see nothing good coming from that."

That was where Opal Davenport had been wrong. Jayden was good, and he'd come from that. Even with that thought Julia knew she should have listened.

"If he makes you happy," her father had said.

Her father's words gave her hope and the impetus to stay. Give love a chance. A chance that she wouldn't have to be alone. Someone to fill the void that had been there since the day her mother had walked out the door and out of their lives, one that had grown only wider the night Nona had done the same.

And Bisset had. He made her happy.

At first.

Flowers after every argument that seemed to arise over nothing and with more frequency. All the compliments he whispered in her ear following his reprimands for inconsequential errors she'd made.

Day after day things got worse, and day after day Julia tried to make it work. Reasoning it was her inner anger inciting these clashing rifts. Not wanting to lose anyone else in her life.

But it all went downhill. He tried to control her. Slither through her mind, weave in it threads of self-doubt. Attempting to make her into something less than what she knew she was.

But Marcus never made her feel that way. She wasn't an ace real estate agent then. No Jayden yet, not a mother who could anchor and be the strength against any storm. She wasn't much of anything back then, but she knew she could be more.

And it seemed to her, so did Marcus.

But to do it, she had to get away from Bisset. From the four years of her life she'd given to him. Even Marcus agreed.

But it wasn't that easy.

Marcus had gotten promoted to bartender, and so much time had passed that his every conversation wasn't about Nona anymore, when Julia told him what she was going through with Bisset.

"I'll never get over Peaches," he'd told her the first night they had a conversation for longer than ten minutes without the interruption of his work duties. "I can't see ever being with anyone else, but if I were, I'd never treat them like that."

And those conversations over a bar top became long telephone calls sometimes late into the night and Julia going over to his small apartment for Sunday dinners.

And maybe that would have been all there was between her and Marcus, a warm friendship, if she hadn't decided to give Bisset Brown one more chance. And if she hadn't used the hurt and shame she'd felt over making another bad decision about him to seduce Marcus so the child she was carrying wouldn't have to have a man like Bisset as his father.

CHAPTER ELEVEN

The . . . tribe had first led the attack because . . . Henry Van Dyck had shot and killed a young Wappinger woman named Tachiniki, for stealing a peach from "his" orchard . . .

—Danelle M. Brown, "The Peach Tree War/A Brief History/Herstory about Peaches & Other Things"

Not even a nanosecond had passed after Nona stepped out that front door before she knew who he was. He had filled out. His beard—something new—was sprinkled with gray, but it was him.

Marcus Curtis.

Nona's heart dipped into her stomach. Setting off a full migration of butterflies that flitted about chaotically inside of her. A smile started to form around her lips to match the one that had flashed across his face, as she went to step down off the porch and go to him. But then she remembered what Jayden had said.

He had come with his father.

Marcus was Jayden's father.

That realization sent her spinning. She grabbed on to the post holding up the dilapidated porch and held on tight.

"Hi, Peaches," Marcus said. He was standing in the yard, and as he spoke, he took a tentative step forward. Closer to her.

But she couldn't answer him. Her throat was tight and dry. And she would have taken a step back, away from him, if kudzu vines hadn't seemingly come through the loose floorboards of her grandmother's porch and wrapped tightly around her ankles. She found she couldn't move. The air, knocked out of her lungs, made it hard for her to breathe.

She swung around to look at her grandmother. She couldn't read the look on her face. But it wasn't remorse or shame for not warning Nona what she was walking into. And it wasn't surprise. Shock that should have mirrored Nona's, because surely if her grandmother had known, she would have told her what Julia had done.

Jayden's startled look let Nona know he had no idea how she'd just been blindsided. What his innocent introduction had done. And then her eyes traveled back to Marcus.

He wanted to say something more. She could see it in his eyes. But he didn't. He waited for her.

But he would just have to wait.

Nona saw Ruby's car pull into the driveway. And knew that was her way out.

She stepped off the porch, thankful that she'd slipped on her sandals before she'd followed her newfound nephew out the door. There'd been a time she could have walked barefoot across any kind of surface, but those days were long gone. She was happy she was able to walk at all. Get away. Escape.

Down the steps and halfway down the walk toward the driveway, she remembered her manners. If asked later, Nona would have said that she wasn't cognizant of any of her actions other than making it to Ruby's car. But she turned around, went back up the porch steps, and hugged Jayden.

"I am so happy to meet you," she told him, wrapping her arms around him. Squeezing him tight. "We're getting together real soon.

Proper-like." Then, not giving him time to answer, she said, "But right now, I really have to go. I'm so sorry, but I have to go."

Nona gave Opal the stank eye, the one Nona had often been warned against using as a child when it came to her grandmother. Heading back down the steps, she locked eyes with Marcus, and that surge of tangled-up emotion she'd been having ever since she first walked onto the porch nearly engulfed her.

His eyes were confused. Hurt. But nothing in them told her that this was a lie. That none of it was true.

She headed down the driveway where Ruby was starting to get out of the car. She waved him back in and ignored the callings of her grandmother's nosy neighbor, Miss Gus, sitting on that porch.

"What's wrong?" Ruby said, standing, one foot in the car, the other on the crumbling driveway.

Can't he see? was what Nona thought.

"Just get back in the car," was what she said. "We need to go!" She hopped in.

"Go where?" he said, but obliged by getting back in.

Nona patted the steering wheel. "Go. Go. Go." Then pushed his leg down, as if that would connect to his foot. "Please."

"Okay," he said, and started up the car. "But you need to tell me where to go." He backed up into the street and put the car in Drive.

"I don't care," she said, turning in her seat to take a last look at Marcus. He was walking toward the street as if he was going to follow the car. "I just don't want to be here."

He hadn't said anything most of the way down Cemetery Road. Not asking his question until after they passed Natchez City Cemetery, the one her father would be buried in the following day. The one where the Turning Angel was. A stone monument overlooking five headstones which seemed, with the glare of a passing car's headlights, to turn and watch as travelers drove by. She hoped it was watching her now.

She needed an angel on her shoulder.

"Are you going to tell me what happened?"

Nona waited until the curved road changed into Maple Street and Ruby put on a blinker to turn onto Clifton Avenue before she answered with a question of her own. Streets she wished she didn't remember. Streets she'd been on so many times, with her father. With Julia. With Marcus.

"Why didn't you tell me?" she asked.

"Tell you what?"

"About Marcus."

Ruby glanced at her, lifted a questioning eyebrow, and, putting his eyes back on the road, gripped the steering wheel tighter. Ruby remembered the scene on the porch when he'd arrived and knew that was what she was talking about.

"Are you saying you didn't know about Jayden?"

"No," she said. "Jayden. Julia and Marcus." She shook herself, disbelief still reeling around inside her head and heart. "Julia and Marcus," she said again, her volume low, like she was trying to process it. As if she was trying to let it settle in. But her being settled about all she'd discovered was not what her stomach and trembling leg signified.

Nona, shifting in her seat, looked at Ruby, her eyes pleading. "I didn't know about any of it."

Nona's mind went to Eli. He would have protected her from this. He always guided her through the disappointments and faced them with her. Although there hadn't been many. She hadn't allowed herself to get tangled up with people or situations. She had when she was younger. Stronger. The old Nona would have been able to handle it herself.

The most frustration Nona had felt was when she'd had trouble getting a research grant. The one she would give her right arm for. It was to delve into archival records, search data of undocumented slaves, and form a pathway to identify their descendants. But Eli had handled that, too, certainly not how she had wanted—she didn't speak up much for herself anymore—encouraging her to step back and let her idea rest.

She'd listened to him and given up on her dream without even a hint of a fight. That, too, was characteristic of the new Nona. One she realized, since she'd been back home, perhaps she shouldn't have let go.

"There'll be a lot of traveling involved," he had said. "And you're trying to get tenured. You just need to slow down."

And she had decided perhaps he was right. He had told her just how to handle it. She needed him to do that now—handle this—because she knew she couldn't, no matter how much it hurt.

"I don't know what I'm going to do," she said to Ruby, leaving those distant thoughts behind, concentrating again on her present pain.

"About what?"

"About this."

"*This*," he said, "or rather *that*"—he looked over his shoulder as if he could see clear back to Nona's grandmother's house—"is already done. There is nothing to *do* about *that*."

Leaning forward to place her elbows on her knees, she used her cupped hands to cover her face.

"I can't believe no one told you about Marcus and Julia."

"Are they still together?" she asked, her words muffled by her hands.

"No. They've been divorced for years."

"Divorced?" The word came out almost in a whisper. Her arms fell into her lap, and her head bent forward to meet them.

Nona hadn't let the disappointment of her life's history make her angry, take to drink, or lose herself in someone else's insecurities like her sister had, although she hadn't learned that part about Julia yet. She had taken the hurt of Julia's betrayal and the heartbreak Marcus had perpetrated and squeezed it and mashed it and shaped it into a little hard ball. A ball she'd thought she'd discarded the day she vowed to never come back to a place where people she loved didn't love her back. She hadn't realized until the moment she set foot on that porch that

that ball hadn't gone anywhere. It had, all this time, been buried deep inside her, and now it had started to unfurl.

"I can't remember ever seeing you like this."

"What?" Nona turned to look at him.

"I don't think I've even ever seen you cry. Not even when you fell down in the Punchbowl and broke your arm."

"I'm not crying." Nona's tone was defensive. She pushed herself against the door, wishing she could melt into it. "I don't cry."

"Why did you leave?"

"What?"

"Why did you leave? In the middle of the night." Ruby glanced over at her. "Without telling me."

"To marry Marcus. I left to marry him."

"And then what happened?"

"I don't know what you're asking. Pushing me for. Everyone should know why I left."

"Because you didn't like us?"

"I didn't know what Julia and Marcus were up to when I left. I liked them just fine. Then."

"What about me?"

Nona looked at Ruby. He took his eyes off the road long enough to meet her gaze.

"You never told me why you were leaving."

"I just told you." She flapped her hands in her lap. "I left to marry Marcus. Everyone knew that. I figured you knew that, too."

Ruby shrugged. "I didn't know. You never actually said it, or for that matter implied it. And you never called me or wrote me. Not once. You want to tell me what I did to you?"

"You didn't do anything." Nona drew in a sharp breath. "I wanted to go. To get married in Chicago. To see my mother. To have an adventure." Nona blew out a breath. "Back then, I loved adventures."

"You couldn't stay here and do that?" he asked.

"Julia was mean to me back then and we . . ." Nona turned and looked out the window. She remembered how Julia watched over everything she did, what she wore, who her friends were. Acting as if she was the mother. Nona hadn't liked it. She'd always been independent, and Julia seemed to want to stifle that. Nona had wanted to open her wings and fly. Julia seemed to want them clipped. "Marcus," she continued. "Me and Marcus didn't want her to put a damper on our happiness. Although, now I'm not so sure if that was why Marcus agreed to go."

"He didn't go."

"I know," Nona said, sarcasm in her voice.

"And even though he wasn't with you, you decided to go anyway?" Ruby asked the question he had waited all this time to have answered. "To stay and not ever talk to us again?"

"I was coming back. I didn't plan not to come back."

"But?"

"But then I found out what Julia and my father did. And because"— Nona hung her head—"Marcus didn't come with me. The man I loved more than any adventure I'd ever taken."

"Right." The sarcasm in Ruby's voice matched hers.

"What does that mean?" They looked at each other. "'Right'? I do love him." She shook her head. "Did love him. And how did this conversation get turned around?" Nona thought she might hyperventilate. "This isn't what we're supposed to be talking about."

"And you come back like this?" He seemed determined to forge ahead, stay on his topic like she hadn't said anything.

"Like what?" Nona asked, exasperation evident in her response.

"What happened to you up there?" He asked another question without answering hers.

She frowned. "Nothing happened to me."

"You've . . . I don't know . . . changed."

"People change, Ruby."

"Usually for the better."

That made Nona sit up straight. She lifted an eyebrow. "You don't think I'm *better*?"

"I think you're different."

"You don't know what I went through."

"In Chicago?"

"Here."

"Tell me about it." He turned to look at her, keeping his eyes trained on hers much longer than it was safe to do. She turned her gaze first, putting them on the road ahead in his stead.

"Julia told my father I was eloping," she started again after a few moments of pause. There wasn't any more prompting from Ruby. Giving her room, he waited for her to speak. "That was how my father knew to stop Marcus from meeting me. He probably threatened him."

Nona remembered the anger that had risen up inside the day Jasper had turned up at her school to bring her home. Only she wasn't feeling it now. Perhaps, she thought, because he was dead and that hurt crowded out all the other feelings she had about him. Or maybe it was because today she'd learned about something new to add to her anguish.

Ruby ran his fingers through his hair. This time he didn't turn to look at her as he spoke. He kept his gaze on the road. His words ragged as if he didn't have enough breath to get each one out. "Is that what you think happened?"

"It's what I *know* happened," Nona said matter-of-factly. "Julia was the only person I told."

"The Peaches I knew would have let that hurt make her stronger."

"How do you know it didn't?"

"I know you better than anyone."

"You *knew* me better. I've changed."

"We're back to that." He tapped the side of his nose. "Was that change for the better?"

"It was. I am. Better. I went to school. I made a life for myself in a whole new city. I'm a professor at a university. I'm waiting . . . I possibly might be receiving . . . well, applying for a research grant." She cleared her throat. "I'm tenured."

"And you're fragile."

Nona wanted to say she wasn't. But of course, that wouldn't have been true.

"Letting things that happened years ago"—he finally allowed his eyes to look into hers—"things that you don't seem to know much about at all, turn you inside out."

─

"What do you care?"

Her grandmother was sitting at the kitchen table, icing the red velvet cake when Nona got back. She'd been able to walk right into the house. No barriers. Not even a locked screen door, even though now Nona got what Opal had meant about not trusting people anymore.

Ruby had driven her around for what seemed like five minutes. He said it had been an hour. He'd tried to keep her mind off of things. Asking her about her work, what her research grant was going to be used to study.

"If I get it," Nona had said. "I haven't applied for it."

"You'll get it," he assured her. "I'm sure all that determination that is a part of your DNA is still there, waiting for you to turn it loose."

Ruby noticed, with his pronouncement, there had been a glimmer of a spark in her eye.

He'd taken her to Liberty Road at the intersection where it meets St. Catherine Street to the Forks of the Road Monument, something he'd said she may like, seeing the kinds of classes she taught. A memorial in stark contrast to the area's usual choice to commemorate the Civil War. There were shackles, once used to imprison blacks, embedded in concrete. A grassy hill with display boards spelling out for all who took the time to read about Natchez's lucrative slave market.

And Nona, Ruby seemed to notice, took interest enough that it curbed the sting she'd been reeling from. So he told her they'd gotten a new flag, too. Promptly drove her downtown to South Pearl Street to see it flying over city hall, hoping to see a spark of the feisty Peaches he knew come back to him.

And what Nona noticed about Ruby was that her man Friday wasn't so much the follower he'd been when they were little. Back then, he'd let her make the decisions, not often offering any opinions of his own. But now, he was full of them, and that made her uncomfortable because it made her curious as to whether any of *that* Nona was still left inside of her.

"What do you mean, what do I care?" Nona asked her grandmother. Standing in the doorway to the kitchen. Fists balled at her side. "I was supposed to marry Marcus."

"You left." It was the first time Opal looked up since the conversation started. Her spatula covered with the buttery cream-cheese frosting. "You're the one who made the choices. You could have turned around and come back that night. But you didn't. And you didn't come back when your father came to get you. When Marcus sent him after you."

"Marcus?"

She didn't believe that. She didn't remember that her father had mentioned Marcus when he came to Chicago. She did remember that she hadn't. She shook her head. There hadn't been any need to do that— inquire about Marcus when her father had come—just like now. No need to ask her grandmother what she meant about what Marcus supposedly did. Nona knew the truth with the revelation today—Julia and Marcus getting married, having a son.

And then it struck her. Punched her in the gut. Realization rushing in, she wasn't sure now whether the whole thing hadn't been planned in the first place.

Perhaps Julia already knew about what Nona was getting ready to do that night she left. Before Nona even told her. Maybe the teasing was because Julia knew it wasn't going to happen.

Nona had always felt that if she hadn't told Julia about what she was up to that night she left Natchez, her father wouldn't have known and couldn't have stopped Marcus. Now, with this, the scenario that Nona had played over and over in her mind of how she'd gotten to *this* place, to being *this* person, might not be the way it happened after all. Marcus hadn't been stopped from meeting her by Jasper. Marcus hadn't ever planned on coming in the first place.

And Opal. Telling Nona all this had been her decision . . . Putting the blame back on Nona.

Nona had come back to her grandmother's only to get the car. Thanking God on the drive back with Ruby that she'd left her suitcase inside of it and wouldn't have to go in to face her grandmother. That was the best way to do it—the same way she'd done for the last twenty years—the way she faced her frustration and hurt was to not face it at all.

Ruby had suggested a hotel for her, a newer one, he'd said, on par with the ones they had in Chicago. Hinting, but not confirming, that perhaps he'd been to Chicago. Like he knew about the classes she taught or the life she had there. But those thoughts left the moment she stepped out of his car. Something began to churn inside her. Standing in that pockmarked driveway. The smell of muddy waters coming atop of a breeze. The hot Mississippi sun and Ruby. The things he'd said to her. Him standing by, waiting to see what big thing they'd do next. She felt that old mischief stir, and without a second thought, she strolled into the house. To talk to her grandmother. To confront Opal on how dangerous and hurtful it was to others for her to keep her little secrets.

Nona had talked to Opal nearly every week since she'd left. Getting church gossip and family recipes that Nona rarely used, but as instructed, had written down. Inquiries from Nona's only familial comrade about her work and eagerness to find out news about Eli.

Yet Opal hadn't much mentioned family goings-on, something Nona certainly appreciated.

Although Opal had told Nona when her father had had that first stroke. The first news she'd heard about family.

"But he'll be fine," Opal had said. "Don't you worry none."

So she hadn't worried. She put it out of her mind, like she did everything else related to Natchez. At least, the things that concerned the people she'd known there. But not once had Opal even hinted about what Nona had learned that morning.

Jayden.

Marcus and Julia.

Why hadn't Opal told Nona about her sister's happy nuptials? The birth of a son? Nona had been determined to find out as she marched into the house, letting the screen door slam behind her. But by the time she left, she wasn't feeling that gravitas. She held that door and eased it shut. Closed it without making a sound and walked onto the front porch.

And that was when it started to rain.

Gray clouds hanging low had displaced the once-sunny day. She braced herself under the porch's tin roof, taking in a breath before sprinting to the car. Puddles already forming inside the holes made in the broken concrete. Climbing in, she shut the car door and put her head down on the steering wheel.

Looking up at the house, rainwater dripping from her hair and face into her eyes, Nona was leaving Opal's house no better than before going in.

CHAPTER TWELVE

Jasper Davenport's wake was going to be from five to seven p.m.

And Julia hadn't gotten anything done. Finding out about her father's will and getting that card from Bisset Brown had set her back. And then Marcus showed up at her house. All her men, one from beyond the grave, had her nerves on end and deflated the determination she had started the day with. Finally able to muster up some energy, she showered and dressed, all set to run her errands.

But as she was leaving home, trying to lock her front door and juggle an armload of aluminum pans and a box at her feet filled with foil-wrapped casserole dishes, Raymond Donaldson showed up at her door with a smile as bright as the morning sun.

Another man in her way.

This one, as she suppressed a bigger smile than the one she gave, didn't bother her as much.

"I just stopped by to check on you and let you know I'd be there tonight, you know, at the wake." He took the stack of pans out of her hands as he spoke. "You know, if you need me for anything."

"Thank you, Mr. . . . . Raymond." Julia corrected herself and smiled at him. "Won't you be working?"

"Yeah, but I'll have time for you." An awkward silence lasted a moment between them. "C'mon," he said. "Let me put this stuff in the car for you."

"Okay."

Raymond balanced the pans he had on top of the ones in the box and picked it up. "Hope you didn't mind me stopping by unannounced," Raymond said as they crossed the grass to the driveway. "Like I said, I wanted to check on you, see how you doing, and well . . . I wanted to see you, too."

Julia didn't mind at all, to her surprise, that Raymond Donaldson had stopped by. Because nothing else that morning seemed to be going right, and seeing him had made her hopeful that things might get better.

Maybe she could get it right this time.

She hadn't been the best girlfriend. Or wife.

Too unsure of herself to stand up to Bisset. Seducing Marcus so he could stand up for her son.

Being with Raymond was going to be for the right reasons. If it turned out they'd get together. If it turned out he was sincere. If it turned out he really did like her.

She was in a better place now. Mentally. Emotionally. She was more sure of herself and who she was. She could be the woman a good man needed. No lies. No cowering. No cover-ups. Over the years, she hadn't thought about having a man or even a man wanting to have her. She'd concentrated on raising her son. But she discovered, when there is death around you, it makes you want to live life more. And maybe Raymond was a life she could have.

Often, in the years since their divorce and even now, Julia had thought about Marcus. Dreamed about him. Wondered what if. But Julia knew, even during the short time they were married, that Marcus' heart had still belonged to Nona. And she was willing to bet it still did. She'd made a mistake lying to him, but up until the day he found out and left, she had never regretted it. A mother will do anything for her child, and Julia wasn't any different. She needed to protect her son from his real father. Marcus had been her best bet. And then there were those feelings she had for him. The ones that had snuck up on her when she spent all that time with him at the bar. Nursing her wounds. Pouring her heart out to him. Then he had seeped in.

And that was all the more reason to make a go at a new relationship that could truly be something real. Mutual.

As she pulled out of the driveway and waved to Raymond, Julia ran through a mental checklist of the things that were irritating her.

First, she still hadn't heard anything from Nona, which agitated her. Julia had vowed, years ago, never to speak to her sister again, yet she had found herself looking forward to her coming. She had crossed her fingers, thinking maybe they could jump right back in and work things out between them. Be the sisters they should be.

Second, she'd been fretting over that card that arrived in the goldenrod envelope ever since she'd opened it. She didn't want Bisset Brown showing up at her doorstep with his suspicions and accusations. Especially not when the family was trying to bury Jasper.

And with that, Julia remembered that she needed to stop by the funeral home to make a final payment on the bronze casket and the extra car service Opal insisted on having.

And then there was Marcus and Jayden. She couldn't find them. They'd left again that morning, readying Marcus' bar for the repast on Saturday. Or so they'd said. But when she stopped by, the place was locked up tight, and the two of them were nowhere in sight.

"Hey, Miss Curtis." A man walked up and gave her a quick hug.

"Hi, Keith." Pulling away, she smiled at him. "How your mama 'n 'em?"

"We good. Can't complain." He mirrored her smile. "You doing okay?"

"Yep." She gave a curt nod.

"We all sorry to hear about your daddy. I didn't really know him, but you good people, Miss Curtis. Hate to see good people hurting."

Julia gave him a warm smile. "Thank you, Keith."

"If you need anything, you just ask, now. Hear? I don't mind helping with whatever you need."

Julia gave him another smile, this one tight. Then glanced back at the doors to the Starlight Lounge.

"Looks like they're closed," he said, pointing with his head.

"I see," Julia said. "And I've got a back seat full of food."

"Oh, for the repast? I heard you were having it here."

"People been bringing so much food to my house. It's too much for us to keep." Especially, Julia thought, since it seemed she wasn't going to have any houseguests. "I don't know where they could've gone off to," she spoke her thoughts out loud. "They said they were coming here. Maybe I should call them . . ."

And that was when it started to rain.

Julia, holding her hand over her head, went back to her car. Keith took off, jogging.

In her car, fingers tapping on the steering wheel, Julia flicked on the windshield wipers and blew out a breath.

"Shopping. Find something to wear to Daddy's wake," she mumbled. That, she thought, would be a good way to get her mind off the things that were stressing her out. But she hadn't been at the mall twenty minutes before Sanganette called. Not even enough time to comb the racks. Maybe talking to Sanganette would send her mind in a different direction, and she would stress less over everything that was going on around her.

"I don't have much time to talk," Julia said after answering the phone and the two went through the perfunctory greetings.

But that didn't stop Sanganette. She seemed to be leading up to something, only Julia didn't have the emotional capacity to deal with her. Not today.

Balancing the cell phone on her shoulder, Julia gave the appropriate "uh-huhs" and "oh yeahs," waiting for an opportunity to cut off Sanganette's banter as she went through the section of the rack with her size. She wasn't sure she wanted to wear black. She didn't know if she wanted to wear a suit. She had a black suit in her closet, and still she was in the mall. Just finding something to wear was harder than she had imagined. Nothing seemed right.

Julia had to be at her grandmother's by 4:15. The funeral home was sending the car to Opal's house at 4:45 so the family could all ride together. But it seemed as if it was only going to be the three of them though in the car—Opal, Julia, and Jayden. Nona hadn't shown up.

Julia would need to find her son to make sure he was dressed and ready to go on time. She had offered a seat in the limousine to Marcus, but he had refused.

"I'll be coming a little late to the wake this evening. I have to put myself in the right mindset for your daddy's service," Sanganette said. "Preston has a thing. You know he has to be with me. I couldn't do it without him. This is such a sad ordeal."

"Yep," Julia said. It was a hard ordeal for her to get through.

"You know Preston thinks I can't do a thing without him. But in this instance, he's right. I probably wouldn't be able to stand upright at the wake if he wasn't there. I'd be a blubbering mess."

"It'll be fine," Julia said. "You'll be fine. I know I'm all cried out."

"I doubt that," Sanganette said. "You're a crier. You need someone like my Preston. Someone to be your rock."

"Oh. Did I tell you what happened?" Julia interrupted, zoning back into the conversation.

"Oh Lord. Something bad?"

"I don't know. Not sure."

"Well, tell me."

Sanganette was a gossip. It was the reason that everyone knew that a pie made by Carmella Burkes, using the fruit taken from the peach tree in the back of Jasper Davenport's rental property on North Rankin Street, had caused him a fatal stroke. Telling Sanganette something was like telling the entire city of Natchez. But Sanganette and Julia were girlfriends.

"Raymond Donaldson told me that I could call him if I need *anything*." Julia mimicked how he'd said the word.

"Oh good Lord!" Sanganette laughed. "Maybe he can be your rock. Is he after you or what?"

"I don't know," Julia said. "And I don't need a rock. I do fine on my own."

"I don't think that man knows what he's saying to you," Sanganette quipped. "Telling you he'd give you anything you need." Sanganette let loose a sinister little laugh. "You been single a long time. He might not be able to live through what you can put on him."

"Sanganette!" Julia blushed. "It's not like that."

"Could be. You just need to give it a chance," Sanganette assured her. "Sounds like he was making a pass at you."

"He came to pick up my father's body. Who flirts with dead bodies around?"

"Evidently Raymond Donaldson does."

They both giggled.

"Didn't you tell me he's been accidentally running into you all the time?" Sanganette asked.

"Yeah, but I'm sure that's just a coincidence. I mean, I see lots of other people around, not just him. He's out and about, and I'm out and about."

"Mm-hmm," Sanganette said, sarcasm in her voice. "I'm sure that's it."

"He just needs to stay in his lane," Julia said, dismissing Sanganette's teasing, although she did appreciate the conversation having taken a jovial tone. Having something to laugh about was what Julia needed. "I have other things to worry about." Julia switched the phone to the other ear and pushed past another dress on the rack. "Things like burying my father and tying up all those loose ends. The idea that he had a will really sent me for a loop."

"Speaking of which," Sanganette said. "I've got some news, too."

It was the intonation and change in her voice. The waywardness in her tone. Julia knew Sanganette had what she probably considered some juicy tidbit up her sleeve. Julia knew the conversation was going to take a turn, and she'd be back in the sour mood she'd been in all morning.

"Y'all been over to your grandmother's house yet?" Sanganette asked.

Where that question came from Julia had no idea. "I'm trying to get everything done so I can get there now."

"You haven't been there yet?"

"Since when?"

"I don't know," Sanganette said, her tone teasing. "Since y'all's daddy died."

Julia blew out a breath and pushed the next dress on the rack aside. "Maybe once or twice. Toward the beginning of the week."

Julia knew Sanganette wanted her to ask why.

It had been a game Sanganette had long played.

Ruby and Nona had been friends long before she and Sanganette. Sanganette and Julia's friendship had been forged by the duties of being an older sibling.

"Do you know where your sister is?" Sanganette, as they were growing up, had often shown up at their door with that refrain. Hand on hip, lips pursed.

Julia remembered those times well.

"Whatcha doing here?" Julia had asked the first time Sanganette showed up. She stood, one foot out the door, one foot in, the screen door resting on her hip.

"Looking for your sister."

Julia had just stared at Sanganette. She hadn't wanted to know why she was asking about Nona. Julia just wanted her to go.

"You want to tell me why your sister dumped all the peaches on the floor at Mr. Grayson's fruit and vegetable store?"

When Sanganette couldn't get a "why" out of Julia, she had proceeded with her story anyway.

"She did no such thing!" Julia had said and started to pull the screen door shut.

Julia didn't know for sure that Nona hadn't done what Sanganette accused her of, because Nona was prone to not thinking before she acted. But Julia did know—for sure—that Sanganette liked to exaggerate. She was one to tell tales. Her truth was often questionable.

"How do you know it's not true?" Sanganette had tilted her head.

Julia snorted.

"Anyway, she done dragged Ruby off somewhere. She'd better not have my brother doing anything that'll get him thrown in jail."

"They don't throw seven-year-olds in jail," Julia had said. She wasn't sure about that either. "And"—she put her weight onto her foot—"she don't need to drag him anywhere." Julia mimicked Sanganette's stance and expression. "The two of them are joined at the hip."

Julia had heard her grandmother say that often, and it was as good a thing as any to say to the rude girl who stood at her door.

"Well, Ruby's got to come home. We've got someplace to go. Someplace important." The reason was always the same, and so was the smirk on Sanganette's face. "And he's got to have time to clean up because I am sure your sister has gotten him into some kind of mess."

And it was with having to clean up after Ruby and Nona's mess— literally the store floor full of peaches—and Sanganette finding out that their two younger siblings were equal culprits, that she and Julia became close allies and eventually friends.

Sanganette's accent wasn't as thick back then, but much else hadn't changed about her. Through the years, having learned how to get a handle on the mess people got themselves into—in particular, Julia—Sanganette had become a good friend to Julia.

Sanganette had been there many a night when Marcus had called from the bar because Julia needed a ride home. Or when Marcus had found Julia asleep on her doorstep, too drunk to make it inside, she'd come to help get her to bed. And Sanganette never once reminded her of any of her transgressions. What she did do was help Julia get over them.

"Ruby stopped by Mama's this morning while I was there," Sanganette was saying when Julia's phone beeped.

It was the funeral home.

"Sanganette, this is Mackel's on the other line. Let me call you right back."

"Make sure you do, Julia. I need to tell you something."

"I will. Bye."

Julia clicked over. Ann May was on the line.

"I was on my way over," Julia said, without waiting for the funeral home director to even speak.

"No problem, Julia. We just need the payment before the family car goes out this evening."

"I should have dropped it off this morning."

"It's okay."

"Didn't know this could be so hard. I can't even figure out what to wear."

Ann gave a light chuckle. "Wear something with a jacket. The cool of the air-conditioning might give you a chill, and the heat of people moving around you and the grief might make you heat up."

"Should I wear a hat?"

"Save that for tomorrow."

"I see you're more than just a funeral director."

"Fashion director as well."

They laughed.

Then Ann May said, "I didn't get a chance to say hi to Peaches yesterday. I got caught up on a telephone call, and by the time I got off, she'd left already. It was so good to see her. She ain't changed one bit." Ann May chuckled. "Don'tcha think?"

CHAPTER THIRTEEN

Her mouth still dry. Her heart still racing. Nona signed the receipt at the Natchez Grand Hotel with shaky hands. Gripping the pen, she felt she might have a splinter from clutching that post on her grandmother's porch so tightly.

The flimsy sundress she'd borrowed from Opal soaked from rain mixed with perspiration and frustration. It stuck to her, making her hot and self-conscious. Nona adjusted her overnight bag on her shoulder, then wrapped an arm around her torso. The other she used to balance her suitcase on its wheels. She hadn't let Ruby come in with her, telling him she didn't need any help.

She made it to her room. Somehow. 207. She had wanted something higher up. Farther away. But although the lobby was empty and the cars in the underground parking garage sparse, Nona was told there wasn't anything else available.

Opening the door, she looked around and noted it did look like a room in Chicago. But it could be a room anywhere, and that was where she wished she was, anywhere but there. Dropping her things at the door, Nona walked over to the bed, crawled into the middle of it and curled up in a ball. She stared at the wall and wondered what she was going to do. Thoughts of the morning were nearly consuming her.

Nona turned on her back and closed her eyes. Hurt from the secrets and lies in her family that had brewed over the last two decades creeping through her, settling deep, leaving a sharp, lingering ache. She didn't know how she was going to make it through the next few days. Having to see Julia. Talking to Opal. Being blamed by her as if it were her fault.

Nona's job was telling the truth. The truth about slave history. The truth about black history. To set the record straight. And with that grant—fingers crossed—she was going to get, she would take part in having missing pieces of that history documented.

But after the revelations of the day, for the first time since she could remember, Nona wondered if it wasn't better to keep some secrets and truths buried.

Using what little motivation she had, she let her hand search the bed. Patting around, she tried to find her purse without having to move her body, but it was out of reach. She felt wilted and heavy and numb, like driftwood. Grunting, she angled her body and tugged on the coverlet to pull her purse closer to her. With all the effort she could muster, she pulled her purse to her by the shoulder strap, took out the phone, and punched in one of the only three numbers she knew by heart.

"I don't know how it feels to lose a parent," Eli said, his voice low. He had answered on the first ring. Like he was waiting for her. Like he knew she would need him.

For some reason that hadn't set well with her.

She hadn't told him what was actually wrong. He just assumed. Which, she reasoned, shouldn't bother her as much as it did, because, after all, her father's death was why she'd come to Mississippi.

"But, babe, I know it can't be easy. You're hurting, and that hurts me." He paused. "You should have let me come with you."

"No, it's not easy," Nona said. "It's just, you know, seeing everyone . . ." She blew out a breath. "Things have changed so much."

"Good thing you're getting out of there soon. You just have to make it through the funeral tomorrow. Then you can get your plane back home." Nona could hear the smile he was wearing in his voice. He assumed that was all it took for her to be okay. "Back here to me," he persisted. "And everything can get back to the way it was."

"Yeah," Nona said, but she wasn't sure if everything could be the way it was again. She had let the world go on around her. Without her. The people and things that had mattered to her.

"You need me," she heard Eli say.

And wasn't that why she had called him? Because she needed him. To help her through her pain. Around it. But she hadn't said what was causing her the pain, and he hadn't asked.

Unlike Ruby, who, for some reason, still cared. Cared enough to ask and to want to help her to help herself.

Nona ended the call, pulled herself off the bed, and shed her damp dress. Letting her clothes drop to the floor, she went into the bathroom to take a shower. Hot and steamy, Nona let all the gusts of emotion overwhelming her rinse off with the soap. And when she finished, she decided she was hungry.

Wrapping the towel around her damp body, she walked over to the window and opened the thick drapes. The sun, breaking through the clouds, rushed in. Bringing the warmth of a day after the rain.

She found her Nivea lotion in her carry-on and spread it over her body. It seemed like ages ago, she mused, the smell of sizzling bacon and biscuits baking in her grandmother's kitchen. But that had been the closest she'd gotten to food.

She recalled seeing a restaurant across from the funeral home after she had visited with her father. New to her, it looked well seasoned—the air around it smoky from a grill, a neon Diner sign flashing, beckoning passersby in. And, through the big plate-glass window of the storefront eatery, she had taken note it was filled with people. Crowded around tables and booths, having a purpose.

She reached behind her back to fasten her bra. Tilting her head, she thought, if she remembered correctly, it was called Lander's. She nodded. Lander's Bar-B-Q & Diner.

In that shower, covered with the suds made from the creamy white bodywash supplied by the hotel, she'd become resolved. All on her own, or so she thought. But if Nona had been honest, she would have taken into account the impact Ruby's words and actions had had on her. Nonetheless, she had decided to "not care." She did give credit to her grandmother for that sentiment, as that had been the question Opal had posed to Nona.

Why do you care?

Not caring would be the attitude Nona would adopt for the remainder of her stay. She wouldn't care how her family had continued to disappoint her. Still betray her. Still lie to her.

She would sit through it—next to them in the limo, during the wake and funeral, at the repast—and do what she came to do. Honor her father's memory. And she would grieve. But only for him.

She had come upon this single-minded purpose because, during her phone call with Eli and her shower, she hadn't been able to determine what you would say to a sister you haven't seen in twenty years. What words would you use to talk to a sister who married the man you were supposed to marry. A sister who stole your whole life to make it her own.

There were no words. None she could think of. And that would be the premise she would act on.

119

It had long troubled Julia the reason Nona hadn't ever contacted her after she left. And maybe the basis of the absence of their relationship wasn't completely one-sided. Julia certainly could have tried to reach out, but she'd been easily persuaded not to pursue Nona's election to leave by her father. He'd almost insisted she not look for her. Anger had only come second to the frenzied state she'd suffered when Julia first learned her baby sister was gone. All by herself. She blamed Marcus for not going with her. Going after her. Herself for not trying to stop her. For keeping a secret that caused her to lose someone else she loved. Although Julia hadn't ever said those things out loud to anyone.

And then, those same feelings of being alone and abandoned and angry that Julia had felt after their mother left began to shroud her conscious thoughts and memories of Nona.

And once Julia's own problems began to take form and she was entrapped in the weeds she'd sown, she saw no open road to take to get back on track with her sister.

Julia's life was entangled with the likes of a Bisset Brown. The marriage and a life with Marcus Curtis she never could explain. Including the reason why, after they'd divorced, Julia and her son still carried his name.

But there were many days, as Julia had driven down Cemetery Road, before she'd learned not to let her eyes stray toward the Devil's Punchbowl, that she'd thought of her sister and wished for her. To talk to her. Visit with her. See her. Even with all the secrets she'd been forced to keep.

And now Julia's sister was here. For two days. And she hadn't reached out to her. Hadn't stopped by or called her.

Julia could see why Sanganette had been so coy. What juicy bit of news she wanted to share. Julia wouldn't give Sanganette the satisfaction. And there would have only been one way for Sanganette to know that Nona had come to Natchez.

Ruben.

She found him at his law office. A storefront with a big glass window. Two rooms. The smaller one for his assistant. Blue carpet, wood panels up half the wall, a beige paint covering the rest of the way up and the ceiling. Twin ceiling fans were always on, but an air-conditioning unit in the window in the back office where Ruby hid out helped to keep the place cool. The air of a struggling, pro bono practice taking on the Supreme Court in landmark cases—it was far from it.

"I know why you're here," Ruby said, rising from his seat.

Julia hadn't even gotten inside the doorway.

He held up his hands. "I told San, and I saw it in her face. Her eyes just lit up. The way she gets when she's got some gossip."

"Ruben."

"You don't have to say it." He toggled his hands back and forth like they were windshield wiper blades. "I already know what you want." He put his open palms down on the paper-littered desk. "I'm gonna tell you where she is. She didn't tell me not to, and the old Peaches would have been steaming that I am. But . . ." He shook his head. "I don't know . . . I think you need . . . the both of you need . . ." The knot in his throat bobbled up, then back down. "To talk."

Talk, Julia thought as she left the law office.

She did have a lot to say.

When Julia left Ruben's office, the rain had stopped. The sun, breaking through the clouds, brought the warmth of a day after the rain.

She went first to the funeral home to pay her family's bill. Careful to avoid any conversation with Ann May about Nona—how Nona looked now or what she had to say about why she'd stayed gone so long. Julia couldn't answer those questions, and she felt embarrassed at that fact. But she knew she was going to fix that. She was going to find Nona. Julia, with determination and some nervousness, was going to go to the hotel where Ruben had said her sister was staying. Because, and maybe it had been brewing inside for a while, she missed her sister.

And even with the hurt she still carried about Nona abandoning her, she realized she was excited to see her and couldn't wait to get to the hotel.

But wouldn't you know. After leaving the parking lot of the Robert D. Mackel & Sons Funeral Home and stopping at the light on the corner at Martin Luther King Jr. Street, who did she see but Miss Nona Davenport herself sitting in the window seat of Lander's Bar-B-Q & Diner.

CHAPTER FOURTEEN

*The letter . . . read in the First Church Houston, and . . . a
well-known member of the Church . . . broke into tears and
cried out, "That is my sister, and I have not seen her for thirty
three years."*

—*The Southwestern Christian Advocate, 1877. Successful
reunion comment from ex-slaves. Lost Friends column.*

Lander's Bar-B-Q & Diner, established 2013, was a friendly place—
from the staff to the atmosphere and right down to the menu prices.
There were benches covered in maroon-colored faux leather, worn, but
scrubbed clean. Tiled floors scattered with square tables and a long sit-
down counter. A lone cook manned the indoor flattop, searing juicy,
greasy burgers and dropping fries into sizzling hot oil. Straight back,
past the display cases filled with shiny-topped pies and cobblers and
thickly iced cakes and on the other side of the wood-framed screen
door, a grill could be seen. The sweet smell of the brown sugar in the
sauce mixed with the pungent acidity of the vinegar. Made from a
black barrel, it huffed and puffed the charcoal-imbued steam through
its makeshift round steel chimney.

Inside there was chatter and laughter and forks clanging on plates, spoons on bowls, and cups. Nona, upon walking in the door and seeing all the people, felt relaxed. Even comfortable. And at home. And since she felt like that, it made sense that among the many patrons there was someone there who knew Nona. Rather, knew of her.

She had gotten a coveted booth set in front of the big picture window, only feet away from the electric neon blue sign. She felt a cool draft from a noisy air-conditioner and heard the *shoosh* of overhead ceiling fans as she slid into her side of the booth.

"Aren't you Dr. Davenport? Nona Davenport?"

A man stood at the side of Nona's table. Appearing just as she'd gotten settled. She looked up from the menu she held and smiled.

"Do I know you?"

"No." He shook his head. "But I know you." He stuck out a hand. "Jeremy Houston. Local historian."

"Historian?" Nona shook his hand. "Nice to meet you."

"I've read your papers," he said, and slid into the seat across from her. "You don't mind, do you?" He pointed to the booth he now occupied.

"No." She gestured with her hand, welcoming him to take the seat, even though he'd already taken it. "You're fine."

"Yeah. Someone told me about your published articles. Because . . . I . . . uhm, write, too. I've got a few books up on Amazon about Natchez's history."

"You do?" Nona's stomach lurched. "A book." She hadn't ever been able to accomplish that.

"Yeah." His smile wide. He drummed his fingers on the table like a bugle announcing his accomplishments. "And after I found out you were from here," he said, "I googled you and kept up with your work."

"Did you now?"

"I work for Miss-Lou Tours—"

She interrupted him. "That's short for Mississippi and Louisiana?"

"Yep. I conduct tours for them. Talk about our history. You know, I take them to the Forks of the Road. Over past the site of the Rhythm Club fire." He rubbed his hands together. "Down to the Devil's Punchbowl."

Nona chuckled. She had hoped to erase even the thought of that place from the minds of everyone. "You take people down there?"

"Yep." He was quite proud of his contributions to setting the record straight. "And sometimes, I quote some of the things you wrote about. Because, as you've said, 'It's up to us to stop those that want to revise our story.'"

Nona blushed, and Jeremy found it satisfying that he had grasped her teachings and shared them.

"We have to stop letting other people's wants twist our history," he continued.

"You have read my work," Nona said.

"I have." Jeremy smiled and rubbed his hands together. "What are you doing down here? Research?"

"No." She pulled her lips tight. "My father died. I came to help bury him."

Jeremy closed his eyes and nodded. "Mr. Davenport. Yep. I knew that. I knew him. Your whole family." His head still bobbing. "So sorry for y'all's loss."

"Thank you, Jeremy."

"No problem." He patted the table. "Hey, I'ma let you eat." The waitress had come and stood, waiting to take her order. "Plus, my food is getting cold. I just wanted to say hey." He slid out of the seat and stood up. A smile beaming on his face. "I couldn't believe it was you."

"It's me."

He had started to walk away but stopped, turning to ask his question. "You been to Melrose yet?"

"I don't know what that is."

"It's a place. An estate." He pulled out a business card. "You need to go there. See it." Pushed it into her hand. "This my number." He pointed to it. "I'll take you down there. Introduce you to Barney. He runs the place."

"Don't know how long I'll be here." Nona cleared her throat. "In Natchez."

"Don't leave without going there. You'd find it interesting. Worth the time."

"Melrose, huh?"

"Yep." He gave a single nod to Nona, then placed his hand on the waitress's shoulder. "Sorry for the interruption." He directed his words to her. "But she's famous, and I had to come say hi."

The waitress looked down at Nona. "You famous?"

"No." Nona chuckled. "Far from it. It just seems he likes history as much as I do." She watched Jeremy go back to his seat before she glanced back down at the menu. "What do you recommend?"

"Everything," the waitress said. "Everything is good here." She tugged at the buttons pulling on her shirt. "That's why I can't fit nothing no more."

Nona laughed. "Okay. I think I'll try the ribs."

"What's your sides?"

"Uhm. Macaroni and cheese and . . . uhm . . ." Nona shrugged. "I don't know. I guess I'll have the baked beans. And collard greens."

"You want sliced onions and tomatoes?"

"Yes, please."

"Okay. Good choice," the waitress said and collected the menu. "What can I get you to drink?"

"I'll have a coke."

"What kind?"

Nona laughed to herself. She'd forgotten where she was. In Mississippi, "coke" was synonymous with "pop."

"You got orange?" Nona asked.

"Yep."

"Okay. I'll take that."

The waitress left, and Nona turned to look out the window. After the rain, the day seemed to be turning out to be a hot one.

Across the street, the white stucco-faced building trimmed in the same green used in the stripes of the white awnings sat ominously. It was where Nona would see her father later that evening. Laid out for all to view. To mingle. To talk. A ritual Nona planned to quietly endure.

When Nona's eyes turned back to the interior of the restaurant, she saw Jeremy again rise from his seat. He stood in front of a woman who had just walked in. After speaking with her for a few moments, he stepped aside, and Nona saw that the woman he had spoken to was Julia.

"Nona." Julia spoke to her sister after walking up to her table. "Look what the wind blew in."

"Julia," was what Nona said. Nothing more. She kept her eyes straight ahead, although her heart did flutter. It was her sister. The person who had taken care of her after Cat left. Nona tried not to let her eyes stray, but she wanted to see Julia's face. She would have known her anywhere. The small moles under her eyes. The little gap between her teeth. She hadn't changed one bit. At least not in the way she looked.

But Julia didn't seem to notice Nona's lack of conversation as she slid into the bench across from her. She had planned, revised, and practiced what she was going to say to her little sister when she saw her. She hadn't expected it to be out in the open, at a busy diner. Julia had planned on it being in the room at the Natchez Grand Hotel behind closed doors. She wanted to clear the air—get all she wanted to say to Nona out before it was time for the family to gather.

"I felt a little foolish not knowing you were here, and everyone else did."

Nona didn't say anything, but Julia smiled and stared at her sister, a notable gleam in her eye.

"I mean, my goodness, Sanganette and Ann May knew before I did." Julia looked down at her hands and noticed they were shaking. She clasped her hands together. "I thought you might stay with me at my house when you came to town."

And even though Nona hadn't responded—she didn't know what to say—Julia drew in a breath and started another monologue.

"To be honest, I realize . . ." Julia looked into her sister's eyes. "Now. Sitting here. How much I've missed you. That I can't . . . I don't want to be mad at you anymore."

"You? Mad at me?" Nona spoke to her sister but only because she was confused by Julia's words.

"Yes. Yes. Mad. Angry." Julia shook her balled fists back and forth and squeezed her eyes tight. "For leaving. For abandoning me, like Cat Montgomery did."

"Cat Montgomery?" Nona spoke under her breath, repeating Julia's words and wondering why she would call their mother by that name.

"I don't think I ever got over her leaving. Even now." Julia hung her head. "It was why I treated you the way I did. Tried to be your mother. But it just made me seem . . . mean. I know that now. It took me years to figure it out. Doing things the wrong way, to learn what was right. To parse out what was wrong with me.

"I was grieving, and I took it out on you." Julia laid her hands on the table facedown and slid them toward Nona. "Can you forgive me for that? Make amends for those bad times?" Julia drew in a shaky breath. "You know how children suffer when they lose a parent, right? And I know you were younger than me, but it had to have hurt you, too, right? For her to leave us and we never see or hear from her again." Julia drew in a sharp breath. "I don't know. Maybe she's dead, too."

Even though it had been her plan, even with all her might, Nona couldn't not respond to that. It was what else Julia said that caught her attention. "You've never heard from Mom?"

"No! Of course not," Julia said, and with that Nona felt something inside her loosen. "She didn't care about us," Julia continued. "She evidently still doesn't, if she's still out there somewhere, breathing. And back then, I blamed you for her leaving."

"Me?"

"Yes. You. You encouraged her to take an 'adventure'"—Julia used air quotes—"after Daddy went to Vidalia, the law chasing after him. But it wasn't you. I know that now. I've known it for a long time. It was her. She didn't want us, and I shouldn't have blamed you for that. I just got stuck."

Nona squinted, and her words were hesitant. "So is that why you drifted apart from me?"

"Yes. It is. And I am sorry." Julia closed her eyes and again made tight fists. "So, so, so sorry. I took my anger"—opening her eyes back up, she shook her head and swallowed hard—"my hurt about losing out on you. And then you left." Julia turned and stared out the window.

Nona noticed how Julia was wringing her hands and how her bottom lip trembled. Unlike Nona but much like their mother, Cat, Julia was prone to crying.

"And then I lost you, too, and I didn't have anyone to help me through all the bad times I went through. I just waded through the muck and mire for the longest time . . ."

A tear rolled down Julia's cheek.

"All the pain." Julia's words came out barely audible. "No one to tell me it would be okay." Julia turned back and looked at her sister. "No sister to help me." She swiped away the tear. "It seemed like I had no one. No one to love me." Julia tugged on her bottom lip with her teeth.

"Now I've lost my mother *and* my father. Forever. And I don't want to lose you. Not again. It's been too long. It hurts too much."

"I'm here now," Nona said, feeling a burst of sympathy for her sister. Even the anger Nona still needed to hold on to felt small and inconsequential. It wasn't enough that it stopped the pain that Julia felt from seeping into Nona's heart.

"Yes, you are." More tears popped out of Julia's eyes, but they came with a smile. "Here, but not even telling me you're here. Where are you even staying?"

"Last night I stayed with Mamaw."

"You did?" Julia swiped at her tears. "Well, that old lady didn't say a thing about it to me. And how did Ruben know?"

"He was at Mamaw's when I got there."

"Hmph." Julia shook her head. "Those two have been conspiring for years. Don't know what they've got cooking, but they should have learned their lesson by now." Julia grinned at her sister. "But you can stay with me. I've got much better accommodations than those half beds in our old room." Pride showed in her eyes. "My house is on Linton Avenue."

"Actually," Nona said, "I slept on Mamaw's couch."

"Oh no!" Julia laughed.

"But I've checked into a hotel now." Nona paused, wondering if she wanted to share where she was staying with her sister. Even with the emotion of Julia's words, Nona didn't plan on giving in. Giving up on the hurt she'd carried for the past two decades. And the new hurt Nona had discovered. But she wasn't going to be rude to her sister either. "The Natchez Grand Hotel." At that moment, she saw no reason not to share that information with her.

"Yes. I've heard," Julia said. "I wouldn't think you'd like a place like that." Julia shrugged and waved a hand. "But what do I know. You've been gone so long, I'm sure you've changed so much."

According to Ruby, Nona thought, *those changes hadn't been for the better.*

"Nona," Julia said, her voice quiet, her words not so rushed. "Why didn't you ever come back?"

Nona's plan hadn't ever been to go to Chicago and stay. It was just to get married and spend her and Marcus' honeymoon there. She had wanted to be in Natchez with Marcus. To raise her family there. She'd only gotten the full scholarship and the college acceptance when things had fallen through. School in Chicago, after she'd met Marcus, had no longer been a path she'd even wanted to consider.

It was only after she arrived and started working on a degree that she learned of the history of the Devil's Punchbowl and wanted to make what she found out known. And she knew she wouldn't be able to do it there, not in Natchez. The memory of the foolishness and gullibility of her six-year-old self wouldn't let her.

"I thought you'd come back," Julia said.

And with those words, all kinds of things popped up in Nona's head. She wanted to lean in toward Julia, reach across the table, and shake her. To tell her sister that she hadn't come back because Julia had betrayed her. To tell Julia she knew she had been the one to tell their father about her plans to leave. Everything Nona had been holding inside all the years she'd been gone, she wanted to spew all over Julia.

But something more heartbreaking loomed over her and was evident in the answer she gave.

"It's a good thing I didn't."

Julia sat up. "What does that mean?"

"Like you don't know."

But before Julia could ruminate on what Nona meant, she told her. "I met your son. And his father."

And that same uneasiness Julia had felt when she first approached her sister came back. Luckily for her, so did Nona's waitress with Nona's lunch in hand. The waitress busied herself placing the food on the table and asking if Nona wanted hot sauce or vinegar for her greens, and Julia took that opportunity to leave. She didn't want to face any more of the things she'd done. And she didn't have the words to explain at that moment what had gone on between her and Marcus.

Julia had mumbled a goodbye, she was almost certain, although she wasn't certain that Nona had heard it.

Julia hadn't wanted Nona to find out about Jayden from someone else. But if Julia was completely honest with herself, she hadn't even thought about actually telling Nona about it at all. Out of fear. Out of remorse. Because she had broken the "sister code." Would Nona understand the choices Julia had made? Julia couldn't be sure, because sometimes she looked back at those choices and couldn't understand why she'd made them herself.

And had that been where Marcus and Jayden were earlier when Julia couldn't find them? With Nona?

She'd wanted to find her sister to make amends for the bad times they'd had after Cat Montgomery left, she knew that as soon as she got wind of Nona being in town. And while Julia never thought Nona wouldn't find out about her son, she never thought she'd have to face Nona knowing what happened after she left so soon. At least not on their first encounter. But it was only stupidity on her part, Julia realized, that made her think she wouldn't have to face any of the things she'd done the next time she had to face her sister.

Julia got in her car and turned the ignition. She drove around for a bit, not sure where to go. She ended up at the same mall she'd been earlier, when she first learned that Nona was home. But she couldn't bring herself to go in. She decided to go home.

Julia, over the years, had learned to be strong. Resilient. She'd been able to overcome every tribulation. And there had been many. But wasn't that what life was about? Rebounding. Moving forward. But she didn't want to move forward from this point, she knew for sure, without her sister in her life. Just the sight of Nona had filled her heart with love and joy.

Julia decided she'd wear the black suit she had in her closet to the wake, she didn't have time to shop. Because, she had also decided, she needed to figure out a way to apologize to her sister. Again. This time about something that was unforgivable.

CHAPTER FIFTEEN

Nona decided she couldn't ride in the family car provided by the funeral home. Not with Julia. At least not yet.

Nona had picked over the food she had ordered after Julia left. There hadn't been anything wrong with her food. She'd just lost her appetite and had her waitress put everything in a doggie bag.

There were so many mixed emotions coursing through Nona's veins and into her heart and the gray matter of her mind. Grief for her sister's hardships, her struggles, and a relief to know Julia had worked to overcome all her misery. But the disgust Nona had harbored hadn't been eroded with Julia's words or the telling of her past predicaments. How, Nona wondered, could she feel so much love and commiseration for Julia and so much resentment and hurt at the same time?

Driving back to the hotel, she thought about the anger that had festered over the years and how she felt it had multiplied when she had learned about Jayden. But Nona couldn't help but see the pain Julia had carried around because of the absence of family—her mother and sister—in her life. And without even giving it a second thought, Nona's heart went out to Julia.

Their mother dead . . .

Nona sucked her tongue and shook her head. How could Julia not know? Their mother was alive and well, a loving parent and a part of her children's life—well, evidently at least one of them. But Nona couldn't tell Julia that. It wouldn't serve any purpose other than to make Julia feel more isolated. Forsaken. Left out. But she didn't want Julia not to know either.

And how could Nona and their mother's absence have had such a big effect on Julia, at least one that she'd held on to for so long? It was common when they were coming up that a parent would leave. Die. Divorce. Escape. Lots of kids they'd known had been raised by grandparents, even, especially grandmothers. Nona remembered an old woman who lived down the street from them whose daughter-in-law had dropped her five-month-old baby off, saying she was going to the store to get milk, and didn't return for ten years. That kid grew up fine.

Well, as far as Nona knew.

But Nona did know how important family was. How the lack of it can change a person. How, in an almost laughable irony, it had changed her, too.

Maybe, Nona thought, she should be more understanding and sympathetic to Julia. Needing family—*maybe everyone needs their family*—was the reason she'd kept some of hers close by. The ones she could trust.

Even though she'd left them when they were young girls, Cat was one of those family members Nona did trust. Nona hadn't felt the same way about Cat's absence as Julia evidently had. She hadn't felt abandoned—well, not until she discovered Julia, their father, and Marcus had left her out to dry. But never by Cat.

Nona didn't speak with her mother every week, like she did her grandmother. And they weren't as close as, say, Eli was with his parents—taking vacations together, calling just to chat, or sending cards and notes through the mail. Nona hadn't often gone to her for advice, and, even though the distance between them short, they hadn't spent many Sunday dinners together. But that was more on Nona than on

Cat. Cat was always there for her. It was that Nona was distant. It was just who she'd become.

Nona just wasn't one to be around people. That had made Eli the perfect companion for her because he was often off on assignment. She was left alone with her books and her writings. Able to think of all the things she wanted to do. Plan how to get them done, even though she was quite aware she didn't have the stamina for such endeavors.

That was another thing missing in her and Cat's relationship as of late—spending time together. And now when they did spend time together, Nona didn't share much of her life with Cat. Again, on Nona. She didn't want anyone else to see the frustration she carried with not fulfilling what she thought she was meant to do. Nona's mother knew where she worked but not her dreams. Cat knew and had met Eli on several occasions but didn't know how Nona relied on him. How he was a crutch for her inadequacies.

But Nona had a mother. Living. Present. Everyone Nona knew, knew that. Everyone but Julia.

And even more than that, how could Nona not know that their mother's leaving had caused Julia so much pain? It hadn't caused Nona as much. But with Julia's words today, about trying to take Cat's place, to be the mother who'd left, maybe Nona never had that same void.

Cat Montgomery.

That was what Julia had called her. She had used Cat's maiden name. Cat wasn't a Montgomery anymore, and she didn't use Jasper's name either. She had adopted Hawthorne, her friend Willie's last name, dumping Davenport soon after she arrived up north. But Julia wouldn't even give her that.

It had been happenstance that the two of them met up. The powers of the universe, Cat had said, tears in her eyes, had brought them together.

Cat, a nurse at St. Luke's, a hospital some thirty minutes away, had helped to create, plan, and then volunteer at a health fair at the college

Nona attended. Cat had made the initial contact and took a lead role in the one-day event, including forwarding a list of students who had visited St. Luke's for medical treatment and might like to be a part of it. Nona hadn't ever visited the hospital, but her name did appear, though Nona hadn't given that a second thought. Something, if it had ever crossed her mind, she'd thought she was required to do—volunteer—as part of her scholarship requirements. The list was sent to one of the co-sponsors of the event, the university's Black Student Union, and per Nona's email of invitation, that had been who tapped Nona to volunteer.

Nona hadn't joined any of the college's organizations and worried more about which classes to take. She'd declared her major in history but wanted a concentration in African American Studies, which the school, at the time, didn't offer. But one school counselor told her she could frame the major herself through classes they did offer and independent study courses.

She'd been surprised when asked to participate in the health fair. The only thing she had to offer was good grades and showing up to class prepared and on time. Her only standout feature. Surely that had been the criteria for them asking her to work, because it couldn't have been based on her outgoing personality. That trait of hers had long been buried.

Nona had gone to the orientation meeting only with the plan to decline the invitation, then quietly duck out. She'd cite her course load and the narrow path she'd tread to carve a major out of a curriculum that didn't exist if asked for a reason.

But they'd seen each other at nearly the same time. Cat recognizing her, she'd later tell Nona, and heading over to her just a few seconds before Nona looked up to see her. It was the story that Cat had recounted with Nona a few times—how astonished she'd been to find her there and how it had been an answered prayer. Their both taking part in the event was meant to be.

And then Nona knew that it wasn't by chance she'd been picked to help out at the health fair, although Cat never knew she'd figured it out. That Cat had had her name added to the list. And Nona had never figured out how Cat knew where she was. But that hadn't mattered. She was elated to see her mother. Missing her more than she'd realized, she was eager to reconnect. Comforted. Satisfied.

Afterward, they had formed a friendship, not a mother–daughter relationship with advice given and memories of a life together shared, but one of respect and admiration. Still, over the years they had become close and found that the love they shared had never died.

They didn't talk about the people back in Natchez. They both had run away from there to start a new life. And while Cat had asked after Julia initially, it soon became moot to question Nona about how Julia was doing. Nona didn't speak of her and had told Cat she didn't care to know how Julia was.

But now Nona realized she was going to have to talk to Cat about Julia.

Nona got back to the hotel, put her plastic bag of food and her purse on the dresser, and called Ruby. She asked if he would come and pick her up for the wake that evening.

"To take you to your grandmother's house?" he had asked.

"No," she had told him. "To the funeral home."

He had agreed without any inquiry and added he had something to ask her.

"What?" she had asked.

"I'll tell you when I pick you up," was all Ruby would say.

"Tell me now," she said. She needed something to ease her mood.

"Well," he said. "I was thinking that on Sunday morning we could drive over to Jackson."

"Mississippi?"

"Yes. You been gone that long that you don't remember that that's our capital."

"What are we going to Jackson for?"

"I went to law school there, you know."

"No. I didn't know," Nona said, feeling puckish. "Is that what you want me to see, your law school?"

"No. There's a Freedom Trail there. They have markers that designate places pivotal to the Civil Rights Movement."

"Oh, like the ones you showed me at the Forks of the Road."

"Yeah. But what I really wanted to show you . . . what I thought about after you told me you wanted to get a research grant . . ." Ruby was excited about what he wanted to share with Nona. "I wanted to take you to the civil rights museum."

"What's there?"

"They have an oral history room."

"A what?"

"Tapings of blacks from post-slavery through the 1970s."

"An oral history." Nona understood what he was saying. Blacks telling their own story. The documented history she taught about. What she wanted to write about.

"It's in its infancy. They really haven't done anything but collected the histories before the money ran out on their grant."

"So how are we supposed to view or even hear it, then?"

"I know a guy who knows a guy."

"You know a guy?" There was levity in Nona's voice.

"I told you, I went to law school there."

"I would love to go," Nona said.

After she hung up with Ruby, Nona mindlessly ironed one of the black dresses she'd packed to wear. It had been in the suitcase since she had arrived and was filled with wrinkles. She took another shower, this one not as long, not as cathartic. She got dressed, slipped on her four-inch black heels, and sat on the side of the bed. Holding her cell phone in her hand, she stared at the screen.

She had an hour or so before Ruby was going to pick her up.

Planning an outing with Ruby, especially one to see things she was passionate about, had helped her mood, but it hadn't cleared it. Nona thought about lying down, taking a nap. Perhaps that would help. Only she didn't want to mess up her newly pressed dress. She had considered taking it off but knew that would take more energy than she cared to expend.

She also considered that perhaps the reason she didn't nap was because she needed to be awake to figure out what to do about Julia and Cat.

CHAPTER SIXTEEN

Ruby and Nona pulled into the parking lot of the funeral home at the same time as the limousine. After they'd parked, Nona opened her door and swung her feet outside of the car. But she didn't get out. She stayed seated and watched as Opal, Julia, and Jayden piled out of the long black Cadillac.

The same gray clouds that had burst earlier with rain had returned. They hung low and made the evening dark and dreary.

Julia emerged first from the car. She looked nice in her black suit, Nona thought. The slim skirt hugged her hips and the bolero-style jacket showed her slim waistline. It had white stitching around the collar and down the front and a ruffle at the bottom of the sleeve.

Nona could see from where she sat that Julia had been crying. Her eyes were swollen and, like her face, red. She held a crumpled tissue in her hand.

And that broke Nona's heart.

Jayden came out next. Wearing black pants and a white shirt, he tugged at the tie as if it gave him discomfort. His face, like his mother's, showed the strain Jasper's death had caused. Nona wondered what kind of relationship the two had had. Those thoughts, along with watching her sister wrap an arm around her son's, caused Nona's heartbeat to stumble.

Ruby, leaving Nona where she was, sprinted over to the car just as Opal's leg emerged. Ruby held out a hand, an offer to help her out. Opal, in a pale-pink raw silk dress, graciously took his hand. She stood outside the car, calm and composed.

All out, the three, as if it had been rehearsed, turned to Nona and waited. Nona took heed of the unspoken call, got out of the car, and joined her family.

Family.

That word made her proud. It gave her strength.

Among tears and smiles and the heavy scent of fragrant roses and sweet lilies, people mingled, offering condolences and memories, a dance coordinating with the organ music piped from the speakers on the walls. Lining up to greet the four of them as they sat at the front, sentinel to that bronze casket where Jasper was contained.

A tidal wave of people came through. Kissing, hugging. Holding hands. Nona had no idea that so many people knew her father.

Most who came by remembered Peaches, although Nona only could recall the faces of a handful. At one point, Nona, who sat to the left of her grandmother, had to place a hand on Opal's arm to tell her that it was fine for the people who stopped by to give their condolences to call her Peaches. Opal was admonishing everyone.

"I thought you don't go by that name anymore." Opal squinted at Nona. She didn't like people making her out to be a liar.

"I don't, but it's okay not to tell everyone that." Nona leaned in closer to her grandmother. "At least not here. Not now."

"They need to know," Opal insisted. "So they don't be calling you by the wrong name."

Nona lowered her voice. "I don't mind them calling me Peaches."

Opal made a clucking sound. "You need to make up your mind."

Nona hadn't fully made up her mind about being upset or not with her grandmother for not telling her the goings-on at home in their weekly conversations. But whatever her thoughts, she'd never be disrespectful.

"Sorry." Nona leaned into her grandmother and said, "It just feels right. You know. Since I'm back home."

Ruby was always close at hand during the evening, as was Ann May, the funeral home director, whom Nona remembered from high school. She had tissues that appeared when tears came and fans for those who were hot. And then there was Raymond Donaldson. She hadn't known him, not that she could remember, but like the others in attendance, he knew her. Walked right up to Nona and told her his name, telling her he worked for the funeral home and, he emphasized, was a friend of her sister's. Nona might not have paid any more attention to him after his introduction, but she had noticed all evening that he kept an eye—both eyes, actually—on Julia more than he did the happenings going on around him. Julia, on the other hand, was keeping her eye on the door.

Nona followed Julia's gaze and wondered whose arrival her sister was anticipating. Nona supposed it was Marcus. She wasn't sure how she felt about that, but the fluttering in her stomach should have given her some indication.

People came and went, some sat for a while. And then appearing at that door Julia had been watching, about half an hour before the wake was to end, was Marcus Curtis.

Julia noticed him first when he arrived. Standing at the wide doorway to the chapel room where Jasper's wake was taking place.

Nona didn't notice him until he walked up to the casket. She held her breath, it seemed, the whole time he was there. He turned, eyed her, then let his eyes scan the first row. Nona knew that, like all the others in attendance had, he was going to come over to speak to the family.

That made her nervous.

Fortunately for Nona, before he stepped more than a few feet from the casket, people came up to speak to him. Circling him. It gave Nona time to get away.

"I have to go to the restroom," Nona whispered as she leaned toward her grandmother.

"You can't wait?" Opal asked.

"Mamaw," Nona said and patted her hand, "I'll be back."

Although she'd said it, Nona had no intention of returning. She would hide out in a stall until the wake was over, clear of Marcus, and then scramble as quickly as she could under the cover of the throng of people leaving, right into the safety of Ruby's car.

On her way out of the chapel room, Nona had to go through the foyer where the front entrance was located. As she walked by, out the corner of her eye, she saw Sanganette come in the door. Their eyes met, and there was no denying Nona had heard Sanganette when she called out "Peaches" and waved a hand to get her attention, although Nona acted as if she didn't. She didn't have time for small talk. Or time for more lies.

Nona made it into the small restroom, shut the door, and searched for a lock. There wasn't one. Hearing rumblings outside the door, she went inside a stall. Locking the door, she let out a breath. But that calm hadn't lasted long.

"Why do you keep running away from me?"

It was Marcus. Standing outside the stall Nona was seated in. Nona clutched her chest, not sure if she could speak. Or even what she should say.

"You still not talking either?" he asked.

"This is the ladies' room," Nona said, her voice shaky.

"And I'm looking for a lady. You seen her? Her name is Peaches."

Nona didn't answer.

"Or is it Nona that she goes by now?" Marcus emphasized her name, making his voice go up.

"What do you want, Marcus?"

"You."

Nona held her breath.

"To talk to you."

"I don't have anything to say to you."

"You don't have to talk back."

"I'm at my father's wake. This is not the right place, and I don't have the time. Not for you."

"You been in here fifteen minutes. I'm thinking you must have had enough of that wake."

"Can you please go away?" Her hands shaking, she worried her voice was, too.

He blew out a breath, placed the palm of his hand on the stall door, and, leaning into it, said, "Okay."

Nona waited until she heard other people coming into the small bathroom and figured the wake must be over. She needed to make her way out and hope Ruby wouldn't be hard to find so she could get into the car. Then she remembered that perhaps the door to the car wasn't locked. She had been the last one out, and Ruby had been making his way inside to help Opal.

Nona made a beeline to the car, carefully keeping her eyes trained on her destination and tuning out any disturbance around her. But as she reached out for the door handle, another hand beat her to it.

Marcus.

"Oh!" Nona jumped, startled.

"You don't have to be afraid of me." He had a smile on his face.

Nona didn't know if she should cry or laugh. "I thought you were going away." She huffed out the words.

"I did. Go away. I came back. And it didn't take me twenty years to do."

Nona groaned.

"Come on," he said and tried to clasp her hand, but she pulled away. "Come take a walk with me."

"No." He made her so nervous. She felt she wouldn't be able to concentrate, think, let alone walk if she had to do it with him. It seemed he still gave her butterflies.

"Just for a minute."

"I'm riding with Ruby. He'll be out any minute." Nona glanced toward the door of the funeral home.

"You can do whatever you want, you know."

Nona had to swallow to keep her voice from trembling. "He'll be looking for me."

"I told your grandmother I was going to bring you over to her house. And I'm sure she'll tell Ruby."

"I'm not going over there. To Mamaw's house." The thought of being with Julia and Marcus together made Nona's mouth go dry. "Why would I go over there?"

"Then I'll take you wherever you wanna go."

Nona didn't say anything. She didn't move.

"C'mon now," Marcus said. "The last time I saw you, we were getting ready to run off and get married. Isn't there anything you want to say to me?"

Nona had a lot of things to say. She was bubbling over with things to say: Why hadn't he followed her? Had he ever really loved her? And why had he chosen Julia over her?

But first she decided she wanted to hear what he had to say, so she started walking.

Marcus fell into step with her, not saying a word. And when they got to the end of the parking lot, Marcus turned to walk down the sidewalk toward Martin Luther King Jr. Street.

"Thought you wanted to talk," Nona said as they reached the corner. Lander's Bar-B-Q & Diner was across the street to her right. She could see the window seat she'd occupied earlier. Where she had been when Julia had walked in on her.

Marcus turned left, and they walked in the opposite direction. "I also said I wanted to take a walk with you."

"Where are we going?" Nona said. "These aren't walking shoes."

"Not much farther. Just down the block." Marcus looked down at her feet and chuckled. "I can carry you the rest of the way if you want."

"No, thank you."

They walked another seven or eight minutes before they stopped. "This is my place," Marcus said, pointing to the double glass doors.

Nona looked up. "The Starlight?"

"Yep."

"Didn't this used to be—"

"Yep," Marcus interrupted her. "But it's my place now."

He opened the door and gestured for her to go in.

"When did you and Julia start dating?" Nona said, not budging. She was anxious. Too edgy. She wasn't sure if she could maintain her composure around him. If she could keep up her restraint. Or if her knees were going to keep holding her up.

"Wow. Is that the first thing you wanna say to me? After all this time?"

"Might be my only question, other than where is your car parked. Because I don't want to have to walk another ten minutes to get a ride back to my hotel."

"It's parked out back." He pointed through the interior of the bar. "We can go this way to get to it."

"You're not fooling me, Marcus."

He grinned. "How about I get you something to drink." He nodded, as if trying to convince her that was what she wanted. "Take a seat at the bar," he said and went around back of it.

Nona sat down, trying to make it seem as if she were reluctant. But she was ready to have an answer to her question.

Marcus filled up a tall glass with the orange bubbly drink, placed a straw in it, and slid it in front of her. She didn't have to explain to him what kind of coke she wanted. He had remembered.

She took a sip, smacked her lips, and repeated her question. "When did you and Julia start dating?"

Marcus scrunched up his nose. "I guess I better answer that question if I want you to say anything else to me, huh?"

Nona took another sip of her drink.

"Okay. Okay," Marcus said. "We never dated. We got married because she was pregnant."

Nona blew a noisy breath through her nostrils. "Don't play with me."

"I'm not." He held out his hands. "We slept together. Once." He wanted to make a point of that. "And we never went on a date."

"You were married," Nona said, ignoring the lie about not ever dating. "You telling me you only had sex with her once?"

He grunted. "I mean before we got married." Frustration in his words. "Once *before* we got married."

"And she got pregnant?" Nona shook her head, signaling she didn't believe him. "After one time?"

"She was already pregnant."

Nona took a moment to process that and then frowned. "Jayden isn't your child?"

"Nope. I married her because I thought he was. She told me he was. I divorced her when I found out he wasn't."

"But he calls you his dad."

"I *am* his dad. I'll always be his dad."

"What about you and Julia?"

"What about me and Julia?"

"You two being in love?"

"In love?"

"Yeah, people get married because they're in love."

"I just told you, I married Julia because I thought Jayden was mine and—"

"It's not 1958, Marcus," Nona cut him off. "People don't get married because the girl gets pregnant."

"And, if you'd let me finish," he said, tension in his voice, "because Julia was in such a bad way. That's what I was going to say. That's why I married her. Not for love. I wanted the best for my son. And for that, he needed me there."

"How did you find out Jayden wasn't your son?"

"He got sick. When he was just about a year old. He was going to have to have surgery, and I went to donate blood. To have just in case."

"And?"

"And my blood type couldn't have produced him. At least that's what they told me. So I asked Julia."

"And she told you she'd lied?"

"No. She told me the hospital did."

"Oh my." Engrossed in it all, Nona was unable to know how she felt about what she was hearing.

"I know, right? But I told her it didn't matter. Jayden was always going to be my son. I hadn't lost anything."

Nona remembered the kindness and understanding that seemed to be a part of the fiber that made up Marcus Curtis, one of the things that had made her fall for him in the first place.

"I was going to be a part of his life," Marcus said, still talking. "Both of their lives. She could count on me." He shrugged. "And I guess I helped her get her life turned around." He blew out a breath. "I tried to help her."

"Because she was in a bad way?"

"Yeah. Not so much as when she first told me she was pregnant. By the time she told me all of what she'd gone through, we'd been married for a little minute." He looked out the corner of his eye to gauge Nona's reaction. "She'd gotten a lot better."

"What do you mean 'in a bad way'?"

"The guy she'd been with was bad news."

"People get into bad relationships," Nona said, only half-heartedly dismissing the premise. "*My* parents did. They move on. People continue living. They do okay. *Like* my parents did."

"People don't just move on. Your father loved your mother."

"I'm sure at some point he did."

"He loved her till the day he died."

"How would you know that?"

"Because he told me."

"I don't believe that," Nona said, shaking her head. "I don't think my mother would have left him. Moved a thousand miles. Changed her name. Not if he had still loved her."

"Changed her name?" A confused look on his face. "Why would you think she changed her name?"

Someone else who didn't know Cat was still alive. Still accessible. Still part of Nona's life.

Marcus shook his head and continued without a response. "That was one thing that was tearing Julia apart."

"Our mother leaving."

"Yep." Marcus didn't seem to notice that she hadn't posed what she'd said as a question. "That ate her up. I think she blamed herself. She was on a steady downhill course, especially after you left, too."

"I didn't do it to hurt Julia."

"Don't matter. That's how she felt," Marcus said. "She took to drinking. And crying. All the time. And got into a bad relationship with that guy."

"That guy? Meaning Jayden's father?"

"Yeah, some slick-talking white dude."

"Jayden's father is white?" All of this was a lot to take in.

"Yep."

"Does Jayden know?"

"Know what? His father is white?"

"Who his real father is?" She looked at Marcus. "And who it isn't."

"He knows. But he doesn't know anything *about* the man."

"You two haven't told him?"

Marcus shrugged. "He doesn't seem to care. He's happy with me, and I'm good with that."

Nona smiled.

"Why tell him all the hurtful things that man has done to his mother?" Marcus continued his reasoning. "It would make Jayden hate him without me or Julia ever giving Jayden the chance to make his own assessment of the man. He still is his father."

"He's that bad, huh?"

"Yep. Seemed like a decent guy at first. But man, he did a number on your sister."

"Did he hit her?" She almost feared hearing his answer. This was not the take-charge Julia she knew. But Nona understood: All the hurt had changed her, too.

He shrugged. "I don't know." His words spoken in disgust. "She said he didn't, but he may as well have. The pain she was in. The mental distress. It was equally as bad."

"And if I hadn't left"—Nona licked her lips, they had gone dry— "maybe she wouldn't have gone through that." Again Nona's words formed a statement because she remembered Julia's words from the restaurant earlier that day. How Julia had said she hadn't had a sister to help her through the hard times.

Marcus pushed his eyebrows together. "No one is saying that."

"Good. I'm glad *you're* not saying that, because there wasn't anything I could have done," Nona said.

She didn't want him to know how much she'd let things that had happened to her mold her and reshape her to the point where she was barely able to help herself. Fight for the things she wanted. Or how she had leaned into a man, something she was sure would make him rethink all the good things he had thought of her.

And at that moment, Nona letting herself lean into Eli even gave her pause. Made her think how she'd lost those good traits about her.

"You could have stayed." Marcus leaned over the top of the bar. He put his face close to hers. "You could have stayed. Here with me." Still holding on to her hand, he rubbed it back and forth with his thumb. "You not coming back nearly killed me. You hurt a lot of us by staying away."

"I didn't do it to hurt anyone," Nona said.

"We thought you'd come back."

"Who thought that?" Nona pulled back from Marcus. "No one should have thought that. How was I supposed to come back? I couldn't. Not to be around all the people who betrayed me."

Marcus stood up straight and folded his arms across his torso. "Who betrayed you?" He tilted his head to one side.

"You," Nona said. "My father. My sister."

"What are you talking about?"

"Julia told my father we were eloping, and then he came and stopped you." She bit her bottom lip to tamp down the emotions that had started to brew. "And you let him."

Marcus tilted his head to the other side. "Is that what you think happened?"

That was the same question Ruby had asked her that morning when he was driving her around. As if she was confused about things. She was there. She remembered. It wasn't what Nona *thought* had happened, it was what she *knew* happened. And she told Marcus just that. And, she added, that it might not be Jayden's father who pushed Julia and him together, her hard times, or the loss of a mother and sister. Maybe what really happened was that the two of them had planned it all along. Behind her back. To get together. That maybe Marcus never wanted to marry her in the first place. Nona voiced all the thoughts that had been banging around in her head.

Marcus came around the bar, after letting her vent her mind and sling her accusations, and sat on the stool next to her. He took her hands and stared at her until she let her eyes meet his.

"I have never loved any other woman than you. Not Julia. Not anyone. The only love Julia and I shared then was the love we had for you." He let out a moan. "And now for Jayden." Her hands started to tremble, she tried again to pull away, not wanting him to know how his words were affecting her, but he gripped them tighter. He wouldn't let go. "And I would have come for you if I'd known where you were."

"Why didn't you just come to me? Meet me that night?"

"We were so young."

"What does that mean?" Nona asked.

Marcus chuckled. "It was all your idea."

"My idea?" Nona squinted her eyes. "You didn't want to marry me?" A knot formed in her throat. One that seemed to stop the air from going to it. It made her dizzy. Lightheaded. Her stomach twisted and turned.

"Yes. I did. I didn't care that it was your idea. That's one of the things I've always loved about you. Your adventurous spirit. Your spontaneity. You have so much energy and fire."

Nona knew those were traits she didn't possess anymore. At least not on the surface. She put her head down and didn't respond to his comment.

"I thought we'd be okay," Marcus continued. "You'd not get on that bus and leave for twenty years. Then the next day when I saw you, we'd work it all out. But deep down, I guess I knew that wasn't you. Not once you set your mind to something. Wasn't no turning you around."

"It would have all worked out, just the way we planned—*I* planned it—if Julia hadn't said anything to my father about me leaving that night."

Marcus slid his hand down Nona's cheek and let his finger outline her bottom lip. "Julia and your father aren't the ones to blame." He shook his head, slightly, slowly. "There you go again." Marcus had a lopsided grin on his face. "You got it all wrong, especially the part where you think I didn't want to marry you. I still want to do that." Marcus leaned in so close, Nona thought he was going to kiss her and knew if he had, she would have fainted. Instead, he said, "It's not at all like you think."

CHAPTER SEVENTEEN

Twenty Years Ago

Jasper Davenport had lost his daughter trying to save her.

Chicago, where he'd gone to collect Nona, might have been somewhere he would have run off to as well. Tall buildings. Streets full of people. Everybody in a hurry.

And pretty women were everywhere he looked. He had a thing for a good-looking woman. *That* had been his downfall. What had brought his marriage to a screeching halt. Not the actual *doing* of it but the getting *caught* of it.

In those days, Jasper—husband, father, breadwinner—had been a janitor at the same junior high school he'd attended as a boy. He'd often say, not complaining, that he hadn't come far in life, just gone around in a circle. He didn't make much money, but he'd found a way enough times than not to bring a little extra in.

Drinking and gambling, Jasper's way of relaxing. Having a good time. Saturday nights. After work. A time to unwind. Cuss and spit. Things he couldn't do in a house filled with girls.

And nothing much beat a little Johnnie Walker Red or CC and Coke, a pair of dice or a deck of cards, a couple of buddies, and some fine, sweet-smelling women. Ones who didn't care he was married. Some of them got clingy, but he didn't have no problem shaking them off. Those things were a release, one Jasper claimed he needed, and as long as they weren't done in excess, they were something any good woman might give in to letting her man do.

That had been his reasoning, although at the time he chuckled at the thought that Cat would approve of some of the things he did with those women.

Women. In his later years, especially after that stroke had hampered his mobility and some of his thinking, he'd smile—the only thing left he could do—about the times he'd had with women. A few of those thoughts made him blush.

He was one of the ones who'd admit, after all the mistakes had already been made, that those were the kinds of things a person looks back on and knows he should have done differently. He'd gotten the prettiest girl in high school, but that just made him want more.

He hadn't wanted much of anything from other women. He'd gotten himself a good catch. Other women were just to hang out with. Something to do. Have a good time with. And what most women, Cat in particular, didn't understand was that sometimes a good time meant giving them the satisfaction they were craving.

"Why'd you do it?" his mother had asked him when he came to pick up the girls after Cat had left.

The only answer he came up with was, "Because I wanted to."

"And while you're being so flippant," Opal had told her grown son, "I hope you've learned that the things you *want* to do have consequences."

But he hadn't let it show to her, or to anyone, how much those consequences had deeply hurt. And for years, he blamed it all on Johnny Miller and that botched robbery.

Johnny Miller was the reason he'd left his family and gone to Vidalia, Louisiana, in the first place. Johnny had lost all his money gambling. But it wasn't the first time he had, and Jasper never figured out why it happening that night had made Johnny so desperate.

"C'mon, Jasper. I'm on fire tonight," Johnny Miller had said. Coming over to the bar, Johnny tried to pull Jasper away. Jasper, sitting on the stool, had his arm wrapped around a little bitty thang, dimples almost as big as Cat's but with big hips and big breasts that would put his wife's to shame. She didn't mind thrusting her goods against Jasper's sweaty body. And was eager to push her tongue inside his hot, liquor-infused mouth.

"I just need to get some more money," Johnny Miller said, standing in close to him and the girl, wanting Jasper to pay attention to what he needed.

"I'm all out," Jasper had told him. He'd pushed the woman away, Johnny's interruption making him realize it was getting late. "Time to pack up and leave."

"No, man. C'mon now. It's still early." Johnny Miller held out his hands. Pleading with him. "I know where we can make a few quick dollars."

They were in an after-hours joint in an alleyway off a dark street, even though it wasn't past closing time for any bar. Wasn't past closing time for most grocery stores. It was dark out, though, and the place had the right kind of feel. Slow, grinding music. Weed filling the air. The snap of fingers when the clink across the tile floor meant the dice had rolled someone's way.

They'd come that night in separate cars, but they took Johnny's car to that convenience store. The one on the other side of town. Where no one knew them. No cameras. Lots of money in the drawer. Nobody smart enough to know how to keep a watchful eye over the till. That was the way Johnny had explained it. "And I got this," he added, pulling a .38 snub-nose pistol from his pocket.

"I ain't up for shooting nobody so you can gamble," Jasper had told him.

"We ain't shooting nobody." Johnny stuffed the gun back in his pocket, nestled down in the seat, and smiled. "We just gone scare 'em some. Enough for them to give up the money."

The two of them soon found out the young hundred-and-five-pound, if that, girl wasn't so afraid. She found the courage to set off an alarm.

Jasper, waiting in the car, saw her face looking anxiously out that big plate-glass window long before the hazy cast of the flashing lights on top of the police car came into view. He ducked out of the car, leaving the keys in the ignition and the car running. He walked across the street, went around a corner at a pace like he was out for a Sunday afternoon stroll. He knew better than to run.

It took him two and half hours to walk the ten miles back to get his car. Not once looking over his shoulder.

He packed up that night and left, not knowing if Johnny Miller got caught and if he did, what he would say. Telling his wife only half of what he'd done, and not taking the time to kiss his girls goodbye, he got in the car and pulled out of their driveway, not knowing that night he'd lose his family. Once around the corner, he told the woman lying down in the back seat she could sit up now.

That dimpled girl from the bar he'd left pouting when he went with Johnny was all smiles now. He hadn't been unlucky that night. Unlike Johnny, Jasper had won a few rounds of bid whist. After giving Cat money to tide her over, Jasper had had plenty left in his pocket to show Dimples a good time. Plus, if he did, he thought, she might not be so keen on giving him up to the police if they came looking. She had overheard the whole plan.

It took four weeks for Johnny to get locked up but only three weeks for that dimpled girl to get knocked up. Neither one of the two ever told anybody anything about Jasper's involvement in either situation.

But somehow Cat knew.

It was probably why he never married again. Although he'd had plenty of women try to get him down that aisle. Even his boy's mama. But he wasn't doing it. Because even though he'd lost a lot because of it, he just didn't think he could change his ways. That next wife might not be able to tolerate him cheating either.

Plus, he still loved Cat.

Those were the things that played through his mind on that eight-hundred-and-fifty-five-mile drive to get his daughter and bring her back home. Chicago. She hadn't been gone long. A few weeks. But Chicago was so far and the trip so long, it made it seem that Jasper had drifted through time and had become even more distant. It had been the place half his family had taken off to. Maybe he should have gone there instead of Vidalia. Upped his family and moved north. It had been a thing. Northern migration.

Initially "She was leaving" had been all he'd heard from the conversation that had set him off on his journey. After the two conspirators' plan had backfired, they decided to tell Jasper what happened. "Eloping with Marcus. We couldn't let that happen," he'd been told.

"Where is she now?" Jasper had asked.

"Gone. That's what we trying to tell you."

"With Marcus?" He wished they'd stop *trying* to tell him and come on out with it.

"No." She'd hung her head and shook it slowly from side to side. Remorse showing in her actions. "She left without him."

"Marcus let her leave?"

"Are you listening? We stopped it. We stopped the whole thing," she said.

"Wasn't easy keeping him away," the other one chimed in.

"Yeah, I had to threaten to call the police to stop that boy. Told him I'd have him arrested for messing with a minor."

"Contributing to the delinquency of a minor."

She waved a dismissive hand. "Whatever it's called. It worked."

"Well, that and the lie you told."

"What lie?" Jasper asked.

"I told him you were already down at the bus station to pick up Nona, with a shotgun ready to shoot him dead."

"But I wasn't." Jasper's squinted eyes showed his confusion. "I wasn't there. I didn't even know." Jasper scratched his head. Nervousness filling up his body. "I'm just now knowing. Julia told me Peaches stayed the night at her friend's house."

"Well, that was a lie." She waved a hand. "Or maybe Julia just didn't know. Them girls ain't as close as they used to be." She rubbed her hands together, showing her distress. "We just never thought Nona would leave without Marcus."

"Yeah," Jasper said. "You already said that."

"We thought she'd come on back home."

"You said that, too." He chewed on the side of his tongue. "But it don't seem to be the case, do it?"

Nona had left in the middle of the night all by herself. But it took another two days before the two of them had admitted what they'd done. Holding out on an unfounded hope that Nona would act contrary to who she was. Stubborn. Independent. Determined.

And now, after driving for nearly fourteen hours and searching a whole day to find her, Jasper couldn't get her to come back. She blamed him for something he had no part in.

"You come here after you kept Marcus from coming to meet me?" was what Nona had said on seeing her father.

"Marcus wanted to come. But—"

"But you stopped him," she said, finishing Jasper's sentence. At least she spoke the words she'd thought he was going to say. Not knowing the truth then, she stood firm, her fists balled, and spat the words at him. "You've taken my life from me. All the things that made me happy."

"I don't know what you got in your head that happened, or what kinds of things you think I took from you, but we can talk about it in the car on the way home."

"I'm not going anywhere with you. This is my home."

They were standing in the gymnasium. Jasper had found the sign that said Freshman Orientation and followed the directions given to him by a nice woman with a pretty smile in the bursar's office.

"I don't much understand these things, but how is it that you can go to school here? Didn't I need to sign something? Give the okay? Were you trying to hide this from me?"

"No. I wasn't trying to hide anything. Oh my goodness, Daddy. I didn't do anything in secret. Everyone in the twelfth grade did it. What's the big deal?" Nona held up her hands. "My high school guidance counselor helped me apply to different colleges, like she did every other student. She picked most of them out. With my grades, they accepted me, no problem. They were happy to have me. Gave me a scholarship." She felt her hands clench and thought she might cry. "A full ride. I hadn't planned on coming, but thank goodness I never told them I wasn't. I'd let them know before the deadline." She lowered her head to try to gain her strength. "So there was a spot for me." She lifted her head, now filled with defiance. "*They* want me here."

"I want you, too. At home. With me and Julia."

"I won't go."

"You can't stay here," Jasper said. "Not all by yourself." He swallowed hard and licked his dry lips.

"I will leave here if you try to stop me," Nona said, not knowing how she'd do it or where she'd go. But she had to make him understand. He had done a wrong to her that was, in her young eyes, irreparable.

Jasper almost expected her to stomp her foot like she did when she was younger, insisting on getting her way. But somehow he knew that this was something more.

"If you or anyone," she emphasized, "tries to stop me. And you'll never find me."

It hadn't been easy to find her this time. Chicago was a big city and could easily swallow up a young girl. But he had found her. With Julia's help, who was beside herself after Nona had gone without Marcus, he'd found the acceptance letter Nona had in her room along with several others. The only letter for a school out of town, she'd gotten into a college there. Summer school, extra classes, and extracurricular studies, it seemed, had put her in the top of her class. Jasper had always been proud of how smart his girl was, but now she had used it against him. To get away from him.

But if she left again, like she threatened, he wouldn't have any clues to follow. So, he promised her he wouldn't come back to try and find her. And he promised himself he wouldn't tell anyone else where she was either. No one else except for one person.

Jasper knew why she'd chosen Chicago. It had been the place Cat had gone when she left him. And now, after Nona refused to come back to Natchez with him, he needed to go and find Cat.

And even until the day he died, Jasper never could figure out why his mother and Ruben Gautier did what they'd done. Why they decided to stop Marcus from going to meet Nona that night. Why they thought they could devise a scheme that would keep Nona from leaving Natchez, even if it meant going it alone. And Jasper didn't ever get a grasp on how the two of them, knowing Nona as well as they did, could think they could do anything to stop Nona from doing something once she set her mind to it.

Cat had wanted to divorce him, only he wouldn't have it.

At first it was getting service of the divorce papers on Jasper. The judge said he had to be notified about the court proceedings.

"You just can't divorce somebody without letting them know," he'd said, sitting high behind his bench.

But before she could have the papers served on him, Jasper had a lawyer call her and say that unless she dismissed the proceedings, she would never, he promised, see the girls again. In any kind of official proceedings she initiated, they would be sure to let the judge know she had abandoned those girls.

But she hadn't. And Jasper knew it.

Once he found out she'd left, he had called her over and over again. Saying he was sorry. Begging her to come back home. Back to him. Back to the girls. That he'd forgiven her for running off with Willie Hawthorne. That he would change.

But him changing wasn't going to change the fact that he had a son on the way.

And Cat leaving with Willie didn't even come close to that. She hadn't cared for Willie, not back in high school, not then. Not now. Not the way she cared for Jasper. She and Willie had only ever been friends. A friend who helped her when her life started to fall apart. He had come to save her.

It had been serendipity. Willie was leaving for a job in Chicago at the same time she needed to get away. Once there, he allowed her to use him and his name on an application for a lease for her first apartment. The one that would have enough room where she could bring her girls. And even though that never happened, she kept Willie's friendship and his last name. But never anything more than that.

Jasper getting another woman pregnant had changed everything. He'd done unalterable damage to his family while they waited at home for him. Worrying if he was safe. If he was okay. And if his freedom was in jeopardy. That had been too much for Cat to take. Too much to forgive.

Jasper had broken Cat's heart.

And all she could think to do was to leave. Leave Jasper. Leave Natchez. But never had it entered her thoughts that she was leaving her girls.

She'd left them with Opal only until she could get settled. But the anger and hurt Cat felt against her husband, Jasper took and turned it around and, along with spite, took it out on her. Punishing her for not wanting to live with a man who went out and made a child with another woman while he was married to her.

Back then, the only job she'd been able to get was one that barely paid enough for her to afford her living expenses, let alone enough to fight Jasper in court. Over the years, starting off as an aide in a hospital, Cat took advantage of her employer's education program and studied to become a registered nurse. A few years after she arrived, she'd left Chicago and moved to Indiana.

Cat sent letters to her daughters, some returned unopened, some not, but her gut told her they hadn't seen those either. Cat later found that those letters had been a way for Jasper to keep up with where she was. And that was how he'd shown up on her doorstep some ten years after she'd left to ask her to keep an eye on Nona.

In order to be a part of Nona's life, he made Cat promise two things. One, that she'd never let Nona know he had been the one who asked her to do it. Cat would have to make it seem that she had just happened upon Nona. And two, she would never try to contact Julia. She would never have both of her girls back. Giving up Julia all over again broke her heart, but it was better than not having her girls at all.

Jasper didn't have to ask her twice.

"I promise," she said. Hoping the shame she'd felt for leaving and for letting Jasper stop her from seeing her girls even after they were grown (because then the fear of their rejection clouded her mind), wouldn't be something Nona would easily notice.

CHAPTER EIGHTEEN

Nona had been wrong. For twenty years. She had had everything mixed up. Marcus had filled in the truth to all the bits and pieces of her past that she had assumed. A past she'd thought had been taken away, only now it seemed it was one she had freely given away.

She'd gone back to her hotel room, turned on the shower, the sink, the television and, pumping up the volume to a satellite radio station on her phone to drown out the noise, she screamed. She just opened her mouth and let it out. For as long as she could hold it, as loud as she could do it. Then she did it again and again and again.

It was the first time in her life that Nona could remember that she thought she might cry. To let everything out and release all the feelings she'd been holding back. The ones she had burrowed inside.

She fell across the bed. Exhausted but not purged, only to have to drag herself up to shut off the things she'd turned on to reduce the noises she had in her head.

She'd left a whole life behind—family, love, and herself—all on account of something that never happened.

And now she would have to deal with the truths and the aftermath of it all. Nona had contemplated, more than a time or two, that she *could* have done things differently because maybe, just maybe, she would have turned out differently. Now she was sure she *should* have.

Marcus had told her everything *he* knew. But unknown to the two of them, he hadn't been privy to all that had happened. Marcus Curtis never knew the part about Jasper visiting Cat after his last time seeing Nona. Telling her to look out for their daughter. No one knew about that but Cat and Jasper. And Jasper had taken that secret to his grave.

⌐

"I know what you did."

A secret that was no longer hidden.

Nona looked over the top of her large round sunglasses at Ruby, who stood in front of her. They were at Opal's house. In that crumbling driveway that, it seemed, was in the same state as the friendship between the two of them. At least in Nona's eyes.

Nona had had a fitful night—tossing and turning, throwing the covers off to stop the heat surging through her body. Vivid images casting in her head, sometimes she didn't know if she was asleep or not. And then there was her heartbeat—she couldn't stop it from thumping in her ears.

Nona had had a dream that she was in a colorful garden, all dressed in white, waiting for someone. And when it was Eli who showed up, she'd woken up with a start, jerking into an upright position. That dream had been what started her heart to racing.

The next dream was about Julia. They were walking in what seemed to be the same garden Nona had been in in the dream right before. The two of them were holding hands.

Nona had given up on trying to get some solid sleep way before the sun had come up. She ordered breakfast—scrambled eggs, bacon, pancakes, a bowl of fruit, orange juice, and coffee. It was as if she couldn't decide and didn't possess the strength needed to make up her mind.

She had gotten dressed, putting on a charcoal-gray skirt and a short-sleeved sweater set. Her usual fare at home, but today it just didn't seem to fit her right. She tugged on the bottom of the inside sweater and fluffed it, pulled on the cardigan—buttoned and unbuttoned it.

She changed into a dress. The one she'd actually bought for the funeral.

Then she unzipped a cosmetic case where she kept, wrapped in facial tissue, a necklace Cat had given her when Nona had graduated from college.

It made her feel more comfortable.

After dressing and eating, she sat on the side of the bed, as she'd done the night before when she was waiting for Ruby. But that morning was so different. She felt restless and out of sorts.

No one was coming to pick her up. Even with all the upside-down feelings she had, there was one thing she knew for sure she wanted to do.

She was going to drive to her grandmother's to wait for the limo. Even though she was still mad—upset—or whatever those feelings were simmering inside of her, she was going to ride in it with her family to the funeral.

Yes. It was different than the night before at the wake when Nona hadn't cared to ride in the car with Julia. To even be near her. But today, things were different. She was different. Nona had a clearer picture of what had transpired at the time she left and the twenty years that followed. It was just like she taught her students: know your history because then you'll know yourself. It is freeing. And it stops you from making the same mistakes again.

And Nona had Marcus to thank for that.

He told Nona how it hadn't been Julia who'd spilled the beans but Sanganette. She had overheard Nona's plans when she'd come back to return Julia's sweater. Sanganette had told her brother, Ruby. And Ruby had told Nona's grandmother, Opal. And then the two of them had cooked up a scheme to stop the whole affair.

And then Marcus told Nona how Jasper hadn't known anything about the elopement that night, because, as Marcus explained, Julia had kept her promise and never said a word. Marcus made clear to Nona how he tried to go with Jasper when he'd driven up north to get her and bring her back, but Jasper wouldn't let him. And how Jasper, on his return, had told Marcus that he hadn't been able to find Nona.

"But he did find me," Nona had said.

"Yeah, but you told him if he told anyone else where you were, you would leave, and he would never be able to find you again."

Nona had blown out a breath. That had been exactly what she'd said.

"Jasper only told me the truth much later."

Nona covered her face with her hands. "I never meant you. If *you* came," Nona had said. "I wanted you to come."

Nona didn't go to Julia after her talk with Marcus. She thought about calling her and realized she didn't have Julia's phone number. It had come up on her dashboard when Julia had called to tell Nona their father was dead, but Nona hadn't kept it. Plus, Nona wasn't sure if she was ready to face her. Going against everything Nona believed in. Everything she taught to others about righting the wrongs of the past and telling the truth. Julia hadn't ever divulged her secret. Nona had blamed Julia all these years for nothing. But in the interim . . .

Had Julia done something worse than what Nona had always accused her of?

Could Nona forgive Julia for marrying Marcus? Tricking him. *Should she?*

Nona still needed time to process all the things he'd told her. All the missteps she'd taken that had given all of them this outcome. That had turned Nona inside out. That had led Julia to where she was. And she needed to process how to deal with Ruby and Opal.

Marcus had driven Nona back to the hotel. Nona hadn't talked much on the ride there, just the conversation they'd had had worn her out. Marcus hadn't left from the circular driveway by the time Nona made it to the elevator. She wondered, but only fleetingly, how long he'd waited before pulling off.

After the temper tantrum Nona had after she'd gotten to her room, she had kicked her shoes off, pulled her dress over her head, and ran a steamy, hot bath. Sliding into it, she leaned back and tried to clear her head. When the water cooled, she stepped out, dried off, and climbed into bed. It didn't take Nona as long as she would have thought to doze off, her mind swirling. But it took hardly any thought at all for her to realize, when she woke up on the morning of Jasper's funeral, she needed to be with her family as they said farewell to her father.

Ruby, not riding in the family car with them, had shown up to Opal's house anyway. Nona, just getting out of the car when Ruby pulled up, was tugging on the snug-fitting dress she'd bought for the funeral, wishing she'd tried it on instead of going by the size tag inside.

She had been happy that she'd packed low-heeled pumps, which she decided to wear. Best for the cemetery, she thought, and in case she was to take any more long walks.

"You look nice," Ruby said.

"Don't change the subject." She grabbed the black floppy hat off the car seat she planned to wear at the funeral and pushed the sunglasses up on her nose.

Ruby had caught up with her before she'd gotten into the house. All smiles, he was unaware what Nona had found out from Marcus. But she hadn't let his ignorance continue for long.

With a smirk on his face, and not a hint of contrition, he held up his hands after she, as her grandmother would say, had blessed him out. "I've already done my time," he said.

"What are you talking about, Ruby?" Nona's voice taut. She looked at him out of the corner of her eye. "Because you should have a lot to say for yourself."

He shook his head, a chuckle from the back of his throat barely audible. "You were mad at Julia the entire time you were away because you *thought* she was the one who told your father you were leaving with Marcus."

"And."

"You punished her."

"I did not *punish* her."

"You did." He nodded. Like a bobblehead. "You didn't speak to her. You didn't contact her. You punished her."

"What are you getting at?"

"Even though you didn't know I was the one who had told, you haven't spoken to me in twenty years *either*. You didn't contact *me* for twenty years."

Nona tilted her head and looked at him.

"I've served my time. Right along with Julia. You've already punished me."

Nona opened her mouth to speak, but Ruby cut her off.

"Without knowing I was the guilty party, you gave me the same sentence as Julia. So, I would think if Julia is getting paroled, then so should I." He looked into her eyes. "And for what it's worth, I'm sorry."

"Answer this first," Nona said. "Why did you tell on me? How did you even find out?"

"I told on you because I was scared for you."

"Scared? That something would happen to me? I would have been with Marcus." She held her arms out, palms facing forward. "But even without him, you can see I am fine."

"I didn't know that then. We were young, and . . ."

"And what?"

"I wasn't just scared for you."

"Then what?"

"It was for me, too. I was scared for *me*." There was nervousness in his voice. She could tell that even now he was still scared. "That you'd love someone else for the rest of our lives. That you'd forget about me. That I wouldn't have you here with me. With me."

"What are you saying, Ruby? You did that to me because you thought you wouldn't have me? You never had me."

"You asked me what I was scared of," Ruby said. "And I've told you. And again, I'm sorry."

"Well, I'm not sure I am willing to accept that apology." She made her lips tight and drew in a sharp breath. "Or let you off the hook, especially since I've never said I was letting Julia off, as you say."

"You're here, aren't you?" he said. "Coming to ride with your family in that long black Cadillac. You must be feeling some forgiveness."

Nona didn't know that his apology was worth anything. But she also didn't know how she could blame anyone else for what happened.

It had been her doing.

Her grandmother had been right. She made the decision to leave. She made the decision not to come back and not to reach out or speak to anyone. All based on wrong information. And wasn't that what Nona had based her life's work on—getting things right?

She'd wanted to talk to Julia. To tell Julia how she, too, had blamed her for something—made a decision based on it—that was a fallacy and because of it had pushed Julia away. But then there still was the fact that Julia had married Marcus. Even if Jayden wasn't his child, it was tactless and offensive.

"Peaches!" Miss Gus called from next door before Nona could get up on Opal's porch. She waved a key she had in her hand at her. "I need you to give this to your Mamaw."

Nona glanced over at Miss Gus, on her porch as usual. This time standing at the banister like she'd just come out of the house. As if she'd been waiting on Nona to get there. So she could distract her. Because although Nona was planning to ride with her family and make a go of reconciliation as much as she could, she still had a thing or two to say to her grandmother.

Then Nona glanced back at Ruby, who was on her heels.

"Here I come, Miss Gus." Nona turned around and had to sidestep Ruby. "I'll be back," she said, so that Ruby, if he had the inclination, wouldn't follow her.

"How you, Miss Gus?" Nona walked over and stood in the grass next to the banister.

"I'm good. Can't kill nothing. Won't nothing die."

Nona hadn't heard that saying in years. Unsure what it meant back then, she knew now, ready to go to her father's funeral, that wasn't true for her.

"What is it, Miss Gus?" Nona said. "What you need?"

Augusta McClure was in her late fifties, light skinned with a faint brush of freckles across her nose and cheeks. Her hair was black, and Nona was sure it was due to a dye job, but whatever she did for upkeep, Miss Gus looked good.

"Come on up on the porch," Miss Gus instructed. "Give me a hug."

Nona obliged and walked up the wooden steps. Different from her grandmother's coarsely assembled house, Miss Gus' house was a two-story farm-style. Painted white, trimmed in green, it was fresh and neat.

"I ain't seen you in years."

Miss Gus had just seen her when she'd gotten into town. Perhaps, Nona pondered, Miss Gus meant up close. And with the tight hug Gus gave her, Nona's theory was confirmed.

"Ooo," Nona said. Miss Gus was squishing her.

"Let me look at you." Opal's neighbor pulled away. Holding on to Nona's arms, Miss Gus looked Nona over.

"The car will be coming soon," Nona said in response, although she had no idea what time it was at the moment. She had risen early. No longer able to sleep. And anxious, she determined, to get to her grandmother's house.

"I know. And you need to go. I just wanted to give you this key"—Gus took Nona by her wrist, placed a key in her palm, and folded her fingers in—"to give to your Mamaw."

"What is it for?" Nona asked.

"She'll know. It's the key to her house. I had to come back from the wake early last night and set the food out, so it'd be ready when folks came by."

Nona nodded. Hard to believe, the way Opal talked about her neighbor, that she would trust Miss Gus with a key to her house.

Neighbors and neighborly though, Nona had learned soon after arriving in Chicago, meant a completely different thing in the South.

And proof of that had been that Miss Gus was there to help out in a time of need and bereavement.

"Didn't see you there." Miss Gus' words were chiding. "You weren't hungry?"

"I had a headache," Nona lied. Although in retrospect, what Nona had learned would make anyone's head reel.

"Those come with life. Had one this morning myself, but I knew I had things to do." Miss Gus swiped a hand down her deep-purple sheath dress, then waved that same hand toward Opal's house, indicating the happenings of the day. "This too shall pass." Miss Gus gave Nona a tight smile. "Sometimes you can't hold things inside of you, you know? They'll just fester."

Nona let a small smile appear on her lips, not sure what Miss Gus was trying to say.

"It'll change you for sure," Miss Gus said. "And you can't let that happen."

"Okay," Nona said, politeness in her voice.

"I know you in there somewhere."

"Pardon me."

"That old Peaches. She's in there somewhere. Me and everybody else can see it."

"Okay," Nona said, ready to go. She didn't know who everybody else was or what they'd seen. She held up the key between her fingers. "I'll be sure to give this to my grandmother."

"You do that, please. And thank you. I just need to put my hat on, and I'm funeral ready. God rest Jasper's soul."

"See you later, Miss Gus."

"Family's a fleeting thing," Miss Gus said, not letting Nona get away. She shook her head and sucked her teeth. "Take care while you can."

"I will," Nona said, even though she wasn't sure how she could.

"Cuz ain't no place like home and family, now is it?"

That was probably true, Nona thought but didn't say out loud. Because home and family, seeing them at least, had turned out, Nona realized, something more than she had ever thought it could be.

CHAPTER NINETEEN

Julia stood in front of the bedroom window, a moist breeze blowing in, making the thin curtains with the faint floral pattern flutter. The sweet smell of hyacinth and gardenia blossoms planted around the front of her house wafted in. Tears were running down her face. Today was her father's funeral.

All laid out on the bed were her clothes, ready for her to slip into. She'd checked on Jayden earlier, made sure he was up and put him on track, but she hadn't been back. It often took several calls to get him out of bed and a few knocks on the bathroom door to get him out of there. His forty-five-minute showers as of late were a cost to her monthly bills she was determined to deter him from causing. But not today. She just couldn't seem to get a move on. Not for herself. Not to help Jayden.

It was as if something inside of her felt it could stave off what the day was going to bring just by being still.

She'd gotten up early enough, made coffee, her usual way to start the day, but that was as far as she'd gotten. Instead of showering early so Jayden would have the time he needed in the house's one bathroom they shared, she set off looking through her father's boxes. The one he left. The one she'd taken from his apartment. Looking for the will.

It bothered her that he'd left one.

Julia had called Sanganette first that day she'd found out about the will, as soon as she had hung up the phone from property manager Alex Marchetti, to tell her what her father had done. How he'd thwarted her plans of selling off everything and how she couldn't imagine he'd leave anything to anyone else.

"You don't know, so just calm down," Sanganette had said. "He still might have left you everything."

Next, Julia had called Opal.

Opal hadn't been surprised at the news at all and seemed confused that Julia hadn't known.

"Didn't I tell you you had to be at the lawyer's office on Monday? I could have sworn I did."

"Why do you know about the will and I don't?" Julia had asked. Her tone accusatory.

"I ain't got nothing to do with who Jasper told his business to and who he didn't" was the answer she gave. "Now you know, too. Just make sure you there on Monday. I got that lawyer's address around here somewhere . . ."

Julia had stopped listening.

She didn't know why this was bothering her so much. She'd made it through running into her sister, Nona knowing about Marcus, and the wake without shedding a tear. But the will had put her on the edge.

So she'd gone through those boxes again. But there wasn't anything new to see in them. Only all the things she already knew to be there. She had touched and examined all their contents way before she discovered the existence of a will, and she knew one was not to be found in them. She felt just maybe, though, she had missed it, since she hadn't known it might be in there.

How could he write a will and not tell her?

Jasper had left behind secrets and now that he was gone, Julia had no way to go to him and ask him anything about them.

Not that she would have. She hadn't ever asked about his lunch dates with a "Benny." She'd found out about him long before Jasper died. Yes, it had been a shock to her, but if her father hid having a child, he must've had a reason to do it. And she was the one who had to protect his interests, his physical health, his mental well-being. At whatever the cost. All families had secrets, and most times they were best if they stayed buried. She wasn't even sure she wanted to know more. She had hoped to reconcile that having her father, after everyone else had abandoned her, was enough. She didn't need to pile on more confusion, dysfunction, or hurt.

And she was good at holding her feelings inside.

She'd sat with that box for a long time, holding all that remained of her father on her lap. His things. His life. Consisting of no more than this.

And whatever is in that will . . .

And with that thought, tears welling up in her eyes, again, she heard her father's voice. For the first time since he'd left her. It was clear and strong and directed right at her.

Ain't nothing for you to worry about, Ju-lee. Everything's gonna be like it's supposed to be.

Out her upstairs bedroom window, Julia saw Sanganette's Beamer pull into her driveway. Julia pulled her calf-length silk robe together and tied it. She swiped a tear from her cheek and sniffed back those that were threatening to fall.

"I'm up here," Julia called out when she heard Sanganette push open the front door.

"Well, what you still doing up there?" Sanganette called up to her. The tapping on the steps from her heels as they hit and the clanking of her charm bracelet got louder as she ascended.

"What are you doing here?" Julia asked.

"I came to see about you." Sanganette stepped out of her high-heel shoes. She had on a black-and-white silk wraparound dress and a black raffia crown hat with a dropped sheer brim. Her lips were a glossy rose-petal pink. "I knew you were here by yourself."

"I'm always here by myself," Julia said. "Since my daddy died." Julia closed her eyes and took in a breath, tears streaming down her cheeks.

"Aww. Look at you." Sanganette had gotten to Julia's bedroom door. "You are nowhere near ready."

"I just can't." The words came out with tears that bubbled over.

"Oh now. It's okay," Sanganette said. She opened her arms wide, walked over to Julia, and wrapped them around her. "You just go on and cry." She patted her on her back. "I know this has got to be hard for you."

"I just feel so alone."

"Alone?" Sanganette pulled away, still keeping her hands on Julia's arms. "Even with that sister of yours acting like she's just passing through some unknown place—not speaking to nobody. Not stopping by the house after the wake, which is awful. You are not alone."

"Who didn't she speak to?" Julia asked amid a sniffle.

"Me," Sanganette said, flapping a hand to show the truth of it, but it didn't matter to her. "I know why, too."

"Why?"

"She's feeling foolish about all that nonsense she's been teaching up there. Up north." Sanganette turned up her nose. "The likes of her and her ideas have even invaded my school. You know. You were there when I got the news. New textbooks, ha." She snorted. "But she won't win. I won't let her get to me."

Julia started crying again. "How is this about you?"

Sanganette sucked her tongue. "I'm sorry. You're right. Peaches just gets me riled up." Sanganette sat on the bed next to Julia. "You are not alone." She grabbed her hand. "Isn't that where we were?" Julia closed her eyes. She nodded at her self-indulged friend. "How y'all all alone?" Julia nodded again. "When you're not."

"You just don't understand."

"I do." Sanganette's eyes got wide. "And how could you even say that, sweetie? You got me. You got Opal." Her drawl made the words long and slow.

"Daddy had a will," Julia said through sobs.

"Oh. Are we on that will again?"

"I can't believe I didn't know."

"Well, if it helps, I asked Ruben about it, and he didn't know anything about it either."

Julia frowned. "Why would Ruben know anything about it?"

"He's a lawyer." Sanganette drew out the first half of the word, saying it as if it were obvious that by default of Ruben's profession, he'd have inside information. "And I would have thought your daddy would have went to him. Ruben said it's probably on deposit down at the courthouse, but it's too late for us to look at it now."

"Doesn't matter." Julia swiped her nose with the back of her hand. "And I don't know who the lawyer is. Mamaw just gave me the address. I knew it wasn't Ruben, though, once I saw it."

"We could google him. The attorney on the case," Sanganette said. "We've got his address."

"It's not a case. And it doesn't matter. The will is already done. My father already made his *secret* will."

"Won't be secret much longer."

Tears came bubbling out from Julia. "Oh my God. Can we just stop talking about this?" The words barely made it out around the knot in her throat.

Sanganette batted her eyelids, processing Julia's demeanor. "This is *really* upsetting you."

"Yes. It. Is," Julia said, sniffling. "I was the one here. I was the one who took care of him. I should get everything. Not because I'm greedy." Her breathing was heavy and erratic. "But because it's right."

"I know you're not greedy." Sanganette rubbed her friend's arm. "And it is only right. Peaches doesn't deserve a damn thing."

"It would say he loved me, you know." Julia swiped a hand over her eyes. "That he appreciated me staying here. Being with him."

"Aww, precious. Of course it was you. It was all you." Sanganette led her over to the bed and sat, tugging on Julia's arm to follow suit. Sanganette fished a tissue out of her purse. "I packed these for the service, but it looks like you need them now."

Julia took one and swiped at her nose and eyes.

"Blow your nose." Sanganette pushed Julia's hand with the tissue up to her nose, and Julia blew into it. "Now what is it you think that you're supposed to be getting?"

"His houses." Julia snorted out the words, sniffing, swiping with the used tissue.

Sanganette pulled out another tissue and pushed it into Julia's hand. "Well, who else would get them?"

"Nona."

"Oh." Sanganette lowered her chin to show she sympathized. "I saw her at the wake last night, and she didn't even speak."

"Yeah, you said that." Julia sniffed back more tears.

"Well, it's worth repeating," Sanganette said. "And for her to leave you all alone down here, never call or come back and now get half of the things that belong to you." Sanganette shook her head. "That just beats all get out." She shook her hand. "And it's plain ole awful." The words came out almost in a whisper. She scrunched her nose.

"Don't talk about my sister, Sanganette."

"What's wrong with Auntie getting some of PaPa's stuff?" Jayden stood at Julia's bedroom door, his long curly hair flopping down on his face, a towel wrapped around his waist.

Julia popped up. "Why aren't you dressed?" She turned and looked at the clock on her nightstand next to her bed and back to him. She threw up her hands. "It's nearly time to go."

"You aren't dressed," he said, turning the scrutiny back around on her. And if they were going to get to Opal's house on time, both of them couldn't be having a meltdown at the same time.

"Jayden." Julia closed her eyes long enough to have counted to ten, but her mind couldn't form the cohesive thought needed. "Can we not do this now?"

"Why are you trying to erase PaPa?"

Julia didn't answer him. She turned, walked back over to the bed, plopped down, and covered her face with her hands. She wasn't trying to erase him. She was just getting things in order. Something he was too young to understand, something she didn't have the time or where-withal to explain.

"Jayden," Sanganette said, drawing out his name. "Why don't you go get ready and"—she held up a hand, to stop him from saying whatever he was poised to say—"I'll help your mama get ready."

"But . . ."

"But nothing. You want to be late for your granddaddy's funeral? No." Sanganette answered for him. "I don't think you do. Because I know you wouldn't want to disappoint him."

Jayden chewed on the inside of his lip and let his eyes drift upward.

"Go on, Jayden." Sanganette anchored her hands on her hips. "Skedaddle."

Julia looked up. Jayden hadn't moved. "I don't want to have to take your computer away from you," Julia said. Her scolding only half-hearted. "Your phone. No more games. No more anime on that over-priced iPhone of yours."

"Because what did I do?" he asked, genuinely confused.

"It's what you're not doing."

"Which is?"

"Not getting ready, Jayden. So we can go."

"I just asked you a question. I just want to know why you trying to make my grandfather disappear."

"And my answer was we'd talk about it later."

"When? After you sell off and give away all of PaPa's stuff?"

Julia chuckled through her tears. "He's got a will. I can't do anything to any of this stuff until we find out who he left it to."

"If he left me anything," Jayden said, "I'm keeping it."

"You can keep whatever you want, Jayden. Just please get ready so we can go."

Jayden left the doorway without saying a word.

"What are you going to do with him?" Sanganette asked.

"He's fine."

"Talking back. Not doing what you told him to do." Sanganette's arms went up, her palms flat. "Help me, Jesus. He is not fine. And that's no way for a child to act."

"*I'm* not even dressed," Julia said. "I can't fault him." She looked at her friend. "Didn't you just come in here and say you knew this was hard?" Sanganette blew out a disgusted breath. "It's hard for him, too."

"I didn't say it wasn't, but he needs to show some respect." Sanganette shook her head. "But you're right. You need to get ready. I just hope that boy of yours straightens out and stops giving you grief."

Julia stood up and pulled the belt on her robe.

"Okay. Don't say nothing," Sanganette said. She threw her hands up in the air. "Moving on." She grabbed the dress off the bed. "This is what you're wearing?"

"Yep."

"What happened to the dress I gave you to wear?"

"It didn't fit," Julia lied.

"You have put on a little around the waist." Sanganette gave a confirming nod. She reached down and grabbed the dress from the bed. "Hold your arms up."

Julia obliged.

"Even this is a little snug," Sanganette said, pulling the dress down over Julia's frame.

Julia wiggled to get it over her hips.

"Sit." Sanganette gave her shoulder a little push. She next grabbed the shoes sitting in a shoebox on top of the bed. "Give me your foot."

As Julia stuck a foot out, someone rang the doorbell.

"Who are you expecting?" Sanganette asked, sliding the shoe onto Julia's foot.

"No one," Julia said.

Sanganette stood up. "You stay here and finish dressing. I'll go see who it is."

"Whoever it is," Julia said, "send them away. I don't feel like being bothered with anybody."

Julia heard murmurings downstairs as she put her other shoe on—with a lot less zeal than Sanganette had done—and stood up, ready to try to put some makeup on, when she heard the tap-tap of Sanganette's heels on the wooden stairs. This time at a quicker pace than when she first came over.

"Did you send them away?" Julia sat at her vanity and looked at herself in the mirror.

"No," Sanganette said. Standing behind Julia in the mirror, her eyes wide.

Julia turned to face her. "What, Sanganette? Who was that?"

"Who *is* that you mean, because like I said, they are still down there."

"Who?"

"You are not going to believe it."

"Just tell me."

Now Sanganette was making her nervous. That goldenrod envelope with a message from Bisset that he might show up hadn't left the recesses of her mind. Still lingering there. Still knowing that that was a possibility.

Or maybe it was Nona. Had she come to see her even after yesterday's conversation? She hadn't said two words to her at the wake the night before and hadn't been gracious enough to come to their grandmother's house afterward.

"Who?" Julia asked again.

"Raymond Donaldson," Sanganette leaned down and whispered.

"What?" Julia's eyes darted toward the door. "He's not supposed to be here." Her words came out quickly. "Why is he here?"

"Said he come to take you to the funeral."

"That couldn't be." Julia stood up and walked to her bedroom doorway. She looked down the steps, even though she wouldn't be able to see him from there. "A car is supposed to pick us up at Mamaw's house. Why would he come here?"

"To see you. To be your personal chauffeur," Sanganette said, teasing. She walked over to where Julia stood and cupped her hands around Julia's face. "Didn't he say he'd do *anything* for you?"

"No." Julia swatted Sanganette's hands away. "That's not what he said. He said if I needed anything to ask."

"Same difference," Sanganette said and hunched her shoulders. "And today you need a ride. You are in no shape to drive."

"I can drive."

"Well, you don't have to, because you got somebody to drive for you." Sanganette got behind Julia and gave her a push. "Now go put on some makeup. Your face is all red from crying. Try to look decent. You've got a gentleman caller waiting for you in your parlor."

Julia didn't know whether to cry or laugh. Getting ready had been hard enough this morning, and if it hadn't been for Sanganette stopping by, she might have still been in that bathrobe. But Raymond Donaldson at her door was a pleasant surprise, even on a day like today.

"This is crazy," Julia said. Holding her head down, she couldn't seem to stop the smile that was appearing, although faintly, on her face.

"Ha ha, look at you now," Sanganette said. "Good. So, c'mon. Get a move on, then. You don't want to keep him waiting." Sanganette walked to the door. "I'll go check on Jayden, see if I have to take a strap to him to get him moving."

"Jayden is fine," Julia said, sitting back down at the vanity. "You go tell Raymond we'll be right down."

"You want me to tell him how big that grin was on your face when you heard he was here?"

"I didn't grin when you told me he was here."

"Yeah, but you're grinning now."

CHAPTER TWENTY

When Nona walked into the house, Opal was sitting on the couch. Again, not wearing one speck of black. Nona looked down at her dress. All black. Funeral appropriate. She gave it a tug.

The top of Opal's dress was lavender, with sheer paisley print sleeves of pastel colors—pink and blue and purple. The bottom had small pleats and was the same material as the arms. Opal held a hat in her lap that looked as it had been cut from the same cloth as her outfit, a nest of small flowers resting around the brim. A netted veil hung from around it.

Her right leg shaking, showing her impatience. Or the involuntary movement may have been nerves.

Ruby was in the doorway between the kitchen and the living room, leaning against the frame. Nona wasn't sure what he was waiting on or why he was even at Opal's house. Maybe, like Julia had said the day before at Lander's, the two of them had their heads together. Cooking up something. Certainly they'd been in cahoots when they had decided to interfere with Nona's life.

Nona hoped, as she sat on the couch next to her grandmother, that whatever the two of them were in alliance about today wouldn't involve her.

"What's your story, morning glory." Opal patted Nona on the hand. "We missed you at the house last night."

Opal placing her hand on Nona's and the words she'd spoken were a gesture of endearment, Nona knew that. But it wasn't how Nona was feeling toward Opal. Not that day. And Nona's response to her wasn't the answer Opal was looking for, Nona was sure of that.

Nona did want to share, nonetheless, why she hadn't come to the house the night before. Where people had gathered. Eating. Reminiscing. Comforting each other in a time of grief.

Nona had been doing her own grieving. About her life. About what had truly happened that set her down the path she took. She'd been a happy child—her father had always said he didn't have to worry about her following someone down the wrong road, he knew she'd be leading the way. Even as a teenager, she'd been outgoing. Confident. Popular. All that changed once she crossed that Mason-Dixon line, out on her own, thinking that the people she loved the most were against her. Not having family can make a person bitter. Lonely. Introverted. And being in a relationship with Eli hadn't helped.

But now she knew her life hadn't had to be like that. Marcus, who still made her heart light and sparked a smile on her face, would have come with her.

If only . . .

Nona wanted to have a conversation with her grandmother about how Opal had thought she should be instrumental in shaping Nona's history. She had walked in that door with the same determination she'd had the day she set out to find peaches at the bottom of the Devil's Punchbowl.

Nona said to Opal without any hesitancy or forethought the same line she had with Ruby. "I know what you did."

Opal, perplexity on her face, looked first to Ruby. Directing her question to him. "What is she talking about?"

He shrugged, as if he had no clue. "She said the same thing to me."

"What'd we do?" Opal asked.

"You know."

"She heard about how we tried to stop her from leaving Natchez."

"You trying to leave?" Opal asked. "I done told you, you have to wait till Monday. After the will gets read."

"I'm not talking about now."

"Then when?" Opal asked. She spoke as if she really didn't know.

"The night I left." Nona raised an eyebrow. "When I left for Chicago. The night both Marcus and I were supposed to leave."

Opal waved a dismissive hand. "You wanna talk about that on *this* day? When we're burying your father?"

"You could have picked *anytime* to tell me, Mamaw. Anytime during the past two decades."

"Sooo," Opal drew the word out, "let's do that." She fluffed the pleats on her dress. "Let's talk about it *anytime* other than today."

"Why did you do it?"

"Stop you from running off and getting married?" Opal asked, but her eyes drifted past Nona's and toward the front door. She wasn't going to indulge in that conversation. Her mind was somewhere else.

"You only stopped me from getting married. I ran off anyway."

She brought her eyes back to meet Nona's. "And you've been paying for it ever since."

"What does that mean?"

"You were seventeen, Nona." Opal shook her head. "What did you know?" She glanced at the door again before focusing back on Nona. "Too young to do what you were trying to do. And evidently too naive to know it wasn't the right thing to do, and I wasn't going to just stand by and let that happen."

"I would have been okay."

"You still ain't married." Opal sucked in a breath like talking was making her tired. "Being married is hard. And, yes, you turned out okay—you ain't on drugs or been to jail—but that ain't the question swirling around on everybody's mind."

"What question? Swirling around on whose mind?"

"Didn't I say *everybody*?" Opal smacked her lips. "Everybody wants to know, are you okay?"

"I am."

"Don't seem that way. Ain't the same rock-solid, strong-willed, vibrant girl that left here." Opal patted Nona's hand. This time a demeaning gesture. "Not if you're still upset about something that happened twenty years ago." Opal looked at Nona with sympathetic eyes. "Don't you know you have to move on? That's the only way you can really be okay."

What Nona wanted was to snatch her hand from under Opal's, hop up, and stomp out the door.

But she didn't.

"Ruben, go look out the door," Opal said, done with the conversation Nona wanted to have.

"What am I looking for?"

But instead of answering him, Opal turned to Nona. "Have you talked to your sister today? She's gonna make us late."

Nona glanced at the glass-domed clock on the mantel: 8:15 a.m. The car wouldn't arrive for another twenty minutes. Then she looked back at her grandmother.

Nona wasn't done with the conversation. "I didn't talk to my sister for twenty years because I thought she told Daddy that I was eloping with Marcus."

"Well, now," Opal said. "You had that all wrong, didn't ya? Hope you apologized to your sister about that. But like I said, I meant today. Have you talked to your sister today?"

Nona wanted to roll her eyes and smack her lips at Opal's comment. But she didn't do that either.

"And that's not going to get her here any quicker, is it?" Opal angled her head and widened her eyes. "If you're done with that craziness and you speaking to her now, maybe you can give her a call on your cell phone." Opal wriggled her fingers at Nona's purse. "See where she is."

"Julia's not late," Nona said. "Car isn't here yet to pick us up."

"She needs to be here when they get here," Opal said, pushing herself up off the couch. "Evidently you and her both must think if you can't get here on time, just get here when you can. But that's not how things go around here. Not while I'm still above ground."

Opal Davenport had lived just a little over eighty-seven years on Earth. And in the time Nona had known her, she had taken most things in stride. Nona had learned that Opal would find out the facts and act on that. Rarely had she acted helter-skelter or let her emotions guide her in her decisions.

In many ways, Nona was like Opal. Only, as Nona had begun to learn about herself, not as resilient. Opal, though, had never wavered. She'd always been the same. Through the years, through the upheavals in her life. Her husband's death—even though that had happened years before the girls came along—Opal had always said, was what had made her strong. She had her boys to raise. A home to take care of. And then, like today, she had her boys to bury.

Nona's loss, like Julia's, had sent her over the edge. Julia, rebounding, as far as Nona could tell, came back much the same person as she had started out to be. Nona hadn't. She had filled journals. Trying to put the hurt out of her mind by penning them to a page. Going around the hurt instead of going through it. Instead of dealing with it out loud. And all the while she had just turned herself inside out and buried herself down deep within.

It didn't take long after Ruby had given up watching the door that Julia and Jayden arrived in the limo from the funeral home.

Still, the two of them came into the house. Julia seemed surprised to see Nona and gave her a smile, however small, when she walked in. Julia placed a hand over her heart, a sign of relief.

Without any words between them, Nona and Opal tugged their hats into place, and the four of them left the house, taking the steps at Opal's pace, and climbed into the limousine. Ruby stood close by, waiting, and it wasn't until the funeral car had pulled off, taking the Davenports to say their last goodbyes to Jasper, that he got in his car to follow.

The ornate, steepled church was packed with mourners. And the cavernous sanctuary, even with its spinning ceiling fans, was stuffy and dry. People in overfilled pews frantically waved printed obituaries and cardboard fans to cool themselves. The smell of the circulating air was perfumed, sweet and nauseatingly so, by warmed bodies and ceremonial bouquets.

While the standing-room-only service suggested to Nona that Jasper was well known and well loved, she was surprised that the service was in a church. Nona hadn't known her father to be a religious man. She'd only heard him call on the Lord when he wanted the dice to roll his way or when the level in his whiskey bottle was low.

Sniffles echoed through the room, and the pastor's voice boomed up through the rafters. Opal held on to Nona's hand and squeezed when Sister Eldridge, who said, after the service was over, she remembered Peaches, sang "Pass Me Not, O Gentle Savior." And if Nona hadn't known her grandmother as well as she did, she would have said that her eyes were misted over, as if tears may fall.

Marcus came in right before the service was called to order and left before the obituary was read. Nona knew because she had held her breath, it seemed, the entire time. And so it confused Nona that Julia, as she had done the evening before, was still watching the door. It had occurred to Nona during the wake that Julia might be keeping an eye out for Marcus. And once he'd come through the door, Nona had made a quick retreat, unsure if his arriving had satisfied Julia's wandering eye.

But today, after Marcus left, Julia was still watching the church doors.

And then even under the cover of a large black umbrella that kept them from the drizzle of rain that had started to fall once they reached the cemetery, Julia kept glancing toward the roadway. Out beyond the plot, past the Turning Angel that kept watch over the wrought-iron gate.

And then, although Julia hadn't seemed satisfied with what she saw, Nona noticed that her interest piqued as a black Lexus pulled up. Double-parked on the road nearest to the grave, the car door swung open and a man emerged.

Nona, turning to see what had finally caught Julia's consideration, knew the person who had just arrived surely wasn't who Julia had been expecting.

Nona's gaze shifted to look at Julia, and then Nona drew a breath and glanced over at the Turning Angel. She was sure it was watching, taking everything in.

And maybe even knowing what she'd thought when she saw what Julia had seen.

Exhaling noisily, she gave another look at those who had gathered around Jasper's bronze casket, standing just at the edge of the green covering underneath it overflowing with flowers, before heading to meet the man walking her way.

It was Eli.

CHAPTER
TWENTY-ONE

Julia was tired.

The wake and the funeral had been more draining than she had imagined.

And she missed her father. He had been a good man. And as much as Julia didn't like to admit it, she was so much like him. His pull-yourself-up-by-your-bootstraps mentality mirrored hers. His ability to forge ahead was who she'd become. The only trait she'd felt he hadn't shared and was indeed far removed from her was his doggedness when it came to family. Forgive. Forget. He didn't hold a grudge against anyone he called blood. Julia had. She'd worked her way around those things that had caused her grudges in her life instead of through them and had moved on. But they hadn't ever been erased. The list filled with the things she was bitter about over time had only dug down deeper, planted roots, and grown.

Like how she'd felt about Cat Montgomery and about Nona.

But now, after Jasper's death and the return of her sister, she felt that maybe some of her hard edges that existed within her might be melting.

Maybe that part of Jasper's spirit, his indulgence in letting things go, had found its way into her. Or maybe it was the arrival of Raymond Donaldson at her doorstep, literally and figuratively, that had begun to soften Julia up.

Certainly, he'd been the bright spot in her morning. Heck, she'd thought, in her week.

"I figured you might need a little something for yourself," he'd said when Julia and Jayden had climbed into the back seat of the stretch limo. It was shiny and black on the outside and smelled, Julia noticed as she sank into the leathery seat, like lemons and lavender inside.

And then there was him.

"It ain't far, I know." His eyes met hers in the rearview mirror as he turned the ignition. "But this way, with me driving you over to your grandmother's, you can take a breath. You know, one less thing for you to do."

"Thank you, Raymond," Julia had said, hoping her genuine appreciation showed in her eyes. "This does help. We were having a time getting started this morning." Julia patted her son on his hand. She could see, out the corner of her eye, the smirk on Jayden's face. He wasn't too young to know what the banter between them may have signified.

"And I'll drop you back home after the funeral service."

"Okay. That'll be nice of you." Julia smiled. "And will I see you at the repast?"

"I'll be there," he'd said. "Looking for you." He took his eyes off the road again to find hers. "You'll save me a seat?"

"I'd be happy to."

⌒

That unencumbered ride over to Opal's that morning made it easier to go inside after seeing Nona's rental car parked in the driveway. Knowing she'd be there.

And then her spirit had lightened even more when Nona smiled. Walking in Opal's front door, seeing Nona sitting next to their Mamaw, had only cemented the melting of the hurt and resentment Julia been carrying around all those years.

Julia had hoped it wasn't an empty gesture on Nona's part, spurred by the occasion of the day. Especially now that Nona knew what lengths Julia had gone to to give her son a decent father. But Julia had determined to move on that act of kindness by Nona and give an impossible apology she'd lain awake the night before memorizing.

Julia didn't know that Nona had held a grudge against her the entire time she'd been gone. And if she had known how Nona felt, Julia would have found Nona herself and straightened things out.

But as it was now, Nona had good cause, as Julia's actions amounted to so much more than Nona's anger. Feelings Nona had that were based on a lie. But if Julia took her cue from how her sister had greeted her, Julia felt as if maybe they were on the road to mending their relationship.

The morning had been hectic, Jayden moving slow. And the dress she'd decided to wear, evidently hanging much longer in her closet than she remembered, didn't fit the same way it had the last time she'd worn it.

And she had worried ever since the start of the services that Benny would show up.

Worried not only if he came, but if he did what he would want. How he would act. Would he even care about the loss of their father or becoming acquainted with his two sisters?

And why wouldn't he? she reasoned. Jasper was his father, too. A secret—knowing about his son—she'd kept from Jasper, just like Jasper had kept from her. Finding proof of his existence only when she'd cleaned out Jasper's apartment in Vidalia.

There hadn't been much for Julia to find—a tattered address book with a scattering of names, *C. Hawthorne, M. Perry, J. Miller*. A pocket calendar, the entries barely legible. Deeds to property he owned. A business card from one Alex Marchetti, property manager. And a small box with pictures inside. Of family. But then came proof of another child. A birth certificate. A brother who didn't share the same mother with her. All nice and neat in a manila folder. When she found that, she had abandoned the rest of the search through the box.

Julia had folded in the flaps on the top of the box, securing it and putting it in the trunk of her car. If Jasper wouldn't show her all the leaves on their family tree, she'd shake it herself to see what fell.

Her father's illegitimate child was part of their family history that had long been buried.

Undocumented. Unreported . . .

She'd read those words in an article Nona had published, and they fit their family perfectly.

Perhaps, Julia wondered as she headed to the Starlight for the repast after leaving the cemetery, her errant half-brother might show up there.

Also like her father, she was always chasing ghosts.

Benjamin "Benny" Eanes was a dentist. That hadn't been hard to learn, a simple Google search did it. He'd grown up in Vidalia but had moved to Baton Rouge after graduating from school. His office was white and crisp and modern. His office staff friendly and talkative. Dr. Eanes, though, was terse and efficient. Tall and dark with a cute dimple in one cheek, he had Jasper's smile and deep voice. Finding that part out had taken a bravado that she knew she could muster. The problem had been she didn't know how long it would hold up once she came face-to-face with him.

But Julia had needed to see what he looked like. Find out what kind of man he was. To see if she could learn why her father kept him secret.

Using the address of a house in the area that was up for sale, Julia made a dental appointment. She used the people skills she'd honed as a real estate agent to make conversation with the front office over the phone and after she arrived. She'd told them how there were horror stories she could tell about her last dentist and the pain he'd caused her and used that as a segue into asking what they thought of Dr. Eanes.

They were forthcoming. Raised by a single mother, he had worked his way through dental school. Hardworking and industrious, he opened his own practice not long after graduating. He was unmarried but a mentor and dentist to inner-city kids, always wanting to give back.

A son any man would be proud of. One certainly to brag about. But Jasper had taken his existence to his grave without mentioning him to anyone. Only he hadn't known that she'd found out.

And Julia surmised he had told someone because of that folder filled with all the vital information on Dr. Benjamin Eanes. And then there was the calendar she'd found that had dates marked, "lunch with Benny."

So where was Benny?

Julia couldn't understand why Benjamin hadn't showed up for the funeral.

Hadn't he loved his father? Hadn't he been raised to show respect for the dead? Especially when the dead was kin.

And, Julia thought, *hadn't Benjamin realized that there was family that possibly wanted to see him . . .*

Julia couldn't reach out to him. What if he rejected her? Wanted to be distant like Cat and Nona had been all those years. No. She'd wait to see if he turned up on his own. Out of obligation. Or maybe love.

After riding back home in the car provided by the funeral home, Julia picked up her car and drove to the repast. She pulled around to the back of the bar and parked her car in the lot. It was already nearly full. Jayden had left the cemetery with his father to go back to the Starlight. They had left the funeral early to start getting things ready, but both had shown up at the cemetery.

The funeral car had dropped everyone back at Opal's for them to take their own cars to the repast. Raymond had taken Julia back to her house.

Opal opted to ride with Ruby, who, it seemed to Nona, was never too far from Opal's side.

But Nona had left in the black Lexus with the man who had shown up, without so much as an introduction to anyone as to who he was.

Julia pulled open the door to the crowded space and was met with bright light. She'd never seen it like that, it looked more like a banquet hall than a bar.

But before she could get inside, Julia heard her name being called.

"Miss Gus," Julia said, turning around.

"Can you help me, baby?"

Augusta McClure was standing by her open car door. She'd lost the big floppy hat and sunglasses she'd worn even during the rain.

She waited for Julia to come close to her. "I've got some string beans and ham hocks and some corn bread I wanna take in."

"Oh, Miss Gus," Julia said. "We have more than enough food."

"You can never have enough food at a repast. People want to take food home." She piled food in Julia's arms as she spoke. "And you'll need some at your house." She reached back into the car with a grunt. "You carry that, and I'll bring this chef's salad."

"Oh." Julia shook her head and chuckled. "Okay."

Julia walked behind Augusta, juggling her load when they got to the door so she could open it for the older lady.

"Oh!" Miss Gus said as she walked in and turned around, nearly bumping into Julia.

"What?" Julia said.

"Come over here." Miss Gus walked back toward the car. "Come here." She waved at Julia.

"What?" Julia asked, coming over to Miss Gus reluctantly.

"I think I just saw somebody."

"Who?" Julia said, turning back to look toward the door. Miss Gus stepped into Julia's line of view.

"I don't know if you should go in there."

"I need to take this food in." Julia raised her arms to draw Miss Gus' attention to the pile of it she'd given to her. "And I need to greet the people who came to pay their last respects to my father."

Miss Gus leaned in close to Julia and whispered, "I think your old boyfriend's in there."

"Who?" Julia asked again. She furrowed her eyebrows, exhausted with Miss Gus and the hot sun that had come after the morning's rain.

"You know." Miss Gus turned up her nose. "The one Marcus had to run off."

Julia's head jerked up slightly as the realization of what Miss Gus was saying set in. "You mean Bisset? You saw Bisset Brown in there?"

Julia nearly dropped the pot of beans as Miss Gus stepped aside. For there he stood, a man she hadn't seen in nearly fifteen years. He was standing in the doorway, holding it open, waiting for her.

CHAPTER

TWENTY-TWO

Nona held her breath as she pushed through the front door of the Starlight.

"Let me get the door for you."

She heard Eli speak, but her hand had already been on the handle and she was already one foot in the door. Once inside, her eyes searched the room. Scanning the faces. Save for Opal, Ruby, and a few cousins, there weren't any others she knew.

Not even Marcus.

Nona had seen him in passing at the church service, and he stood nearly behind her at the graveside until she'd changed positions after Eli arrived. She had planned on talking to him at the repast, when things were more relaxed, and Nona realized she still wanted to do that. Spend time chatting with Marcus. Although Nona wasn't sure how she was going to feel with Marcus when Eli was going to be by her side.

It had only occurred to Nona now, after Eli had arrived, that Eli and Marcus knew her as two different people. One thought she was reserved. Yielding. Gullible. The other knew her to be outgoing. Defiant. Tough.

But to Nona she was straddling the fence, something she hadn't seen in herself. It seemed since she'd been home, some of her old attributes were coming back. When first returning, the mirrored reflection of her was filled with misapprehension and embarrassment. But being around the people who knew her as something else—someone else—had started making her feel differently about things. Inside. An evolution she hadn't realized until Eli got out of that car at the cemetery.

Eli had just shown up. Not giving Nona a clue beforehand what he had planned. At the cemetery. In the rain. And she hadn't liked it.

His appearance sent all kinds of thoughts through Nona's brain. The first one had been that it was hard to believe that he'd walk across the wet grass—in a cemetery, no less—in his shiny, expensive shoes. She'd watched as he walked her way. She edged her way to the back of the crowd to meet him, where he put down his umbrella to stand under hers. Then he'd wrapped his arm around her shoulders.

And that evoked another thought. That Eli was intruding. In her life. In her family. It didn't feel to Nona that he was supposed to be there. That he *should* be there. He hadn't been invited. He had a grip on her life like the grip he had on her shoulders.

It made her want to step away. Take his arm from around her.

But she didn't.

And that, reflexively, she realized, made her eyes go to Marcus. She had wondered what he would think about Eli being there. Or would he believe that the Peaches he knew had learned to live with someone like Eli? Controlling. Arrogant. Things about him she hadn't just learned about, but things she just realized she cared that he was. And would he believe how she had so easily succumbed to it? How it had been exactly what she wanted?

Those hadn't been pleasant thoughts.

Not stopping to introduce him to anyone, Nona got in the car with Eli after the graveside service and rode with him in the rental car he'd come in to the repast. He was chatty enough, she felt, perhaps even too much so.

Happy to see her. Wasn't she surprised? *I'm here now for you, babe* . . .

His arrival had already distracted her from saying goodbye to her father. And now his words and sentences and questions were invading the loneness she wanted to process it all. And to be around the people who felt the same way she did.

At the repast, he pointed to a table, one close to the center of the room, and headed to it. Nona knew he expected her to follow. But she didn't. Not at first. She stood there, not wanting to do it. But not knowing what to do instead. Opal and Ruby, sitting at a table closer to the bar, were her only option. Other family members present were less familiar to her, and she knew sitting with them would require pleasantries and small talk. She wasn't up for that. Sitting with Opal and Ruby, whom Nona wasn't quite through having a conversation with, would require her to introduce them to Eli. She didn't want to do that either.

Nona went and sat with Eli.

"You want to grab some food?" Eli said after she sat at the table. "I'm starving." He looked around the room, rubbing his hands together, then over toward the bar. "Something smells good. I can't wait."

"I don't know what time they'll be putting the food out." She looked at him and gave him a sweet little smile. "How about I go check?"

She popped up without waiting for his answer and headed toward the back of the room. She'd seen a hallway the night before when she'd been there. Maybe that was where Marcus was.

It was the third door down that hall where she found the kitchen, past the two restrooms—one marked Gents, the other Ladies. Nona opened the door and found a few people moving around the kitchen. A nice-size room, there was an aluminum prep table in the center of it, an oversized sink, a six-burner stove, and a refrigerator. Nona hadn't remembered seeing a menu out front. And she hadn't expected to see anyone in the back but Marcus. At least that had been the only person she'd come looking for.

"Hi, Auntie Peach—uhm, Nona. Auntie Nona."

It was Jayden. Nona hadn't had a chance to talk to him again after she'd run off the porch the day she'd been told Marcus was his father.

Nona held her arms outstretched. "Hi, Jayden." A big smile appeared on her face. "Come give me a hug."

Jayden put down the aluminum container he had in his hands, wiped them down the front of his pants, and came over to Nona's open arms.

And as she hugged him, she spoke in his ear. "You can call me Auntie Peaches. It's fine." She loosened her embrace and asked, "So, are you the cook for today's feast?"

He blushed, giving her a big grin. "No. I can't cook. I'm just helping my dad."

"Well, aren't you a good son." They both looked toward Marcus. Nona held on to Jayden's hand. "And I bet my dad would be proud of you, too."

"I miss him," Jayden said and hung his head. "PaPa. He lived with us, you know."

"No. I didn't know," Nona said.

"Yep." He nodded in confirmation. "I got to see him every day." Nona saw his eyes mist up, and she squeezed his hand a little tighter. "He used to say I was the boy he never had but always wanted." Jayden chuckled. "I told him that was corny."

"How is that corny?" Nona laughed. "I think it's sweet, and I'm glad you were right there with my father. He was stuck with two girls to raise. I know he loved having you around."

"Hey, Peaches." Marcus gave her a big, wide smile. "Did you come back here to help?" he said without stopping what he was doing—taking pans out of the oven, putting other ones back in. Stirring pots on the stove and directing the other helpers.

Nona wasn't sure why she'd come back. Was it to see Marcus? Or was it to get away from Eli?

"Do you need help?" she asked.

"A couple more hands never hurt."

Nona smiled at him, then pointed back over her shoulder. "Eli's here. I don't guess I should leave him alone out there too long."

"And who is Eli?" Marcus asked.

She hesitated, at a loss for words. She didn't take her eyes off of Marcus, and he waited for her answer. Only she didn't know what answer to give.

Hadn't she told Marcus about Eli the night before?

Had she told anyone about him since she'd been there?

And in that moment, she realized she hadn't talked about the usual things that family do when they hadn't seen each other. Things they've been doing. How they've been doing. How they are doing now.

She'd avoided those kinds of conversations, maybe not even thought about having them. With her extended family, her cousins—children of Jasper's deceased brothers. Missing that opportunity completely by not going over Opal's house after the wake. She knew people would be gathered there. Socializing. With Jayden. With Julia. Everything she found out about how Julia had been, what she'd been up to, about Julia's life, her own sister, had come from someone else.

"No one," she said. Perhaps not intentionally, she later thought. But it was what had come out. "No one special. But I do have to get back out there."

She let go of Jayden's hand. She let her eyes meet his. "Tell your mother I'm going to stop by and see you two tomorrow."

"At our house?"

"Yep." She smiled. "At your house."

"You leaving?" Marcus asked. He'd been paying attention to everything Nona had said since she'd walked into the room.

Nona nodded. "Yep, we're going to head out."

"But the food is almost ready," Marcus protested as his eyes scanned the crowded prep table. "You gotta stay and eat." He crossed his arms across his chest. "Plus, don't you want to introduce me to this Eli person?"

"I'm not hungry," Nona said. "And neither is Eli. And he's no one you need to meet." She smiled at him to let him know she wasn't being mean or secretive. She didn't want Marcus to think that of her.

But Marcus followed her when she left the kitchen. Not saying anything, even when she looked back and asked where he was going. Nona noticed that he stopped and stood by the doorway to the small hallway, watching as she made her way over to Eli.

That made her nervous.

And then Eli was reluctant to leave. He was hungry. He hadn't met her family. They had just gotten there.

"And I met Ruby," Eli said. "Came right over and introduced himself to me. Wanted to know who I was." Eli raised an eyebrow.

Nona glanced over at the table she'd seen Ruby and her grandmother sitting at when they'd first came in. Opal was chatting away with someone standing over her. Ruby was looking at her. Her eyes went around the room, and she saw that Marcus was, too.

"Let's go," Nona said, and tugged on Eli's arm to get him moving. "We'll go and find you something to eat somewhere else. This is too much for me."

"Oh, honey, I'm sorry. I know this has to be overwhelming for you."

"Let's go," she said more sternly than she'd ever spoken to him.

Before she could prod him out of his seat and out the door, Marcus came over.

"Hi," he said, sticking his hand out for Eli to shake. "I'm Marcus Curtis, Peaches' old boyfriend."

Nona did a hasty introduction, leaving out Eli's present position in her life before rushing the two of them out the door.

"You didn't want me talking to your old boyfriend?" Eli had asked once they were in the car.

"What would you talk to him about?"

"For one, why he called you Peaches."

"I told you, it's a childhood nickname."

"And why he felt compelled to tell me who he was to you."

Nona smiled at the thought of Marcus' actions. "He was just being polite."

"Sounded more like he wanted me to be jealous," Eli said and glanced over at her. "How close were the two of you?"

"Marcus Curtis was the reason I came to Chicago in the first place. We were going to elope."

CHAPTER
TWENTY-THREE

He had on a suit that looked like he'd bought it from a 1950s vintage shop. A short-brimmed straw hat and his brown shoes were dusty. He looked thin and worn, but amusement, Julia noted, danced around in his eyes.

Julia had first taken in Bisset Brown when he had walked over to meet her at the back door when she'd arrived with Miss Gus.

Her eyes flitted back and forth from him to the dishes she was carrying. She didn't want him to see her looking, wanting to avoid him and his gaze, but her eyes kept being drawn to him.

She'd seen the dinginess of the collar of his yellowed white shirt. There were sweat rings visible under his arms when he pulled off his jacket. He wiped the sweat from his reddened face with a paper napkin as he stood in the doorway, waiting for her.

How could she have let a man like that into her life.

Julia didn't stop to ask why he'd come. She walked past him, keeping her eyes down, through the door he held open. She just wanted to get away from him. And she needed to find Jayden. Find out if that no-good lowlife had said anything to her son.

But her hands were trembling. Her feet felt as if she were walking barefoot over rocks—unstable and unsteady—she wasn't sure how far she'd make it.

"What are you doing here?" Julia heard Miss Gus hiss at him. "You have some nerve. You're not welcome here, you know."

"Lady, do I even know you?" Julia thought his voice seemed to slur. She hoped he hadn't been drinking. That was when he was at his worst. "You better keep away from me."

If that was possible.

"You don't scare me none," Miss Gus said. "And ain't nobody in here going to put up with your shenanigans."

It had been a long time, but Julia hadn't forgotten all the things he'd done to her—all his shenanigans. Or like the other time he'd locked her outside, this time only wearing her underwear. He wouldn't let her back in until she apologized correctly. But she'd already said it. A thousand times. And it took two hours for him to decide she could come back in. She'd sat on that back stoop the whole time and cried. Too ashamed to go for help.

Shame was his favorite weapon.

And it wasn't that she didn't think she couldn't handle whatever he planned on dishing out this day. She wasn't that person anymore. The one who cowered and gave in and went back because he'd convinced her that no one else would ever want her. That she was stuck with him.

But with all the things that had been going on, she knew she wasn't at her strongest.

Keeping her eyes forward, she saw Sanganette coming her way. *Good,* Julia thought, *in case my knees give way.*

"Now let me take some of those things you're carrying," Sanganette said as she looked past Julia and scowled at Bisset. "What is all this you got?"

"Just some . . . Miss Gus made . . ." Julia turned and looked at Miss Gus, not being able to form the words.

"I made some beans and ham hocks," Miss Gus said. "You help her carry that. I'm going to find Marcus."

Julia looked at Sanganette. It was where she'd been trying to get to. To Marcus. But at that moment, Sanganette would do. "I'm okay," she said. Happy the words came out, her voice sounding normal. "I just need to get these back to the kitchen."

"I just want to talk to her," Bisset interjected, although no one had spoken to him directly. "I want to find out how she was doing, that's all. Her and Jayden."

"She's not going to talk to you," Miss Gus said.

"Then maybe she'll let me talk to Jayden."

Sanganette went and stood in front of Bisset. "I think it's best that you leave."

"I'm not going anywhere," Bisset said, his voice going up a decibel or two. "I came to check on her." He swung a finger at Julia. "What's the harm in that?"

"You're making a scene," Sanganette said. "Have some respect for the dead, we're here because of Julia's father."

"And so am I."

"I can talk to him," Julia said. She couldn't see any way out of it, not wanting to cause a ruckus. People were already looking. Then she'd seen her grandmother stand up. It appeared she was ready to come over and join the ensuing clamor, too.

And Julia knew, too, that Bisset's apparent concern was nothing but a deceptive façade that, to Julia, was as obvious as his dusty shoes.

She shoved what she was holding into Sanganette's arms and turned around to face him. Not saying a word, she gave him a nod and pushed past him, out the door she had entered only moments before and back out to the parking lot.

She felt the heat from the midday sun beaming. The air was still and quiet. Beads of sweat started to form on her top lip and across her forehead. She could feel the moisture of it.

Bisset followed her out and about as she walked to a far corner of the asphalt space. Julia wanted to get as far from the building as she could. She didn't want the blowout from Bisset Brown, talking on about this and that. Nothing relevant. Nothing worth hearing. It turned into white noise for Julia, who was praying that he'd get to whatever he came to say and go away.

She wasn't going to give away her strength. Especially to the likes of him. She had worked too hard to find it to have it trampled on all over again.

She watched him as he talked—he was sulky, the shimmer of the heat rising from the asphalt coming up behind him. It made the outline of his body indistinct. Hazy.

The Starlight was filled with the ghosts of her past, long buried, Julia thought, yet here, now, she felt whiffs of the things she had suffered through swirling up around her. Trying to devour her.

She was frustrated and struggled to stand there and not scream at him. Yell at him for coming there, for trying to drag her down because that was all he'd ever done to her. Tried to make her less than what she was. Listening to him had taken her back. To the place where time had stood still. She couldn't move forward. Her pulse felt as if it were spiraling, and it all was starting to blur.

She closed her eyes to block him out. To gain her composure. But he got in her face, his hot breath too close for her to breathe. These had been the times, when he was standing in the way of her getting out, that she'd started to drink. It filled the hollowed-out crevices of her soul that had been filled with loneliness and loss. And she thought how much she'd like to have a drink right now. For that moment to drown him out. To make him disappear. To stop the pounding in her head that started the moment he'd begun to speak.

Jayden. He was saying her son's name in every sentence he uttered. Wanting to see him. Wanting to know why she'd kept him from him. Spouting his rights and her inadequacies.

He was, after all, he spewed, Jayden's father.

Julia had known all along she couldn't hide from the fears of her past. Not for long, anyway. The suffering Bisset had caused her was mixed in and inextricably intertwined with the joy she got from just her son's existence. No more hiding from it. Being broken made you feel like an outsider. Not belonging anywhere. And she had decided long ago she wasn't going to be in that place anymore.

"Julia. What's going on?" It was Marcus. He'd come to her rescue.

"I'm okay," Julia said, knowing now she was ready to stand up to Bisset. "I can do this."

"You don't have to. Come on," Marcus said. "Come inside."

"Where's my son?" Bisset said, his lip curling like a rabid dog. "I wanna see him. I got a right to see him."

"You don't have a son. Leastways not one here," Marcus said. He stepped away from Julia to face Bisset. "And you ain't got no rights to anything here. I suggest you move on."

"You can't take him away from me."

"He's never been yours," Julia said, interjecting. He was going to know that she'd found the voice she'd lacked when they were together.

"And he won't be yours either." Bisset spat his words at Julia. "Not for long. You ain't never been good at nothing." He stepped back from Marcus to face Julia. "Long as I've known you. And I know with you that boy ain't got nothing but shit for a mother. But I'm gonna fix that." Bisset nodded. "You best believe that."

And there he was. The Bisset that she knew.

"Look here," Marcus said and grabbed a handful of the grimy shirt Bisset wore. "It would be best if you crawled back under whatever rock you slithered here from under." Marcus pushed Bisset hard, letting go of his shirt, making Bisset fall back. "Because when it comes to protecting my family"—he gestured toward Julia—"Jayden and Julia, I don't have no problem taking you out. Permanently."

"You don't scare me, Marcus," Bisset said, keeping his distance. "You can't waltz in when you want and steal a man's child."

"What man?" Marcus crossed over to Bisset in two long strides, nearly bumping chests with him. Taller than Bisset, Marcus lowered his head so that they were nose to nose. "I don't see no man standing out here. Only you, Bisset. A sick and sorry human being."

"You can't stop me from seeing him."

"I can put a stop to you, period." The muscles in Marcus' jaw tightened, his hands clenched into fists. "And if I ever catch you anywhere near *my* son, believe me, that's exactly what I'll do."

"Is that him?" Bisset asked. He looked past Marcus. Then Marcus and Julia followed Bisset's gaze. Standing at the door of the Starlight, holding it open, just as Bisset had done earlier, was Jayden. "It's a shame I don't know him."

"No, I think it's a blessing," Julia said, moving to stand in Jayden's line of sight. She didn't want her son to even have to look at this man. "What is it you want with him?" She squinted her eyes, trying to understand him.

"I've been absent from his life too long."

"You weren't ever present," Julia said. "You left before he could even get here. Before you ever saw him. Telling me that he might not even be yours. Making me the bad guy so you could shirk your responsibility, just like you always have."

"Yeah, well, I'm here now. And whatever he got is part mine because he's a part of me."

A sick chuckle erupted from Julia that made her chest heave. "Is that why you're here? You think Jayden has some kind of inheritance?"

"I just want to see my boy. Get to know him." Bisset started to walk toward the door, but Marcus stepped in front of him.

"I think it's best if you leave. Now." Marcus squinted and straddled his legs. "Otherwise, man, they gonna be carrying you outta here in a bag."

CHAPTER

TWENTY-FOUR

"I've been wanting to do this for a long time." Eli had finished most of his meal when he lifted his hip slightly from the chair and dug down into his pants pocket. "But now, with all the men down here chasing you, I thought I'd better do it now."

After Nona and Eli had left the repast, they found a quaint little Italian restaurant that the two of them had compromised on. Eli, pulling into the parking lot, expressed his surprise that she had an opinion on where she wanted to eat.

"That's so unlike you," he commented. "All day you've been acting strange."

Everyone seemed to think that about her lately. Somehow, she wasn't who she was supposed to be.

She wondered who exactly that was.

Seated at a table covered with a white tablecloth and a candle burning in the center of it, Nona stared at the menu. She wasn't hungry, and she felt uncomfortable sitting there while Eli asked her a million unwanted and unwarranted questions.

"Now why is it they call you Peaches? . . . Why did your old boy-friend—what's his name? Marcus?—come and introduce himself to me? Is he trying to talk to you again? . . . Was Ruby a boyfriend, too? I wouldn't think he'd be your type . . . I want to meet your family. Are you trying to keep them from me?"

Nona could feel the stress in her neck, right behind her ear. Rubbing her hand over the area, she could feel her pulse and noted it was racing.

Maybe she had anticipated what had come next.

"Will you marry me?" Eli asked. He'd taken a small box out of his pocket and held it open in front of her.

Nona felt dizzy.

She stared at the ring and up to Eli's face.

"I hope I'm not too late," he said and chuckled.

But it was too late.

She'd realized she'd mistaken the shield Eli provided for her for love. Marcus was more than a yardstick to measure Eli up against, and without Nona knowing it, she had done just that. Put the two of them next to each other, and Eli had fallen short.

Being home had given Nona a new sense of worth. Something she hadn't felt in a long time. She didn't know if it was because of Ruby and Opal expecting so much more of her and the two of them not being hesitant about voicing it. Questioning the whereabouts of the missing parts of herself. Or the strength Julia seemed to expect of her, thinking that Nona could have saved Julia from the downward spiral she'd taken. Or Marcus' love. A love that had lasted through years of not seeing her, a love that was created within him by the girl she used to be.

Nona wanted to be that girl again. She just wasn't sure she knew how to do it.

She glanced into Eli's eyes. And he looked back into hers.

"Maybe I shouldn't have let you come down here and stay the whole time by yourself." Eli noticed a difference in Nona.

"Is that part of the proposal?" she asked. Nona didn't like that he thought he could have stopped her from coming home.

"No." Eli blushed and let out a chuckle. "Guess I'm just kind of nervous. This day isn't going quite like I planned."

But Nona thought about how he had been there when she needed someone to lean on. So she reached in and gently pulled the ring from where it was perched.

"It's beautiful," she said, turning it so the light would hit the emer-ald-cut stone.

"Best diamond they had in the store." He put the last forkful of food in his mouth.

"Really?"

Still chewing, Eli took the ring from her but held on to her hand. "Here," he said and slipped it onto her finger. "I made sure it would be a perfect fit."

"It certainly is that," Nona said. "And a surprise."

"C'mon now," he said. "You knew I was going to propose to you. You knew I wanted to marry you."

"Just didn't think it would happen now. Here." Nona, placing her hand in her lap, looked up at him. "I didn't think you'd be here."

"I decided to come right after I hung up with you," he said. "I knew you needed me." He wiped his mouth with the cloth napkin.

She squinted at him. "How did you know how to find me?" She hadn't told him anything about her father's funeral arrangements. And certainly not the cemetery where the interment would be.

"I found out the particulars from Cat." He lifted a hand to wave the waiter over. "You want more wine?"

Nona shook her head no. She wanted to be clear-headed. She had slipped so far from being who she really was, she knew that to get back, she needed all the wits she could muster.

"I had just missed you at the church," he continued. "The proces-sion had pulled away when I got there." He stopped his conversation with her long enough to order another glass of wine for both of them. "I thought funeral processions were slow going. I had to pick up some speed to catch up."

"My mother?" Nona wanted to hear that part of the story. "You talked to my mother? Why would you do that?"

"Yeah." He held up a hand of surrender. "I know. I know. I could have just called you, but I wanted to surprise you." He smiled. Pleased that he had. "And I got a seat on your flight back tomorrow. We can fly home together."

Eli never answered the *why* to her question. Why he'd contacted her mother. He continued with the itinerary he'd swooped in and expected her to follow.

She didn't like that he had talked to Cat, but she didn't dwell on it. Instead, she explained to him, feeling quite satisfied having to do it, that she wouldn't be going home with him on Sunday. And after her explanation why, he agreed that she probably should have told him when she'd spoken to him the day before that her plans had changed.

"Why would you do something like that and not tell me? What's going on down here?"

As the waiter set the Cabernet Sauvignon in front of them, Nona could see in his eyes as he fingered the base of the wineglass that Eli was honestly puzzled. And she could tell by his words that he was also suspiciously perturbed.

"It has nothing to do with anything else down here," she said, remembering that Marcus had made his presence known to him. She at least didn't want Eli to think anything along those lines, especially—she glanced down at her hand—after what she seemingly just agreed to.

"It appears my father had a will," she said. "I didn't know it before I came. My grandmother didn't tell me until after I got here."

She felt odd explaining herself to Eli. There usually wasn't anything to explain. She went along willingly, letting him run the show. He didn't like that that wasn't going to be the case.

"You should have told me," he said again. "This just isn't like you."

And with him there—Eli interacting with the Nona she'd become, the person she'd embraced and allowed to replace who she used to be—Nona could see why people thought the new her wasn't necessarily a good thing.

CHAPTER
TWENTY-FIVE

Bisset Brown left in a huff, but nothing had been blown over. He didn't have that much bite.

Marcus watched Bisset drive off and then marched to the back door of the Starlight, where Jayden had long disappeared, stopping only after he'd gotten to the door, turning to look at Julia, and asking without words, "Are you coming?"

Julia dawdled across the parking lot and walked past Marcus.

Opal, Miss Gus, Sanganette, and a couple of cousins were standing near the doorway.

"You okay?" came a murmur from a few.

"I got Marcus and your Mamaw as soon as you went out that door with him." Miss Gus was rubbing Julia on her back in what she thought were soothing circles.

"I'm okay," Julia answered to no one in particular. She didn't quite know where to turn, which way to go. She wanted to get to Jayden, but there were too many people around to have a conversation with her son about something she should have said years ago—an explanation of why his real father wasn't in his life.

"I've got Jayden," Sanganette said, wrapping her arm around Julia's shoulder, tugging her away from Miss Gus and nodding toward the table where she and her husband, Preston, were seated.

Opal caught Julia's gaze and gave a firm nod and went back to her seat.

It had surprised Julia that Opal hadn't come outside. She'd faced down Bisset more than once when Julia hadn't been able to stand up to him.

But whether Bisset knew it or not, those days were over. She had braced herself for his onslaught of words of manipulation and bullying, but she was prepared to chuck it right back at him.

She wasn't prepared, though, for her son to stand witness to the abusive, toxic, and manipulative man that Bisset was. She glanced over at him. He had his head down, hands folded. Julia headed over to him.

But before she could get where he was, Marcus arrived, standing over him. He put his hand on Jayden's shoulder. Jayden stood up, facing his father, they seemed to come to a peaceful understanding without a word. Jayden followed Marcus into the back.

Julia wanted to be the one to have that oneness with Jayden. Marcus didn't have to say anything, and she was struggling to find the words to tell her son what she wanted him to know.

Even with people still milling around—Sanganette and Miss Gus. Cousins. Onlookers—Julia felt abandoned. And she thought, perhaps, unwittingly and unwillingly, she had let Bisset do that to her all over again.

She wandered down the hallway she'd seen Marcus and Jayden go down. She followed it to the entryway of the kitchen and saw the two of them. Moving about, preparing food as if nothing had happened. Both in sync, Jayden following Marcus' lead.

And she somehow found her strength in that.

Turning around, she went back the way she came. Julia would talk to Jayden, a serious sit-down talk, but not today. She mingled with the people wanting to convey their condolences. She sat and chatted with Opal and Ruby and steered Miss Gus' conversation away from what had transpired and back to what was relevant. What mattered. The life of her father and the life all of them who were left had to live.

By the time the food was being brought out, Julia was back to herself and ready to help. With the aid of others, they readied the table, putting out plates and plasticware and napkins. Julia fussed with Opal and Miss Gus on having punch or just serving water and coffee.

"Punch!" They nearly spoke in unison. It was the first time that Julia could remember them agreeing on anything. But that was all they agreed on.

"That's not enough ginger ale," Opal said, tilting up the bottom of the two-liter bottle.

"You don't need no ginger ale in the punch. Just add some fruit," Miss Gus said, reaching for the bottle. Opal smacked her hand away. "Some orange slices would be nice."

"And where you think she supposed to get some oranges from?"

"Behind the bar," Miss Gus said, gesturing over to the long oak counter. "They keep oranges for the drinks."

Opal smacked her lips. "You would know that."

Julia just kept moving, trying to stay clear of the two of them. She took her place, over the protests of others, as a server in the banquet line. Grabbing a plate of food for herself after she'd dished up a plate for everyone else. She found the seat Opal had saved for her at the family table, and in the chair next to her was Jayden.

"You okay?" she leaned over and whispered. She'd sat next to him to eat, saying not a word as to what had occurred earlier. Nervous to start that conversation. She had come to sit in the chair beside him only after she'd helped clear off the tables, took everything back to the kitchen, and grabbed the last piece of sweet-potato pie.

"Yep," he said, wiping his mouth with his napkin. "You okay?"

She smiled and rubbed his leg. "I'm fine." It was nice when your child acted as if he cared about you.

"Sorry I'm late." The voice came from behind Julia and now was familiar to her. "I hope there's some food left."

Julia turned around to find Raymond Donaldson leaning into her. She almost bumped heads with him. She pulled back, and he leaned closer. "I had to get everything squared away at the funeral home."

"It's okay," Julia said. "I'm sure there's something left." She scooted her chair back to get up, and as she stood up, he straightened out. "If I'd known you were coming, I would have put a plate up for you."

Julia went down the hallway, Raymond following her. The busyness over, the kitchen was quiet and dark.

"I just need to find the light switch."

It wasn't Julia's first time in the kitchen. She'd spent many a night there with Marcus before he owned it and it was his job to clean it up. But in those days, her mind had been muddled, and she hadn't paid much attention to anything other than what was going on with her.

"This light switch?" Raymond flicked it, and light flooded the room.

"And there was light," Julia said. She started peeking under the foil tops of the pans of leftover food. "Anything in particular you want?" She looked up at him. "I'll see if I can find some. We had some of everything, but I don't know what's left."

"I'll take a piece of chicken."

"I think we've got some of that," Julia said. "You like thighs?"

"Thigh or a leg, I like 'em both." He grinned at her. "Do you cook?"

"Yep. Got a growing boy. Couldn't get away with not cooking."

"Fine young man you got there." He nodded. "You doing a good job raising him."

"Am I?" Julia said feeling more unsure of herself than she had in a long time. Had just the presence of Bisset done that to her? She stood straight up and turned her gaze to Raymond, a lost look in her eye. "My father used to say that it takes a man to raise a boy."

"It's good to have a man in his life, teach him things," Raymond said, looking into Julia's eyes, "but that don't mean a woman can't raise a fine man."

Julia thought of what Bisset had said. That she wasn't good at anything. And even without Bisset's words, she'd often worried if she was doing right by her son. She wanted to be a good mother. Better than the mother she'd had. She wanted to be there for him. Teach him how to be a man. A black man in today's world. And she wanted him to learn how to treat people. Things she knew he couldn't learn from his father—his real father.

"What's bothering you?" Raymond said. "I can see it in your face. You having a hard time with your boy?"

And without a second thought, Julia spilled everything that was on her heart. On her mind. In her past.

And Raymond listened.

But even if he hadn't, Julia didn't think she could stop talking. Confessing. Venting.

Julia talked about how Jayden had begun to challenge her. At times making her feel as if she didn't know how to do things, that she wasn't doing them right. And maybe, she'd said, that was just what teenagers do, because they had always been close up until now. Then she told him how Jayden seemed to be forming a tighter bond with Marcus. But now, even though she was the one who put Marcus in Jayden's life, she wasn't sure how she felt about that.

And she confessed how she wasn't sure about a lot of things when it came to Jayden.

He told her that lots of mothers feel that way. "Raising kids is probably the hardest job a person can have."

Julia almost felt a smile come on amid the tears that filled her eyes. So then she told him about Bisset Brown.

All the words came tumbling out. Their history of how he abused her and his reappearance and how it made her feel.

"It makes me scared. It makes me think that I am not strong enough to make it through."

"You seem okay to me," Raymond said. He rubbed her arm.

"I do?"

"You do," he said. "From what you're telling me, you've made good decisions. You've protected your son. You've given him a good life. Put good people into his life."

Julia stood up a little straighter and nodded. Maybe she was okay, although that was something else she wasn't so sure about, but maybe her being able to stand there and talk to Raymond about things was proof. Her not cowering to Bisset in the parking lot was proof. Jayden being a good child was proof.

And that made everything seem to clear.

Julia held her head up and looked back into his eyes. "I am happy that Marcus is Jayden's father, however that may have come about. I'm grateful he was there when Jayden and I needed him." She swallowed back her tears. "Really grateful. You know?"

"Yup. I know."

She did appreciate Marcus. Him being in Jayden's life. In her life. And not out loud, she admitted that she felt good about Marcus being there even if it may not have been the smartest thing she'd done. Date a man who was supposed to marry her sister.

"You're doing fine," Raymond said when Julia stopped long enough to take a breath. "Everything is going to be fine."

"You think so?" Julia asked, her eyes misting over. "Most times, I'm sure it will be. That I've overcome so much, you know, that I know I can make it through whatever. And then there are days like today. Where I bury my father and all the demons I thought I'd exorcised"—she coughed out a chuckle—"are back."

"I got you," he said. "I deal with ghosts and demons all the time working at the funeral home." He smiled at her. "I know everything there is to know about them and their little tricks. I won't let them anywhere near you." He gave her a reassuring smile. "And if they try, you just call me." He walked over close to her. "You need anything, you just let me know. I got you."

CHAPTER TWENTY-SIX

It wasn't possible for Nona to go to the airport with Eli the next day. They both had rental cars. He'd need to drop his off before boarding the plane, and if she rode with him in his car, she'd be stuck without a ride back. And if Nona was honest with herself, she was okay with not seeing him off.

Still swirling around in her head were all the realizations and feelings that had come from seeing him here. The faux engagement—because that was what it was. She knew, even if he hadn't, that she hadn't given him an answer. Her yearning to perhaps unbury that Nona from Natchez that everyone else there saw. And her mother.

Nona wasn't sure if she liked that Cat had told Eli how to find her (and even more unsure how she felt that he had). But even more worrisome than that, Nona wanted to talk to her mother about Julia. About why Cat wasn't in Julia's life.

Nona had told Jayden she'd come to visit. And she knew once she saw Julia, she would have to tell her about their mother—she'd learned that not saying anything didn't work. It only made things worse. Tell Julia where Cat was. How she was. And the why of it, at least the part she knew. How could she not? Cat not being around had caused Julia more grief than Nona could have imagined. Julia hadn't had the big sister to step in and fill the gap, like she'd done for Nona. Nona had to fix this for her sister.

And to get the answers to that, Nona knew she had to talk to Cat. But before she could dial her number, Ruby called.

"You left early yesterday," he said. "You okay?"

"I can't go to Jackson," she said, not exactly giving him the information he was searching for. He avoided, Nona could tell, asking directly about Eli. She was sure Opal had probably told him who Eli was. She had told her grandmother about him, and Opal had to have guessed it was him, even though she'd never seen him before.

Nona looked down at the ring on her finger before slipping it off and putting it in the zippered part of her wallet.

She wanted to go to Jackson. To see the museum. To listen to the oral histories. That was her passion. All the things she wanted to do. To be involved in. They revolved around what she had grounded her entire career in. She wanted so much to go see it that she was willing to go with Eli. Someone who would not have appreciated it. So she even asked Eli to go with her. Just for the company. But he hadn't seen any purpose to taking a side trip. Just like she knew he would.

Breakfast in the room and a walk around the area had been his suggestion on what to do with their time together. So that was what she did. Until he'd gone.

Going with Ruby, though, seemed to her out of the question. She still hadn't completely reconciled Ruby's past actions and didn't know if or when she could. Trying to untangle the knots with everyone was going to be hard enough. She couldn't do them all at once, and Julia had to be first.

And to make that happen, she knew she had to talk to her mother. It took some effort, without just being rude, to get Ruby off the phone.

"But we had plans."

"I know. And I'm sorry," Nona said, not wanting to share with him what she was planning on doing. He'd done enough meddling in her life.

"I really think you'd enjoy it," he said.

"I know that I would," she said, wishing she had someone else to go with. "But I can't today."

"Maybe we can do something else. Later on."

"Maybe so."

Nona sat on the side of the bed, shoulders drooping. She bounced her leg on the ball of her foot and dialed her mother's number. She didn't quite know how to start the conversation she wanted—she needed—to have with Cat. How do you ask someone why they had abandoned one of their children? Why she had picked one child over the other?

Childless Nona couldn't ever imagine.

Trying to figure it out, she fiddled with the light switch on the lamp and the cord to the phone, both on the nightstand near where she sat, and listened to Cat make small talk. Nervousness in her voice, Nona thought, and not the usual easy chatting between them.

"How was the funeral?" Cat asked, her voice low and thick. Nona could tell that Cat had been crying. Sniffles surrounded their conversation. She added before Nona could answer how it broke her heart that Nona hadn't been able to see Jasper before he passed.

"I didn't think you ever thought about my father."

"Why wouldn't I think about him?" Cat's voice had a lilt of surprise. "He was still my husband, you know."

"I don't know that you ever told me *that*. That you weren't divorced. I thought you were." Nona sat up straight. Her interest piqued. "I can't remember you ever talking about him to me."

"Because *you* never talked about *him* to me," Cat said. "Maybe I should have encouraged you to do that."

"I was too angry with him, thinking he'd ruined my life."

"And he hadn't?"

"Appears not."

"I could have told you that."

"You knew about him not being the one who kept Marcus from coming to meet me at the bus station?"

Was that something else that Cat hadn't mentioned?

Nona had never asked Cat why she'd left Natchez. Nona didn't want to talk about the past. All the people back in Natchez. But what could have been the reason a mother would leave her children? Nona knew Cat wouldn't have ever done that without good motivation.

On the other hand, Nona knew that Cat knew all about the reasons Nona had changed.

Once she had learned of Nona's new persona, Cat had asked her about it. How she'd become an introvert and not one to share. How she wasn't the same precocious adult as she'd been as a child. And had reminded Nona how she used to climb in her lap and tell her how she was going all over the world and maybe even to Jupiter.

"Why Jupiter?" Cat had recalled she'd asked.

"Because this boy in my class. You know Fred?"

"Yes. I know Fred."

"He said he was going to *our* moon. But Earth only has one moon. Jupiter," Nona had said with a gleam in her eye, "has sixty-nine."

"So you'll be able to go to more moons than Fred?"

"More moons than anyone."

That person was gone. A broken heart can do that. Cat understood that firsthand.

"What I know," Cat said, "is that it's not usually the parent that is the problem when the child is a headstrong girl like yourself."

"Yeah. I probably wouldn't have listened to you if you had told me that. I had my mind made up." Nona exhaled noisily through her nostrils. "Even though now I know I was wrong." Nona blew out a breath. "About a lot of things."

"You have always been so independent."

And with those words, a wash of anger and frustration swept through Nona. That wasn't her. Independent. Strong. Not anymore. Cat must be remembering what she'd been when she was younger. And for the second time in the short span of that day, it bothered Nona. Certainly she'd been reminded of it enough since she'd been back home. But Cat—her *mother*—had known her then and now. Couldn't she tell the difference? See how she had changed? Did Cat want her to stay the same? Because ever since she'd been back to Natchez, Nona wasn't sure she wanted to.

That made her question Eli's surprise visit.

"He showed me the ring," Cat said in response.

"Was that all it took for you tell him where I was? Where the funeral was and everything?"

"He already knew where you were," Cat chuckled. "And why wouldn't you want a man who thinks you would marry him to know how to find you?"

Nona had seen the ring, too, and had even allowed it to be put on her finger. She glanced at her wallet on the bed next to her. And even then, when she took it, she'd known. With each minute she spent in Natchez, something was sprouting inside her. She wanted to see what it would grow out to be. And it would take her mental capabilities to process it. To do it. And she would give it all the time needed. But not now.

"Eli isn't who I called to talk about," Nona said.

"Is it Julia?" Cat said. It was easy to detect the hopefulness in her voice. "Have you seen her?"

Nona felt that same uneasiness she had when Julia talked about Cat. She'd gotten herself in the middle of what could be a tumultuous situation. Someplace she wasn't comfortable being.

"Of course I've seen her."

"How is she?"

"Why didn't you ever contact her, Mom?" Nona asked. "I know we never—*I* never—spoke about her, but—"

"Because you were upset with her?" Cat interrupted.

"Yes." Nona didn't hesitate in her answer, but she felt ashamed. "I was upset with her."

"Why?"

Nona sucked her tongue and fell back on the bed. "I already told you. Because I thought she had ruined my life." She stared at the ceiling. "But why didn't you ever mention her? Contact her? What had she done to you?"

"She's never done anything to me," Cat said, barely above a whisper. "I've missed her so. Thought about her every day."

"So, what happened?"

It was through tears and words mixed with sobs that Cat told Nona the story of how Jasper had twisted her hand. It was why she'd become a nurse, to make enough money to fight back, then he threatened her. Told her she'd never see the girls again if she took him to court. He'd take them somewhere she'd never find them.

"I never meant to leave you girls. Huh." Cat sniffed back tears. "I never wanted to leave my husband."

"Then why did you?"

"I felt betrayed. Lied to by Jasper. Humiliated. I felt ashamed by what he'd done. I just wanted to take you girls and run. Run from the hurt. The pain."

"But you didn't take us."

"I couldn't. I didn't have a place to go. Nowhere to stay. I left you with your grandmother, and she promised to help get you two back to me once I got settled."

"But she didn't. She just helped my father keep you away."

"No. She tried. But she couldn't. If it wasn't for her," Cat said, "if it wasn't for Opal, Julia would have been lost to me forever."

"What are you saying?" Nona felt her heart pounding. She wasn't sure she'd be able to breathe through the rest of the conversation. And wished perhaps she could have folded, like she often did, instead of

231

facing circumstances. But she wanted to know what happened. She wanted to help fix Julia, and now, she also wanted to find a way to ease Cat's pain and the pain that had begun to swirl around inside her.

"She told me things she did, how she was. About her being a real estate agent. About Jayden."

"You know about Jayden?"

"I know. And maybe that's why I sent Eli down there. Because I knew I couldn't come."

"Why not?"

"Not after all this time." Cat got quiet. She didn't say anything for a long while, but Nona could hear her soft cries, even over the throbbing of her own heart. It had been filled with so much—sorrow, regret, love, and disappointment. "Because I know Julia probably hates me," Cat continued. "And wouldn't want to see me, and I don't think my heart could take that rejection."

Nona didn't know what to say. All three of them had done the same thing. Let lies and hurt separate them over the years and across the miles. And now, still, those things continued to leave them stranded and distant. It had to stop. Nona had to figure out how. But it was so hard, and the love she felt for her sister and mother overflowed.

"And," Cat said after a while, "then you came." Cat couldn't catch her breath, and her words came out with sniffles. "I had one of you, but my heart never stopped aching for my other child. For Julia. It hurts so much. It still does. I really have missed my family." She started weeping.

Then, for the first time since Nona could remember, she cried, too.

CHAPTER

TWENTY-SEVEN

Nona wanted to make things right. Between her and Julia. Cat and Julia. And within herself.

Family, like Miss Gus had said, was a fleeting thing. You just can't get angry with them and go on never making up. You can't wait until you've gotten past what set you off in the first place, because people die. And in between, they need you to help make it through.

Being apart from her family, holding grudges, leaning into misconceptions and untruths, had made Nona into someone else. Not necessarily something bad, only something different. It had broken her. And since she'd been home, she realized that being broken made you feel like an outsider. Not belonging anywhere. And now she decided she didn't want to be in that place anymore.

Because of her swearing off her family, she'd lost out.

But not completely. She saw that she'd only shut out her father and sister. A sister who said she had needed her. A father who passed on before she could see or talk to him again. She'd kept close to her grandmother and mother. Kept them in her life. Even if she hadn't been able to see, until now, that she needed all of them. Even Opal, who had lied to her so many times. But each lie, Nona realized, was to protect her. To keep her from making all the mistakes she wouldn't have made if only she had done what Opal wanted her to.

And that was all she could think about during the night. She swiped at the lingering tears that had persisted.

Nona pulled herself up off the bed and showered. Wiping the condensation off the mirror, she studied her face. She didn't look any different, but she was different. She felt different. Things were clearer. The troubled waters seemed to be behind her.

She put on the dress Opal had given her, having had it washed in anticipation of returning it to her grandmother. She put on a little makeup, wanting to look nice for her sister, and flat ironed her short hair. She knew her hair, no longer used to the humidity in Natchez, wouldn't hold a style for long. But it pleased her to put some effort into it.

Trying, that was what mattered.

And she set out in her car to give it a try.

To get back some sort of relationship with her sister and to start one with her nephew.

She wasn't quite sure what she was going to do about Opal and Ruby. But she knew now where she needed to go. She hoped it wasn't too early to visit her sister.

But then she got sidetracked.

Marcus was outside the Starlight. He had hosed down the sidewalk to clean it and was now sweeping the wet sidewalk, forcing the water to run into the street and down the drain.

Without a second thought, she stopped, parked the car, and got out. She walked over to Marcus and couldn't help but to smile at him when he looked up and noticed her.

"Morning, Mr. Curtis."

"Ms. Davenport." He stopped sweeping and leaned against the broom handle. "Good to see you today. You by yourself?"

"I am."

"What happened to you yesterday?" Marcus tilted his head to the side. "Is the guy that bad that you didn't want to hang around if he was going to be with you?"

Nona chuckled. "No. He's not that bad."

"But bad?"

"I didn't say that," she said. "He's my boyfriend—well, my fiancé." A knot caught in Nona's throat with those words.

He glanced down at her hand.

Her eyes followed his, and she wiggled her fingers.

She wanted to say it needed sizing, but that would have been a lie on her part as well as Eli's. He was meticulous. He would have found out the details before making such a large purchase, just as he had.

"It's in my wallet."

"Having second thoughts?"

"I didn't come here to talk about me and Eli."

"Who did you come to talk about? Me and you?"

"No," she said. She could feel herself wanting to giggle. She had to try hard to suppress it. "I didn't come to talk about anything in particular. I saw you out and"—she shrugged—"just thought I'd stop by to say hey."

"Hey," he said, and smiled.

"Hey," she said.

With all she'd found out after she'd gotten back to Natchez, her anger and frustration had hopped from one person to another. Julia. Ruby. Opal. But she realized that she hadn't ever been upset with Marcus. Hadn't placed any of the blame for all the things that had happened on him.

"I gotta go," she said.

"How about a little breakfast"—he glanced down at his watch—"or brunch. I can whip something up in the kitchen. We can sit and chat. Talk about us."

Nona sucked her teeth and started to turn away. That was another thing she needed to process—her feelings about Marcus. She hadn't added that to the list she'd mentally made earlier. Julia. Cat. Her becoming Nona again. But she couldn't have a conversation about her and Marcus until she figured all that other stuff out.

Marcus saw what his words had done. "We can talk about whatever you want to chat about, Peaches." The name rolled off his lips in a way that gave her pause and made her smile. "How about I tell you what happened after you left yesterday. And then you can tell me about what happened with you."

"Okay," she said, her plans changed around, just like that. But it didn't feel the same as when she let Eli dictate the things they did. It felt so much different. "But no talking about what happened to me. Or about Eli."

"Okay." He held up a hand.

"Or about us."

"Us?" He grinned. "I like the sound of that."

"Okay," Nona said, not budging from where she stood. "I'm leaving."

"No." He chuckled, not at all concerned she really would leave. "Don't go." He leaned the broom up against the wall of the building. "No talking about us. Promise." He placed one hand over his heart and reached out to her with the other. She walked past him, and he moved to open the door, gesturing for her to go in. "So, tell me, Ms. Davenport, you still like your eggs sunny-side up?"

"Yes, Mr. Curtis. I do."

CHAPTER
TWENTY-EIGHT

"Hi." Julia's front door was already open when she heard the knock. Standing on the other side of it was Nona. That nearly gave Julia goose bumps. "You by yourself?" Julia asked, pushing the screen open and poking her head out to look around. The last time she'd seen Nona, at the cemetery, she'd had a man in tow.

Nona turned around and looked behind her. "Yep. By myself." It was the second time that day she'd been questioned about Eli's whereabouts. She wasn't sure she wanted to explain him to anyone. He'd been who she'd hidden behind, and she had decided she wasn't going to hide anymore.

Nona turned back and let her eyes meet Julia's, her hands folded in front of her. "Are you going to let me in?"

"Oh!" Julia chuckled. It was a nervous laugh. Although Julia was surprised to see Nona, she was happy about her being there. "Of course." She stepped aside so Nona could enter. "How did you know where I lived?"

Nona ducked her head. "Marcus told me."

Julia nodded and then without thinking glanced up the stairs. Jayden was up there, and if Nona was here to have a discussion about Marcus, Julia didn't want Jayden involved.

Nona followed her glance. "Where is Jayden? I told him I was going to come over today."

"You did?"

"Yep. He didn't tell you?"

"He doesn't communicate much with me unless he's hungry or there is some perceived interference into his life by me."

Nona laughed.

"He's still in his room. I don't know if he's asleep or playing that game."

"Fortnite?"

"Yeah." Julia shook her head. "How do you know?" Julia hoped that didn't sound insensitive.

Nona laughed. "I teach college students. As of late, I've had to include in my syllabus that late nights playing the game is not an excuse for assignments not being turned in on time."

Julia's shoulders relaxed. Whether Nona was there to have that conversation or because she was offering an olive branch, Julia didn't know. But there was no reason to be uneasy, Nona was still her sister, and it was good to have her there.

Standing in the foyer, Nona let her eyes explore the space they stood in. The dark staircase, the chair rail, and paneling on the walls. Then, settling her eyes back on Julia, she nodded toward an adjacent room. One that had a few chairs and a sofa. Julia turned to look at it and then back at Nona.

"Oh." Julia let the word out in a gush of air. "Sorry." Julia gestured with her hand. Her sister's presence made her flustered. In a good way. She wanted to make things right. She hoped they could. "C'mon in. Have a seat. I can get you something to drink."

"I'll take some water." Nona gave her sister a gracious smile. She was full after her big brunch, but she didn't want to turn down her sister's offer. "I'd somehow forgotten how hot it can get down here. Something I'd have to get used to all over again."

"You look cool in that dress."

Nona looked down at it. "It's Mamaw's."

"Really?"

"Yep." Nona pressed her hand down the front of it. "I sent it to her years ago as a present. It still had the tags on it."

"She has her own style."

"And evidently I don't know it," Nona said.

"Let me get you a glass of water." Julia started off toward the back of the house.

"I'll come with you," Nona said and followed.

Julia half turned and talked as she walked. "So. You and Mamaw talked, huh?" In the kitchen, Julia reached in the cabinet for a glass. "I mean while you were gone."

"Yeah. We did."

Nona could tell by Julia's face that she didn't know that they had, and from what Nona could read from her expression, that fact seemed to agitate her.

She hadn't planned to bring it up so soon into her visit, but it seemed the perfect segue.

"And I talked to Mom, too." Nona tilted her head from side to side. "You know, while I've been gone."

"Mom?" Julia asked, her hand on the refrigerator door, looking at Nona, squinting. She blinked several times. Then she turned her head to the side, as if Nona's words had just registered. "Cat Montgomery?"

"Mom's not dead, Julia. Not even hiding out somewhere." Not sure how Julia was going to react, Nona squeezed tight one eye and braced herself. "She's in Gary, and she didn't forget about us."

"You've seen her?" Holding on to the refrigerator door so she wouldn't fall, Julia felt flushed and wobbly. Her stomach was churning over, queasy. She tried to hold back tears she knew were coming.

Julia, wondering why she hadn't been able to run into her, felt a rush of emotions overtake her.

"I *see* her, Julia." Nona stepped closer to her sister, seeing the anguish in Julia's eyes. But Nona knew she needed to come clean. Tell Julia about Cat and not have her wondering what had happened. No more secrets or misinformation. The longer they're kept, Nona already knew, the more they hurt when they're set free.

"She—Mom—drove me to the airport when I came down here. She's even the one who told Eli how to find me."

"Wait. Who is Eli?"

"The man at the cemetery. You remember him. You saw him when he pulled up." Nona sighed. "The man who thinks I am going to marry him."

"You're not?"

"I'm undecided." But if Nona had been honest with herself and her sister, she would have had to admit she actually knew the answer.

Julia waved a hand, a "let's move past that for now" motion. She wanted to get back to Cat.

"Cat Montgomery knew Daddy died?"

"Yep. I thought I was the one who told her about it, but from what she told Eli, she knew a lot more than what I'd said."

"Why didn't she come?"

Nona opened her mouth to speak. But she knew she shouldn't speak for her mother. So she raised her shoulders and shook her head from side to side. "I don't know." Nona held up her hands. "Do you think it would have been okay? You know, with what happened with them? With not seeing you after all this time?"

"To see me? Yes. She should have come to see me." Julia licked her lips, ran a trembling hand across her forehead. "Yes. Of course." Her eyes misted over. She sat down in a nearby chair and then stood back up. Wringing her hands, she tried to get the words out. "It would have been okay to come and see me. I never didn't want to see her." Julia stopped momentarily, opening the refrigerator, breathing hard. When she spoke again, her voice was shaky. "I want to see her. I've always wanted to see her."

Nona took another step closer, happy that both her mother and sister wanted a reunion. "She wants to talk to you."

Julia sidestepped letting the refrigerator door close. "Why hasn't she talked to me all this time?"

"You'll have to ask her," Nona said. "Because I don't have the answer to that. We can call her now if you want." She took out her cell phone and held it out toward Julia.

But before she could get the go-ahead from Julia, a knock at the door distracted them.

"Who is that?" Julia asked.

Nona looked that way, but there was no view of the door from the kitchen. "Guess you'll have to go and see."

Julia shook her head, coming back to herself. "Sorry," she said. "Feeling kind of overwhelmed."

Nona followed her to the door as Jayden came bounding down the stairs.

"You made it," Jayden said, a beaming smile on his face. Happy to see his aunt.

"What are you doing here?" Julia said to the person standing outside the door. She reached over and flicked the lock on it. "Didn't I tell you yesterday I didn't have anything to say to you? I didn't want to see you."

"You didn't mean that," the man said, a smirk on his face.

Even though she'd never seen him, Nona knew right away who it was.

Jayden's father. The one Julia had fled from. Lied to Marcus to keep her son from. And the one person, Nona suspected, Julia had been expecting to show up. Constantly checking the door for his appearance.

He was standing with his hands dug down into the pockets. He wore a straw hat and had a scraggly moustache and goatee. His teeth brown around the edges and yellowing in the center.

Marcus had told her how Bisset had shown up soon after she and Eli had left. Met Julia as she'd come through the door. Per Marcus, all he'd come for was to "start some mess." And how Marcus had to put Bisset out because he and Julia didn't want Jayden anywhere around him.

"What's going on?" Nona said, coming to stand side by side with her sister.

"Nothing," Julia said. "I got this."

"Mom." It was Jayden. "You okay?" He was coming toward the door.

"Is that my boy?" Bisset asked, trying to look around Julia and Nona and into the house.

Julia shifted so that she was blocking Bisset's line of sight. Nona mimicked her sister's movements.

"You need to leave," Nona said.

"Who are you?" Bisset said, disdain in his voice.

At the same time, Julia said, "Nona, get my son."

"I'm not leaving you here with him." Nona nodded toward the man at the door.

"I'm not afraid of him," Julia said, locking eyes with Bisset.

"I know you're not. I've learned just how strong you are." Nona lowered her voice and leaned into Julia's ear. "Physically he has you beat. I don't want him to hurt you."

Julia looked Bisset up and down. He was, as her father would say, "a lightweight." But Nona was right.

"Okay. I'll have someone here while I handle this." She glared at Bisset. "Handle him." She looked at Nona, those old instincts kicking in. "But not you. I don't want anything to happen to you."

"You sure?" Nona asked. "I'm right here if you need me."

Julia nodded. "I need you to get Jayden."

"C'mon, nephew," Nona said. Glancing over at Julia, she turned and grabbed her nephew. "I need you to help me with something in the kitchen." Then she held up her phone, showing it to Julia. "I'll make a call." She gave a firm nod, hoping her sister understood what she was trying to convey.

Nona, too, thought it best to get Jayden away from this man. And to get her sister help. She was going to call Marcus.

"No, Nona," Julia said, understanding. "Call Mackel. Ask for Raymond Donaldson. If he isn't there, they'll know how to find him."

CHAPTER TWENTY-NINE

Nona found a willing Raymond Donaldson on the other end of the line, thanking her for calling and saying he was going to come right over. He told Nona that she might want to take Jayden out for a little while because he knew Julia wouldn't want him in the middle of anything Mr. Brown might start.

Bisset Brown had taken up residence in the room where Nona had first gone when she'd come over. He sat on the couch. Legs crossed, with a large jar of ice water he'd gotten Julia to give him. Nona liked that Julia knew how to keep him distracted until Raymond arrived and she and Jayden could leave. Julia had finally let him in after an exchange that Nona thought calm considering the circumstances.

She'd followed Julia and Bisset into the room, standing by the doorway, her back against the wall.

"Thought you were leaving?" Julia said, walking over to her.

"I told you that I wasn't leaving you here alone with him. Not until you're good." Nona and Julia moved their conversation out into the hallway.

They spoke in strained whispers, far away enough to keep Bisset from hearing. He sat on the sofa, fingers drumming on the arm- rest, assessing his surroundings as if they were soon to be his. Calm. Diabolical. Both sisters afraid of the chaos of what his visit may mean.

And the sisters' conversation was in low tones in an effort to hide it from Jayden, who wanted to protect his mother from the apparent demon who had entered their house. Determined. Unintimidated. Both sisters.

The conversation was interrupted with the arrival of Raymond Donaldson.

"Hello," he called out.

"Is he your boyfriend?" Nona asked, giving a nod toward the front of the house.

"Are you taking Jayden outta here for me?" Julia asked, not answer- ing Nona's question, although it was easy to see how her face had lit up.

"I'm not leaving you," Jayden said.

"Oh my goodness. Not you, too," Julia said. "Mr. Donaldson is here, if somebody would let him in the house." Julia gave Nona an expected look. "He'll help me. I'll be fine."

Nona went to the door and pulled it open. She remembered Raymond Donaldson as soon as he walked in the house, but she had had no indication that there was anything going on between him and her sister.

"Nona," he said, "thought you and the boy were going out."

"We are now," Nona said, liking that this man was trying to protect her sister.

She led him into the room where Jayden stood in a standoff with his mother. His lips tight. Eyes filled with determination.

"See?" Julia said. "Help has arrived."

"I don't know anything about him, other than he drives a car for the funeral home." Jayden gave the man a once-over.

Julia looked at Nona, exasperation in her eyes.

"And we know he came to your mother's rescue," Nona said. She put her hands atop of Jayden's shoulders and guided him out the back door. "C'mon, buddy. You're taking a ride with me."

Jayden looked back at his mother, reluctance covering his face.

"Hello," Mr. Donaldson spoke up. "What's going on?" He leaned forward, taking in the occupant in the next room. Standing back up, he nodded. "Oh. I see," he said and looked at Jayden. "Everything will be okay."

"Yes. You see that? He said everything will be okay. And I'm telling you, *I'll* be okay," Julia said to her son to reassure him. Getting him to leave. Then she turned her attention to Raymond. "You told me to call you if I needed you. I need you."

⌒

"I know who he is," Jayden said. They were walking around the house on the flat stones. "She doesn't need to try and hide him from me."

"Who?" Nona asked the question, not sure which "he" he was referring to.

"I know he's my biological father." A tough-guy persona evident. Nona was sure that it was more bravado than actual capability. This boy didn't seem like a fighter. No street toughness in him.

"Oh." Nona knew he knew. Marcus had told Jayden the truth about who he was. He'd also said Jayden wasn't interested in knowing much else about Bisset. And Nona was raised in the belief that some things shouldn't be shared with a fourteen-year-old, for sure, but who their father is shouldn't be a question debated. Even Julia was wounded when she didn't know about her mother. Nona wanted to talk to her nephew about it, but she didn't want to break Marcus' trust with his son by letting Jayden know he'd told her. So she feigned ignorance.

"How did you find out?"

"My dad told me." Jayden kept walking, not turning to face Nona. "A long time ago."

"Your dad?" Nona shook her head. "Marcus."

"I just didn't tell my mother that I knew. I didn't want her getting upset and crying. You know she cries all the time."

Nona had to keep from smiling with that answer. Julia knew he knew, but she had decided, and it was her decision to make, not to talk about Bisset to Jayden. And that was understandable. Not only would Julia have to explain what kind of man Bisset was but also why she'd let him into her life in the first place and let him stay. And why she'd lied about him being Jayden's father and let him believe Marcus was. It was a lot to confess to someone you wanted to love you and trust you.

"She cries." Nona nodded. "She's always been a crier."

"She has?"

"Yes."

"All the time? Because she cries all the time."

"Well, a lot." Nona chuckled. "I doubt if it's all the time."

"It is. That's why I didn't tell her what I know."

"She has always been the emotional one," Nona said, although that wasn't the word she'd usually used to describe Julia.

"Drama queen," Jayden said.

Nona chuckled. Now that was the phrase she'd use. Although she had recently discovered crying wasn't such a bad thing.

"But she's strong," Nona said. "She's been through a lot, and she's still standing. She raised you, and you seem like a pretty good guy." He blushed at the compliment. "So, what do you think about him being your father?"

"Nothing to think about," Jayden said. They'd reached the front yard, and he stood, looking up at his house. "It's a good thing to know who you are and where you come from. It helps you to see who you are but also who you shouldn't be."

Nona smiled. A boy after her own heart.

"C'mon, nephew. There's a museum in Jackson I wanna show you."

She'd found the right person to go explore the history she loved with. Someone she hoped shared her fervor. And someone who knew the importance of how history helped shape the future.

CHAPTER THIRTY

"Why would you just take my son and just disappear?" Julia said. "After what happened this morning. That man showing up at my door."

Nona and Jayden had walked into Opal's front yard. Stepping up with smiles, ready for conversation about their little excursion to Jackson and the adventure they'd had together. A porch full of people. Opal. Julia. Of course, Ruby. And Sanganette, for some reason, was there, too.

Miss Gus was over on her porch, but everyone knew that distance wouldn't stop her from joining in on whatever conversation was being held outside Opal's house.

The fleeting glance Nona threw Sanganette's way in recognition nearly washed the smile from Nona's face. She'd been avoiding the woman the whole trip. For something Sanganette had done eons ago. Her revisionist theories. Something Sanganette at the time probably didn't understand the meaning of. The history behind the claims of how and why the war that tore the country apart had started or what it really meant to all the people involved. Nona had forgiven everyone else.

"Julia," Opal said. Her tone scolding. "Don't take out on Nona all the hate that man brought this morning."

Nona hadn't quite processed Julia's words or her tone. But looking at her sister, she knew no harm had come to her. She had confidence in Julia's ability to handle Bisset, and Nona hadn't left until Raymond had gotten there.

"Don't 'Julia' me," she said, her words coming at the same time as Nona's. "And this doesn't have anything to do with this morning. I didn't know where my son was. For hours. I don't want anyone else coming up missing on me."

"Okay, Julia," Nona said, unintentionally speaking over Julia, wanting to calm her. "Guess where we've been." Trying to move the conversation forward, Nona glanced at Jayden. He'd already taken in his mother's disposition, evident by the distress showing in his face.

"I shouldn't have to guess the whereabouts of my son."

"Come again?" Nona turned her attention to Julia. "What's wrong?" she asked, noticing the scrutiny in her sister's face. "You just said everything went okay this morning, which I had already guessed."

"You don't know?"

"No." Nona shook her head. "I don't know what's wrong with you. You told me to take Jayden. Did something else happen other than with Bisset?" Nona looked around to take in everyone else's face. Had she missed something?

"Don't say that name in front of my son." Julia walked over to Jayden. Tugging on his arm, she tried to pry him away from Nona's side.

"Why, Mom?" Jayden said. "I already know who he is. I didn't tell you I know, but I do, although I don't know why you think I don't know him. Why you'd think I wouldn't know who was at the door." He took a step away from his mother. "Isn't that why you sent me away?"

"I didn't send you away." Julia's words came from between clenched teeth. "I only asked Nona to get you out of the way because I didn't know what would happen." Julia drew in a breath. "What *may* happen. What he might do." She turned a cold gaze to Nona. "I didn't expect you to be gone all day and to not know where you were."

Julia knew she was overreacting, but the morning had drained her. Bisset showing up on her doorstep had been something she'd always feared. She had handled it. Faced down a demon that had long possessed her. She had even liked the way it felt to have Raymond Donaldson at her side. He hadn't tried to take over the situation, just gave her his reassurances.

But then there were Bisset's threats of coming back again and again to see Jayden, no matter how many men Julia sicced on him. And maybe even take him. To talk to Jayden. How he'd told her she wouldn't always be able to shield him.

And she knew she couldn't. Not after learning the whereabouts of Cat Montgomery. Julia, better than anyone else, understood about a child needing their parent, having some interaction, whether they were a good parent or not.

And how could she do that if he was gone from her protection for hours. With someone who didn't mind leaving. Leaving Julia and staying away for years. That seemed to light a flame under Julia. Bursting open all the emotions she'd felt over all the years Nona had been gone. Floodgates opened, even though she wanted it all to be alright with her sister, Julia couldn't control what she was feeling.

"You could have called," Nona said.

"I don't have your number, remember? You never cared enough about your sister, your flesh and blood, to let me know how you were. Where you were. Or how to get in touch with you."

"Mamaw has my number, Julia." Nona understood about changing emotions and dealing with issues long since buried. She was experiencing the same thing. Julia was being over the top, but Nona was willing to take the brunt of it if it was going to help Julia. She owed her sister that much.

"Or you could have called me," Jayden said.

"I did," Julia said. "Several times."

Jayden pulled out his phone and punched in his code. "Oh," he said. "I had it on Do Not Disturb."

"Why?" Julia asked.

"Because we were in a museum."

"What museum?" Ruby spoke up. He looked at Nona. "In Jackson?"

"I don't know what the heck is going on here," Nona said, not answering Ruby. "What did you think I was going to do with Jayden, Julia? I don't know what you're trying to say. I thought everything was okay with us?"

"I don't know what you might do with him. You like disappearing. Making people worry."

"No, I don't."

"Yes, you do." Julia stepped closer to Nona. "You know that man was lurking around, trying to get to my son, and I didn't know where he was. What if Bisset had found you?"

"You said you were taking care of that. I just took Jayden for a little while."

"It's been all day. I didn't know where you were. Where Bisset was after he left."

"I'm sorry, Julia. I thought me taking Jayden was what you wanted."

"Ever since you came back here, you've turned everyone's life upside down."

"I have not." Nona took a step back. She searched the eyes of the onlookers. Now Julia was going way beyond the hurt feelings she'd been harboring. She was attacking Nona.

"You've got everybody talking about you," Julia said, certainty in her voice. Nona's gaze instinctively moved across the yard to Miss Gus.

Augusta McClure held up her hands, noting her innocence.

"Me?" Nona said. "I get you're dealing with a lot, Julia, and throwing blame around. But you wanna tell me how, pray tell, did I do that?"

She flung an arm at Ruby. "And you got poor Ruben still chasing after you."

"Ruben has never chased after me."

"Only because you were too stuck-up to notice. He tried to stop you from marrying Marcus so he could have you and still is trying to get you. How you think he and Mamaw got so close? Haven't you noticed how he's always around up under her? Mamaw was his only ally in a plan he hatched to get you to be with him."

Ruben stood up from where he'd been seated. "Julia, I don't know what you're sore about." He stepped down off the porch. "But my business isn't any of your business, nor is it for you to tell."

"Ruby," Nona said, "has already told me all of this, Julia. But I can't understand why you're bringing it up now."

"She was just worried about Jayden," Opal said. "She's been in a frenzy all afternoon. Came over here looking for the two of you. We had to stop her from calling the police."

"Oh," Miss Gus said. "You finally got it, Nona? Because even somebody blind could see Ruby got a thing for you." She may have been in spectator seating, but she wasn't going to not take part in the melee.

"Augusta," Opal said, "we've already covered that. Let's not stir up all the pots."

"And then you've got some man coming down here for you that you don't even introduce to people." Julia's voice had escalated, she'd leaned in closer to Nona. "What? Aren't we good enough to meet your up-north friends?"

Nona attempted to interrupt, but Julia wasn't having it.

"You've got Marcus spilling his guts out to you. Him telling you my business—Jayden's business—and ain't no telling what else he done said to you. He ain't yours no more, Nona. Don't think you can come back down here and take up where you left off."

But those words caught Nona, and she could feel the heat rise up her face. She could understand Julia being worried about Jayden. Afraid of Bisset trying to talk to him, take him, or God knows what. She could forgive her sister for lashing out for that. But bringing her feelings for Marcus up, if indeed that was what they were, in front of everyone was too much. So Nona blasted right back at her. "Why, Julia? Because you stepped in as my proxy? He's not yours either. You think you can take the place of me? You can't."

"I wouldn't want to be you."

"Really? Because it seemed that you wanted my life." Nona put her hands on her hips. "You tried to take my man."

"Who is your man, Auntie Peaches?"

"It wasn't one-sided, Nona," Julia said, her anger making her unable to hear her son. "And he didn't even come after you. He stayed right here."

"He didn't come after me because of you or Daddy."

"Of course not. I didn't have anything to do with it."

"But you didn't help," Nona said. "You, Daddy"—Nona pointed to Opal—"Mamaw. All the people I call family. And then when he didn't come after me, you what? Stepped in?"

"I did what you couldn't do," Julia said. "I did what was right. For my family. People you care nothing about."

"Julia!" Opal stood up from her metal porch chair. "What do you think you doing?"

"Stirring up trouble," Ruben said. "And trying to pull everyone down in the mire with her." He narrowed his eyes at Julia.

"Shut up, Ruben," Julia said, snorting. "She didn't want any of us. Including you, and still doesn't. That's why she left in the first place."

"I didn't leave because of *you*," Nona said, emphasizing the word she directed at Julia. "And I didn't know anything about Ruby. How he felt back then. What he did or would do. Believe me." Nona arched an eyebrow. "And Marcus . . . Marcus . . ." Nona flapped her arms. "That's in the past, and we should just leave it there."

"I don't even know why you came back here," Julia said. "You don't care what happened while you were gone." Julia was crying. "You didn't care about Daddy. About Marcus. About me."

Where Wild Peaches Grow

"That is not true." Nona spat the words at her. "I cared—care—I care about all of you. I love all of you. And whether I knew it before or not, I missed all of you."

"Then why did you do us like you did, Nona?" Julia drew in a breath to push her words out with more force. "Why did you do that to us?"

So this was it. All the pain Julia had been feeling, keeping inside about her sister, came pouring out. Perhaps Bisset had been a catalyst, but Nona knew for Julia it was cathartic.

And Nona knew, if things were to ever be right, everything did need to come out. No matter how much pain and regret she and Julia would need to spill out.

For Nona, she wasn't going to let people and situations change the person she truly was. And the Nona everyone in Natchez knew was someone who could take much of whatever was thrown at her.

"I didn't do anything to you." Nona raised her eyebrows and calmed the rise Julia had brought on. She remembered the conversation the two of them had had at Lander's. Julia's hurt because she'd left. "I didn't come back before because of what I *thought* you all did to me."

"We did something to *you*? Ha!" Julia swallowed hard. Her hands trembling. Her voice wobbly. "Of course, it's all about you. When isn't it?"

"I said, I thought. I know it's not true." She stepped closer to her sister. "I came back because this is home," Nona said. "I can come home whenever I want to." She reached out a hand to Julia. "And I came back, I know now, because I've missed you."

"Julia," Sanganette said, "you should calm down." She reached out to touch Julia's arm, but Julia pulled away. "C'mon, sweetie. Jayden's back. That son-of-a-gun is gone. Everything is going to be alright."

Julia wasn't sure for how long. She was sure, though, that she wasn't going to keep anything else hidden and that she was going to handle things and not let outside influences get the best of her.

But Julia wasn't through venting. Turning loose years of pain. "Yeah," she said to Nona, tears streaming down her face. "But I don't want you here if you're going to teach my son about leaving. Enticing him with things away from me. I don't want you around my son if you try and show him that it's okay to leave family. To stay away for twenty years."

"I wouldn't do that," Nona said.

"Teaching him to leave," Julia continued. "When all the while, you seem to be wanting to come back here and act as if you can start back where you left off. With Marcus. With Ruby. With me. Trying to be family to my son, whom you've never met. Telling him about Bisset. Taking the things that Daddy left behind. You don't deserve any of it. And then you go making everything into an uproar." Julia shook a finger at Nona.

"Nona told him about Bisset?" Sanganette seemed to want to get into the argument. "Did she tell him what happened between the two of you?"

"She didn't tell me that," Jayden said, his face filled with confusion. "I don't know anything that happened between the two of you other than making me." Jayden balled up his fists. "And I don't want to know."

"Oh! Your Auntie Peaches left out telling you *that*? All my humiliation? I can't believe it. Because she just been going around talking about me and my life to *everyone* else she runs into."

Nona frowned. "I have not been doing that. You're talking crazy. There is something else bothering you, Julia, and it isn't me." Nona glanced over at her nephew. "I wouldn't ever tell him anything about Bisset. It isn't my place to tell," Nona said. She worried about how all this would affect him. They'd had the makings of forming a good relationship between them.

"Nothing is your place. Not here." Julia's voice escalated. Her words fast. "So, take your useless PhD in something that doesn't exist and all the sandy mess that goes with it and go back home to your mother."

Sanganette snickered at Julia's comment, and then she realized the entirety of what Julia had said. "Mother? Your mother? Nona knows where your mother is?"

"Sanganette," Ruby said. "Mind your business."

"Why are you always taking up for her?" Sanganette asked Ruben, pointing her finger from him to Nona.

"How do you need to even ask that question?" Julia snickered. "It's obvious to everyone but Miss Queen Anne over here."

"I've heard enough." Opal grabbed the banister and took one foot at a time to the bottom of the two steps.

"What's going on?" Marcus had walked up the driveway. "Why is everyone standing outside, yelling?"

"Because they have lost their cotton-picking minds," Opal said. "But I'm going to put a stop to it."

"I hate that saying," Nona said.

"And I *hate* that the two of you have the nerve to stand in my yard, hurling accusations at each other. Disrespecting my house and me. And for what?"

"To set Nona straight," Julia said. "That's for what."

"Straight?" Opal licked her bottom lip. Her hands curled into fists. She stomped her foot. "How you think you gonna do that? Both of y'all just as guilty."

"Guilty of what?" The sisters spoke practically in unison.

"I can't see nothing Julia's done," Sanganette said. "But Nona is guilty of spreading lies."

"Well, ain't that the pot calling the kettle black," Opal said.

"Sanganette." Ruben called her name. "You need to stay out of this." He went and stood by Nona.

"I have a right, a Constitutional right, to say whatever I want to say, Mr. Lawyer. You should know that," Sanganette said.

"You shouldn't be spouting law you don't know or understand," Ruben said.

"Or history," Nona added.

Sanganette, mimicking Opal's actions, put her hand on her hips and stomped her foot. "And she"—Sanganette stretched out her arm and pointed a finger at Nona—"came down here to ruin me."

"Sanganette," Opal said, "nobody's trying to do anything to you. Nona's just trying to set the record straight."

"Something Sanganette knows nothing about," Nona said.

"This isn't about Sanganette, Nona. It's about you. About this family," Julia said. "The one you abandoned. The one you're now all of a sudden so interested in."

"She didn't abandon anybody, Julia." Opal looked at her granddaughter, compassion evident in her eyes.

"Yes. She. Did." Tears still streaming down Julia's face. "Even you, Mamaw. She left you, too. Don't you know that?" Julia bent forward. Her words pleading. "A phone call every now and then. Was that enough?" Julia turned to Nona. "And you still got her"—Julia flung an arm toward her grandmother—"worrying about you. Taking up for you. Even running around, trying to hook you up with Ruben. Probably so she can get you to stay."

"She is not," Nona said.

"Not what?" Julia asked. "Because she is. She is doing all those things. But you wouldn't even stay for me."

"Julia, you need to calm down." Marcus spoke for the first time since arriving. "I thought everything was okay between the two of you. What happened between this morning and now?"

"How can everything be okay?" Nona asked. "When your sister marries the man you were supposed to. The man you love." Nona shook her head. "Loved. And then accusing me of being the one who has caused the trouble. I don't even know what trouble. I thought everything was fine. We were just fine this morning. And she's the one mad. Marrying you and never bothers to tell me. Never even cared enough to see how I felt about it. No. She just hid it from me. I'm guessing thinking I'd never find out."

And the steadiness she hoped to offer to Julia's outburst, despite feeling pricked by the sharp blade of Julia's comments, had taken a turn. A turn, she realized, that came about when Marcus arrived.

Everyone turned to look at Nona. Ruben stepped back from her.

"See," Julia said. "She thinks everything is about her."

"Oh my Lord!" Nona said and stomped over to Julia. "You think it's okay what you did?"

"You left!" Julia shouted.

"And that made what you did okay?" She emphasized the words as she repeated them again.

"I stayed. I took care of Daddy. I lived through Bisset. I stayed," she said again, giving a firm nod of confirmation. "I survived." She waggled a finger at Nona. "And don't think you're any better."

"What is that supposed to mean?"

Julia leaned in close to her sister's face. "You kept secrets. The whole time you were gone. Just to hurt me."

"Me? I kept secrets?"

"Cat." Julia cocked her head to the side. "You tried to keep her all to yourself."

"What are you two talking about!" It was Jayden. "Can you just stop?" He was starting to cry. "What did you do to Auntie Peaches, Ma? What did you do?"

"And now you are turning my son against me." Julia hissed out the words.

"Ma! She is not."

"Oh my Lord, Julia," Nona said. "What is wrong with you? Just tell me so we can get through this."

Julia drew in a deep breath. She took a long moment to look around her, then down at her shaking hands before glancing at her son. She bit her bottom lip and shook her head. "I don't know." She sniffed back tears that had seemed to bubble up. "I don't know. Everything is feeling all tangled up inside of me, and I just can't seem to get out of it."

CHAPTER

THIRTY-ONE

The forty acres and a mule promised in a wartime order wasn't ever directed to the entirety of the population of freed slaves. Although rustlings of such fulfillment, from then until now, have been heard given as reparations. But in coastal regions of rolling hills and lowlands like that of Natchez, off the muddy waters of the mighty river, those promises weren't ever made. At the center of the two-hundred-year-old practices, Mississippi, second to secede from the union, was one of the last to return.

And to give up any land to those who had worked it and made it profitable.

After Cat left, there was no more robbing Peter to pay Paul because Jasper had spent all the household money gambling. He had two little girls to take care of. He couldn't be frivolous. Reckless.

It wasn't that he hadn't been the breadwinner of the family all along, but now that Cat was gone, he had to become the responsible one, too. That had always been Cat's job. Making sure things ran smoothly on the home front and trying to keep Jasper in line.

Jasper Davenport bought his first property in Louisiana. An old, dilapidated one-story that he worked on for nearly a year. Bringing his girls along, he patched holes, added new plumbing, painted the inside white and the outside sky blue. He gave it a yellow door, white shutters, and put in some shrubs and window boxes filled with red geraniums. He was good with his hands. Nona had said it looked like a house in one of her storybooks.

He sold that one, turning a tidy little profit, then it was a while before he bought another one. But once he started, as the girls grew, he bought a few more.

And then just the land.

One piece of land in particular . . .

The lawyer stood as Julia and Nona walked to his office, ushered in by his assistant. He pressed down his tie and buttoned his suit jacket.

They walked in one after another, neither looking the other's way. Today was about their father. Jasper Davenport, a man who'd always been there for them. Now it was time to do the same for him. Nothing could come between or stand in the way of their duty to him.

"Come in. Have a seat." The lawyer gestured to the women.

The law firm on Franklin Street was large. This room spanned over the front half of the building, and its furnishings made note of its prestige.

Both Julia and Nona, surprised that their father would deal with a company of such stature, slid into the upholstered chairs that sat in front of the big mahogany desk.

Nona settled in and put her hands in her lap. Julia turned to look one more time at the door they'd entered before sweeping her skirt under her and sitting next to her sister. She took to staring out the window, although the only view the second-story office gave was of another brick-and-mortar building across the street.

The man seated in front of the sisters smiled. And stood with that smile pasted to his face for what the sisters both thought an uncomfortable amount of time. Then, as if acting on some sort of cue, he unbuttoned the jacket that he'd just fastened and took his chair behind the desk.

"Is anyone else coming?" Julia asked, not turning her gaze.

"Who else would you expect?" the lawyer asked.

"Our grandmother," Nona said. "Shouldn't she be here?" Speaking what she thought was on Julia's mind.

"Just the two of you are all we need," he said, that same unyielding smile reappearing. "Shall we start?"

The sisters nodded.

"So, I'm Alex Marchetti, and I was your father's lawyer."

"I thought you were his property manager," Julia said. Turning her eyes to him, she arched an eyebrow. His being there surprised her. He hadn't mentioned when they spoke that he would be the one handling the probate, even acting unsure as to what had to be done. Never would she have thought from the impression he gave her that he knew anything about the law or her father's estate.

Nona, who'd been staring down at her folded hands, glanced up at Julia, then at the lawyer.

"I was both."

Julia and Nona looked at each other.

"And he left me instructions on what he wanted me to do after he was gone."

"And what was that?" Julia asked.

"He wanted me to make sure that the two of you were together." He paused, looking at the sisters, a slight smile on his face indicating he'd done that part of his job. "And I'm supposed to give you these." He pulled two envelopes out of a folder and held them up.

"That's what he left for us? Letters?"

"No land?" Julia asked.

"No. There's plenty of land. And houses." He sat the letters down and opened a folder in front of him. "And Julia, you get the bulk of the real estate." Julia's shoulders relaxed. She tried not to let her smile show outwardly or have the glance over to Nona be noticed.

"There are two properties for your son." He glanced up at Julia. "And Nona"—he turned his gaze—"he left you a property on North Rankin Street."

"Is that all?" Julia asked. No matter what rifts her outburst had caused, although Nona had seemed fine that day when she left, even hugging Julia and holding her tight, she didn't want Nona to be slighted.

"No." Alex looked back down at the opened folder. "He's left you land on Cemetery Road. And . . ." The lawyer blew out a breath and closed the folder. "Nona"—he picked up a folded document that had been lying on his desk—"Jasper left you and your nephew, Jayden Curtis, jointly, ownership of the real estate known as the Devil's Punchbowl."

~

They had both sat in the upholstered wine-colored chairs in the lawyer's office and signed off on all the paperwork before he gave each the sealed envelope with the letter their father had left for them.

Attorney Alex Marchetti had Julia step into the office next door, and he'd left Nona alone in his.

"Read them over before you go," he had instructed. "If you have any questions, let me know. I don't want you leaving my office and not fully understanding what your father left for you."

"Is it that complicated?" Julia held up the letter.

"No. But sometimes these things—divvying up a loved ones' possessions can be . . . well . . . disheartening. And confusing." He tested the weight of his words with the back and forth of his head. "Certainly sad and sometimes surprising."

It was exactly how the two sisters felt when they read their letters. And for each, they felt, at that moment, alone.

Nona's letter had once again brought tears to her eyes.

He'd called her his *darling daughter*. He'd written how proud he was of her. And the reason he'd left her the Devil's Punchbowl. She'd looked away before she'd read why and then held the letter close to her chest after reading his words.

Because, he'd written, *I know that you have what it takes—the mind, the strength, the understanding—to make the legacy of that land right.*

He told her how much he had missed her and how heartbroken he'd been when she wouldn't come home with him. How he couldn't ever understand her anger with him. But whatever it was, he hoped she would forgive him, for he was truly sorry for anything he had done.

"You didn't do anything," Nona whispered. "It was all my fault." She glanced out the window and up to the perfectly blue sky. "Can you forgive *me*, Daddy?"

And then he told her he hadn't—couldn't have—left her there all alone, and it was him who had contacted Cat to look after her.

> *Don't be upset with your mother about not telling you the truth of how she found you. I made her promise never to tell, and I've given her something to try and make it up to her. But I am breaking that awful vow and telling you the truth. And I hope it makes up, in even a small way, for me keeping her from you all those years ago. I can't take, even in death, telling Julia what I've done. I hope you will remember the good and the happy times and try and love me in spite of all the wrongs I've done. Know that you three—Cat, you, and Julia—are the loves of my life. And I'll carry that love for you even into eternity.*

Nona lowered the letter into her lap. And flashes from her childhood flooded her mind with emotion. Times she'd spent with her father.

The love he'd always shown her. The care he'd given her. How he'd always made everything alright.

And how it shouldn't have been a notion, a thought of possibility, that he would have betrayed her the way she'd accused him of. It made her realize, and probably not for the first time since she'd been back, how much she'd missed home. Family.

A tear rolled down Nona's cheek.

And how much more she understood her sister, Julia.

Julia's meltdown when she and Jayden had returned from Jackson hadn't made a ripple in Nona's feelings for her. Her desire to reconnect and be sisters again. It made her see how much Julia was hurting. Since she'd been home, Nona had also learned how long it had been going on.

Julia had even called Nona after she'd left and gone back to her hotel to say she was sorry. "Sorry for the outburst," she'd said. "I'd just been so worried about Jayden with Bisset on the prowl." And then she'd added, rather sheepishly, "Sorry for marrying Marcus. Sorry for lying to him. Hurting him."

Nona had started to say, "Okay. No worries," until that second *sorry* came out. She didn't know what to say to Julia about that.

"Was he hurt when you told him about Jayden?"

"He tried to be strong, but I knew I'd hurt him. Hurt him deep. He's never said it, though. And to make up, I've always tried not to interfere in his and Jayden's relationship."

"They have a good relationship." It wasn't a question. Nona had seen them together. She'd heard Marcus talk about him. She knew how much he loved that boy.

"They do. But I'm still saying sorry to you for it. I've said it to him enough times."

Today, admitting to all the pain she caused, and over and above the duty they had toward their father, Julia seemed okay. Approachable. Julia and Nona both had reached a point where they wouldn't let things go unsaid or drag on between them. People argued, disagreed, made mistakes, and anger didn't last as long as it had between them. Makeups came often within moments or without letting the sun go down on each other's discontent.

They wouldn't let that happen again.

"Who are you looking for?" Nona stepped inside the room Julia had occupied after the two had been separated. She had prepared herself in case Julia was ready to issue another verbal bashing, even after the apology. Nona had learned that Julia's emotions were on a seesaw.

Nona's sister stood at the window. Staring out. Expectant. Uncomfortable.

The room had the same design as the one Nona had been left in, but in green—heavy curtains, thick carpet. All the woodwork stained dark, a big, thick desk, the top void of any paperwork or files, sat in the middle of the room. The door open, Julia's stoic stance concerned Nona.

Things still felt tight between them from the day before. And because of how things went when she and Jayden returned from Jackson, Nona hadn't been able to find out how things had gone. Showing up at the repast and at Julia's home, both times unannounced, may have meant Bisset didn't plan on retreating. Perhaps Julia thought he had followed her to the reading of the will as well. Thinking he could get from her whatever their father had left.

"You don't think he'd follow you here, do you?" Nona asked. She took a few steps in to get a better view out the window.

Julia turned and looked at Nona. "Who?"

"Jayden's father."

"Hmph," Julia grunted and turned back, her gaze empty. "I don't know what he might do." She stared out the window. "He doesn't seem to be giving up on seeing Jayden."

"Are you going to let him see Jayden?"

Julia shook her head. "I don't want to." She held up her letter. She grasped it tightly. "But it isn't easy not knowing your father."

Nona sensed, from her twist in conversation, that Julia's letter had left her with doubts about something. "You knew Daddy."

Julia gave Nona a small smile. "Yep. Well. But not as well as I used to think." She drew in a breath. "I *do* know Bisset, though. Through and through. And what he wants from me or Jayden couldn't be good. I got nothing for him, but I probably shouldn't speak for my son."

"He just wants to make you stumble," Nona said.

"I know." Julia lowered her head. "But he won't do that." She looked back out the window. "I *won't* let him do that. Him being here can cause me to falter in the progress I've made." Julia lowered her eyes. "It's just a struggle in what's best for my son. You know. Should I let Jayden make the decision about knowing his father—his biological father? Or should I just continue to protect him and not let Bisset anywhere near him?"

"What do you think is best?"

"I sure wouldn't like someone doing that to me."

Nona looked down at the letter from her father. He had said he couldn't be the one to tell Julia how he'd forced his hand with Cat. Made her stay away.

"I just don't want to make the wrong decision."

"I know you won't." Nona, despite not having seen her sister or know the woman she'd grown to be, had confidence in her. That she'd make the right decision for herself. For Jayden. Marcus had told her how low she'd gone and how she'd dug herself out of that hole. Nona knew she'd been part of the reason Julia had lost faith in herself. Now there was so much time to make up, yet the distance between them seemed to be dissipating.

"I think it's all going to work out okay," Nona said. "You've got a lot of people looking out for you. Marcus. That guy from the funeral home." Nona smiled at her.

"Raymond Donaldson," Julia said.

"Yep. Raymond," Nona said. "I liked him. He seems like a pretty decent guy. One that likes you."

"I guess you're right about that." Julia turned back to the window, a blush coming across her face before her eyes searched again the street below.

"So, then, who *have* you been looking for?" Nona turned the conversation around. "The wake. The funeral. Here. You've kept your eye on the door the whole time." Nona cocked her head to the side. "I know it had to be disconcerting with Bisset showing up, but it seems now that that isn't it. Even with reassurances about Bisset, you seem distracted by something. The expectation of something . . . someone else."

"Tell me about Eli," Julia said. "Marcus tells me he proposed."

"Don't change the subject." Nona moved to stand by her sister at the window. "Tell me who you're looking for."

Julia looked down and studied her hands, still holding the letter she'd received from her father.

"Benjamin." Julia gave the letter a shake. "I thought he might come."

"And who is Benjamin?" Nona asked.

"Our brother."

"Whose brother?"

"Yours and mine." Julia flashed a glance at her. "Didn't Daddy tell you in your letter?"

Nona lifted her eyebrow. "No." She adjusted the strap of her purse, where she'd tucked the letter, on her shoulder. "He told me about the Melrose Estate. Told me to go and visit it."

"What is it?"

"I don't know. It's the second time I heard it mentioned." Nona shrugged. She reached in and pulled the letter from her purse. "I guess it is some kind of explanation why he'd leave me that godforsaken place. Although he did explain it in his letter."

"The Punchbowl."

Nona nodded. "The *Devil's* Punchbowl. A pit of lies, just like the devil himself. It made me want to spend my life trying to debunk them.

Now he wants me to have it to set the legacy of it straight. Put the truth of the history on record."

"He left it to Jayden, too," Julia said. "That's what was strange to me. That had always been your spot, so I understand him leaving it to you."

"My spot because I believed what Sanganette said about it. Her and her kind's stories of blacks not believing slavery was all that bad and the Civil War fought for states' rights. All those untruths."

"Yeah." Julia could see the passion in her sister's eyes, hear the conviction in her voice. "I read the article you wrote on it."

"And Jayden—Daddy had to know about Bisset, right?"

Julia nodded. "He met him. Saw him."

"So, Jayden is half black, half white. Daddy knew it and left him land that is smack in the thicket of racial controversy. Slavery and a lost cause . . . mythology. Why? Just seems so wrong to do to him."

"Maybe to form a bridge across a divide," Julia said.

"Maybe." The thought made Nona laugh. "Daddy had his reasons for doing everything." She waved her letter at Julia. "Man, the things that man did. Why?"

"Huh," Julia grunted. "Why did Daddy do anything he did?" Julia looked down at her letter.

"Oh. You got me off subject again," Nona said, following Julia's gaze. "We were talking about your letter." Nona pursed her lips. "Tell me about this brother of ours, or are you the one who is now keeping secrets about family?"

"Look," Julia said. "I'm sorry, okay? For yelling and jumping on you about Ca . . ." Julia closed her eyes and took in a breath. "About our mother."

"I had no idea she hadn't ever contacted you."

"I believe you."

"Are we good on that?"

"We're good on that," Julia said and nodded.

"Now tell me about Benjamin."

"Benjamin Eanes is his name. DDS follows it."

"A dentist?" Nona nodded in admiration. "Oh." It hit her. "Not Davenport?"

Julia shook her head. "Don't know the story behind that, but no, his last name isn't Davenport."

"Oh wow. You'd think Daddy would want to pass that on. His name dies with us girls."

Even with the hum of the air-conditioning circulating cool air though the room, Nona felt hot. She pulled off the cardigan of her sweater set. This was more of her history, all tangled up and undocumented. The very thing she wanted to eradicate. Misinformation. Misunderstandings.

Julia studied her sister's face. "What do you think about us having a brother?"

Nona shrugged. "I like the idea. More family to love." Julia nodded. "So," Nona said, turning Julia's question around, "is that why you said you feel like you don't know Daddy? Because he kept Benjamin from you?"

"Yeah. I guess." Julia shook her head. "But I knew about Benjamin. I met him once."

"But wait." Nona held on to Julia's arm. "Attorney Marchetti said that no one got anything but me, you, and Jayden. Daddy didn't leave him anything."

"Seems not."

Silence fell momentarily over the room, the two lost in thought. "So you've been looking out for Benjamin all this time. Expecting him to show up? Show his face. Demand his inheritance?"

"Or maybe show up for his father." Julia shrugged. "I don't know if he even knows about Daddy dying. I don't know if he cares."

"You didn't tell him?"

"I don't *know* him. I just knew *about* him."

Nona's confusion showed on her face. "I don't get it. You said you met him once. Didn't Daddy introduce the two of you?"

"No. He was Daddy's little secret." Julia flapped the letter. Glancing at it, she shook her head. "Until now."

"Oh," Nona said. "He came clean in the letter?" Nona looked at the paper Julia was holding. Like hers, it was one page. Back and front with Jasper's familiar scrawl etched into it.

Julia looked at it. After a moment of silence, she started to read it. "I've left everything I have to you and Nona, even though I do have another child. A boy child named Benjamin. I'm sure I owe him just as much as I owe the two of you, but the most important thing I could have given him I messed up years ago. That was family. He has all he needs, but I'd like for him to have that at least."

"So Daddy wants us to see Benjamin?"

"I guess. Give him his family." Julia blew out a breath. "I don't even know if Mamaw knows," Julia said.

"Mamaw knows," Nona said. "She knows everything."

Julia chuckled. "You're probably right about that. And she's good at keeping secrets." Julia flapped the letter again. "I only found out when Daddy had gotten sick and I had to clean out his apartment."

"You never told him you knew?"

Julia shook her head.

"Why?"

"Because he wanted to keep it a secret, and if he felt that way about it, so did I." She tilted her head as if weighing her words. "Plus, I didn't want him to know I'd been snooping through his things. Everyone has something they need to keep close in their life." Julia paused. Hadn't she tried to do that? Hide the truth from everyone. Keeping secret who Jayden's father was. But she hadn't been as successful as her father. Too bad, because Jayden's father was toxic. Bad news. Thank God he had Marcus. She smiled at that thought. Then felt a flash in her stomach over the secrets she'd kept. "We all have something we don't want to share with others until we're ready to do it."

"He picked his time to tell." Nona glanced down at the letter, although Nona sensed Julia was talking about something more.

"Yep. That he did." Julia folded the letter and put it in her purse.

"When did Daddy have another child?"

"During the whole Johnny Miller thing." Julia glanced at her sister and blew out a breath. "You know, when he went to Vidalia to escape getting caught for whatever mess that man had gotten our daddy into."

"Oh. Yeah. I remember that. Our lives changed forever after that, didn't they?"

And that pronouncement made something click in Nona's brain. Something about their mother, but she thought better of mentioning it to Julia.

"What?" Julia said. She'd noticed the recognition in Nona's face.

Nona shook her head. "I'd rather not say." She wasn't going to open up that can of worms again.

"Cat Montgomery?"

Nona didn't want to chuckle, but every time Julia called their mother that, it tickled her. Pressing her lips together, she just nodded.

"What about her?"

Nona hunched her shoulders. "I don't know for sure." She paused, reluctant.

"You may as well tell me."

"It's not a big deal now, after all this time, but I think that may have been why she left."

"It's a big deal to me," Julia said. And Nona could see it in her eyes. "Why she left is important to me."

"I'm thinking," Nona said, "now with the information about Benjamin, that it wasn't because of us."

"What was the reason she left?" Julia frowned. "You know?"

"She's never told me." Nona shrugged. "But maybe it had to do with Daddy getting someone else pregnant."

Julia squinted her eyes. "You think that was it?"

"I don't know that for sure," Nona said and shrugged again. "It would make me leave somebody. The timing is right. She left him while he was away in Vidalia. And it makes sense with what she said."

Julia turned and positioned her body to face Nona. "What did she say?"

"That Daddy had betrayed her."

"Hmph," Julia said. "Seemed like he betrayed all of us."

CHAPTER
THIRTY-TWO

Ten Years Ago

"The world's history shouldn't be taken away or added to at the whims of others who want to tell a different story. Tell the story like it happened. And how do we do that?" Standing at the lectern, Dr. Nona Davenport's eyes scanned the rows of students. No hands went up to offer an answer. *Perhaps,* she thought, *it sounded too rhetorical.* "We do that by recounting what happened through the words of those who were involved." She answered the question herself.

"Aren't they all dead?" someone asked.

Even though she was new at creating and presenting her own curriculum, Nona knew what to expect. She'd been a teacher's assistant since working on her master's. Earning an undergraduate degree in history with an emphasis on African American history, she'd been accepted into a dual program, getting her master's and doctorate in one fell swoop.

As a student, she'd been sitting on the other side, in those auditorium chairs, for nearly a decade. Now, she'd been hired as a full associate professor, and it was her turn to shape the minds of others. But she wanted to ensure, from her classes, they got the truth. "At some point they were alive. They wrote down the things that happened to them. The things they saw."

"I heard eyewitness testimony isn't always reliable," another, hand raised, said before he could be called on.

"That can be true." Nona came from behind her podium. She knew that firsthand. "So then we have to compare and take the totality of the information we have."

"So, history, the history we know, learned in school, or wherever, is wrong?" That question came from the back of the hall.

"It can be," Nona said. "That's why it is important to take the time, check your resources, study, get history right. For every person to know the truth of it. The past talks to us. We just have to listen as history speaks."

She had learned that the hard way.

This history class, Civil War and Reconstruction, was an elective for university requirements and had always been an easy A.

Who didn't know about slavery and the war between the states?

A one-semester general rehashing of a history that all Americans knew. But she had added "Perspectives of" to the course name and planned for her students to get just that. To learn and see the different attitudes and conclusions of the era. To help them not make the same mistakes she had.

It would be years before she made tenure, something she was required to do if she wanted to protect the academic freedom needed to teach her subject of choice without the worry of being fired. And it would be even more years before she came to know of her own misguided past, but at that moment in time, she was determined to set the record straight. The first of many.

This would be the first time she tested those waters.

Nona hoped she could pull it off. She didn't have the same gumption she had before she'd arrived in the Windy City. She'd been a loner after her arrival. Not mingling much with others, the only semblance of a friendship she'd forged had been with her mother.

Cat had been around from almost the beginning of her new life up north. An October health fair during Nona's first semester had reunited them, and they'd spent many a holiday and loads of weekends together. But as Nona's coursework became more intense, and the new job at the university making lesson plans and pondering over reading materials took up most of Nona's time, their visits weren't less meaningful but became less frequent.

Especially after Nona found out the truth.

Not about her mother but her history.

The devil is a liar.

A saying Nona had heard often hanging around church gatherings, bible studies, and old-time preachers who'd stop by to see her grandmother. And she found it an appropriate adage for the only devil she'd ever known up close and in person: the Devil's Punchbowl.

None of Sanganette's story about the kudzu-covered canyon had been true. A truth Nona had found out from another student in a class where Nona had been a star student. Nona had initially argued the point—some of her gumption from her life in Natchez coming unburied—but she was quickly shot down. She'd hurried to the library and researched. And researched. And researched. Nothing. No credible information. That false narrative recounted in YouTube videos and pseudo-historical websites. Comments left wanting to know why the true story of it all wasn't known. Wasn't spoken about. So there had been efforts, by her own people, to get that story out.

She was embarrassed. Bothered. And she felt foolish and stupid. She was from there. Been tangled up in its story all her life. How could she have not known the truth?

Nona's knowledge of it had come from Sanganette. A story told with lots of hand gestures and grim faces. A little ten-year-old wielding big knowledge one hundred and fifty years old. False knowledge. The truth came to her from a professor of agronomy with a concentration in fruit and vegetables at Mississippi State University and her own memory. Nona couldn't recall ever seeing a peach tree other than the ones her father had planted.

By Sanganette's account, which she swore to be true, "ex-slaves, more than a hundred thousand, came overnight," in essence foolishly escaping their benevolent masters and coming to Natchez in supplication. To those they thought their saviors—Union soldiers. They approached, as Sanganette's story went, under the mistaken impression that life would be better free. Under this false narrative they had determined that they wanted—no, needed—refuge.

But being overwhelmed by the sheer number of ex-slaves, "Union soldiers," she said, "knew they had only one choice. To get rid of them. So, they sealed them in that canyon and left them there to die."

Sanganette told of their shrieks like she was narrating a horror movie. How they begged to be let out. Vowing to go back to slavery but starvation and disease took them first.

"We're dying down here." Sanganette melted to the ground like the Wicked Witch of the West in *The Wizard of Oz*. So dramatic. Then, popping up, she ran a few feet across the grass to portray the equally-as-wicked soldiers in blue. "Just bury them where they drop!" Her Southern twang not giving an appropriate representation of those Yankee intruders, but the egregiousness of the words still shone through. Nona ate up every word.

"Those blacks soon found out that slavery wasn't that bad," Sanganette had said. She even added that that was what "was needed to be realized today." People talking about the cruelty of it all, she explained, didn't have it right. But most people knew the truth of it all. Even Nona had known that part wasn't true. But the rest she believed.

Sanganette came and sat down beside her rapt audience—Nona and Ruby—and pulled a peach out of a brown paper bag. The only prop she'd needed for her storytelling.

"And now," she said, holding up the velvety, rosy, fleshy fruit. "There's a grove of wild peach trees growing down there." She nodded toward the Punchbowl. "But nobody around here will eat them. You know why?" The two of them shook their heads. "Because it was the blood of slaves that made those trees grow."

And Nona believed it all. Every bit of that big lie.

And why wouldn't Nona believe it? Confederate monuments of the courageous and heroic members of the Confederate army, the real champions for the likes of Nona's forefathers, ornamented Natchez and all of Mississippi.

The term *ex-slaves* should have been Nona's first clue. Why would *former* slaves go to Union soldiers for help—they weren't even slaves anymore.

That made Nona turn into herself even more. Become more isolated. Less sociable. The shame of being so gullible made her less sure of herself.

Granted, Nona was six years old. And the history she learned in school hadn't mentioned slavery at all. Or that no one could have been *trapped* in that canyon. It was on the shore of a narrow bend of the Mississippi River, where the other side, Vidalia, Louisiana, was only a mile away. Anyone could have swum to safety. Although a six-year-old wouldn't have known that.

But it took a lot longer for Nona to learn the real truth of the matter. That at that time there weren't any peach trees in that canyon or anywhere else around. Not in the city of Natchez. And that it was Sanganette who had been spouting tall tales.

Nona remembered thinking, *How could I have been so gullible?*

That upset and embarrassed her. It had been the fuel that drove her and ignited her ambition to make a difference. To get the story straight. To get history right.

That was when she decided to get rid of her nickname. It, too, was built on misconceptions and untruths.

Dr. Davenport's class wasn't going to be an easy *A*, as many thought when they signed up. She knew how hard it was going to be to change the misinformation and prejudices her students had learned. She'd found that out when she defended her dissertation.

So different than the ideas she'd filled up notebooks with since she'd first decided on her major. One based on a subject that had defined her. A paper she later was able to get published in a mainstream journal.

It had been one that described the hotbed of revisionist theories and delved into the myth of the Lost Cause. And one that had nearly lost her the respect of her mentors. That hadn't mattered to Nona. For the chance of its mainstream disclosure, she had found some of the inner determination she'd had as a child but had, somewhere along the way, lost. Steadfast in her intentions, she wasn't going to let others be deceived, like she had been, in the undocumented, letting the true story go untold.

⌇

It had been the cherished purpose of those whose lineage was wrought with the noble and brave soldiers who had defended the South. And into the twenty-first century, their mission hadn't faltered—to preserve and defend their cause until the entire civilized world knew that their fight had been one that was just and right.

The primary focus of those wanting to preserve their contrived history had been to protect and venerate Confederate memory. After all, they, just as much as anyone else, had been part of the honorable heritage of this country's military traditions. And to that end, monuments were erected, textbooks filled only with history loyal to the Lost Cause assembled and distributed to schools to disseminate the "truthful" history of what led to the war between the states.

"How am I supposed to teach my students the truth about their Southern heritage and history when people like your sister print messes like this?"

"Huh?" Julia looked up from her desk. Sanganette Gautier-Preston was standing over her. She'd heard someone storm in through the glass front door and had hoped it wasn't a disgruntled client. She was just learning real estate and had made more than a few mistakes with the stack of paperwork required throughout the process, especially at closing. She'd kept her head down until the quaking footsteps of the tempest had hovered over her.

"Look what Peaches did!" She was waving a magazine overhead, creating a breeze and ruffling papers on Julia's desk.

"Hi, Sanganette." Julia hoped to quell her antics. Her eyes searched the room to see who had noticed.

"Don't 'hi, Sanganette' me! She is a little ingrate."

"Who?"

"Peaches!" Sanganette bellowed. "Are you listening to me?"

"I probably could hear you better if we went outside to talk. Like you tell your students, you're using your outside voice." Julia stood up and walked around the desk. She held on to Sanganette's arm to steer her seemingly furious friend out, but she wasn't budging.

"This is all lies, and she had the nerve to have it printed in a national publication."

Seeing she wasn't going to get her out the door, Julia decided to get through it. "What are you talking about, Sanganette?"

Sanganette flung the periodical at Julia. She caught it as it hit her in her chest. "I'm doing my part to preserve the South's legacy. She seems intent on clouding it up."

Julia stared at the front cover, then back at Sanganette. The journal appeared to be innocuous enough. "What? What's wrong?"

Sanganette snatched it back, flipped through it, and pushed it back to Julia. When Julia looked down at it, Sanganette jabbed a finger into the open journal. "That!"

It was an article by Dr. Nona Davenport entitled "The Devil Is in the Details: Natchez's Devil's Punchbowl Myth."

A proud moment—seeing her sister's name on printed material—quickly evaporated. Julia was recently divorced with a young son to take care of. She'd just started her job at Magnolia Landmark Realty and couldn't afford to lose it. Not for the likes of Sanganette's outburst.

It was a hot and muggy summer, not one that anyone, including Julia, would want to go slogging around in, having to accompany people looking at house after house. Submerged in complaints of clients who didn't like the furniture, none of which came with the houses, or the paint colors, which could easily be changed, Julia found it hard to hold her tongue. Not to yell. To smile and be professional. She had to hold back, being content to mentally scream at her picky potential home buyers and the source of her livelihood.

"Come with me." Julia clapped the magazine shut, snagged Sanganette by the arm, and led her into the breakroom in the back. "What the heck, Sanganette. You trying to get me fired?" Julia asked, after shutting the door to all the staring eyes that had followed them. She threw the magazine on one of the round tables.

Julia hadn't seen hide nor hair of her sister in ten years, and neither had Sanganette. She couldn't imagine how an article about that canyon overrun with kudzu could matter and cause so much commotion. Julia couldn't think what Nona could have done to Sanganette all the way from Chicago. And why would Sanganette think that whatever wrong she perceived Nona to have done would make it okay for her to take it out on Julia?

"I'm here to show you what your sister is doing up there."

"And what do you want me to do about it?"

Sanganette blew out a breath. She put a hand up to her forehead and closed her eyes, not saying a word.

Julia could see Sanganette's frustration. "Where did you get this from, anyway?"

"Ruby," she said, and sat in one of the orange plastic chairs.

"Was he upset about it?" Julia asked. She couldn't imagine how he'd be upset with Nona about anything. After Nona abandoned the family, Julia hadn't cared to keep up with her. She had enough problems of her own and no time to deal with Nona's selfishness. Or whatever it was that had Sanganette in such a tizzy.

"No. He tried to show it to me to make a point." Sanganette shook her head. "Can you believe that? Like I don't know *my* history." Sanganette was getting excited again. Julia sat across from her at the white Formica table, wanting to keep her calm. With her fingers, she slid the magazine over in front of her.

"What did he say?" Julia imagined him taking Nona's side probably set Sanganette off.

"He said that if Peaches said Union soldiers didn't trap slaves in the Devil's Punchbowl, then it probably wasn't true. Finding out the truth is her profession." She sucked her teeth. "Can you believe him? Her *profession*. Hmph." She pointed her finger at Julia. "He has always taken her side."

"You think she's lying?" Julia started flipping through the pages, glancing at it to find the article.

"I think she doesn't know," Sanganette said matter-of-factly. "How could she?" She looked Julia in the eyes. "No offense, but she didn't have anyone who knew the story tell her about it."

Julia raised her eyebrows. "Who do you know that knows what happened?"

"My daddy. I learned that story at my daddy's knee." Sanganette shook her head. "Your sister has it all wrong. She doesn't know anything about her history." Sanganette snatched the magazine from Julia's hands and waved it at her.

"What are you talking about?"

"No offense, Julia. Don't take it the wrong way, but she doesn't know who her people are." Sanganette slammed the magazine down on the table. "I got it firsthand. Ruby heard it, too. He knows it's a fact. But he's gotten brainwashed because of a childhood friendship."

"With Nona."

"Yes. I had to tell him, 'So what if the story isn't true?,' which I know it is. 'So what? Because slaves' blood is everywhere in Natchez. Just because it's not bleeding from those peach groves in the canyon doesn't mean their blood hasn't fertilized peaches everywhere else around the city.' And you know what he said?"

"What?" Julia asked.

"That there aren't even any peach trees in Natchez." She snorted. "Or in Mississippi."

"I don't know about anywhere else in Mississippi, but he's right. There aren't any peach trees in Natchez, other than the ones my daddy planted." Then Julia asked Sanganette, "Why don't you know that?"

"I do know that," Sanganette said. "And he said the same thing. But there were peach trees in 1865."

"What happened to them?"

"I don't know," Sanganette said, sputtering. "But why would my daddy lie?" She cocked her head and stared at Julia.

"Maybe because he's got it all wrong," Julia said. She stood up, walked over to the door, swung it open, and went back to work.

CHAPTER
THIRTY-THREE

*I was born in slavery and when I was eight years old was
bonded out to Sam Briggs of New London. Mr. Briggs was a
good master . . .*

*—William Black, Hannibal, Missouri. Born in Slavery:
Slave Narratives from the Federal Writers' Project,
1936–1938*

The guided tour took two and a half hours. The self-guided tour that
Nona took, took four. A historic landmark, Melrose Estate was built in
the mid-1800s. The antebellum Greek revival-style mansion was well
preserved, a step back in time. Tall columns having circular capitals
on top. Nona walked up the stone steps, her hand running along the
delicate railing.

The inside of the estate was nearly intact in its structure and fur-
nishing—painted cypress doors, smooth Italian marble fireplaces,
French scenic wallpaper. Nona strolled through, lightly letting her eyes

roam over the French gold-rimmed mirrors and the bronze chandeliers. She fingered the heavy draperies hung up to the high windows.

Out back, the estate spread out over eighty acres of well-manicured lawn and open space. Nona breathed in the history as she followed gravel roads and paved paths. She walked past the two-storied kitchen, a dairy and a barn, the smokehouse, a carriage house, and of course, the slave quarters.

And then, to Nona's surprise, there was an orchard. In it were planted two peach trees. Nona stood staring at them, lost in thought. Soaked in memories. Adrift in the meaning of all the history.

There are records there . . .

Nona held open the letter her father had written her. Her eyes brimmed with tears.

That will help you tell the story you want to tell . . .

Walking the grounds gave Nona a sense of place. A connection with the things she'd seen and heard in Jackson. The stories. The people. The history.

Just as coming back to Natchez had shown her hers. How easily and mistakenly things had gone awry. How much she'd had a hand in it, whether she knew it or not.

And how much she'd gotten wrong.

It had caused her to be estranged from the people who meant the most.

Her father, it seemed, still knew her. He remembered what pushed her buttons. What got her going. He'd been right, in his last letter to her, to tell her about Melrose. It was just as good, if not better, than Jackson because for her, there was a connection to her own roots. Jasper understood that about her, even in his last wishes for her.

The purpose of the place was to acknowledge the diversity of the people who lived and worked there. But it also was an accounting of the overlooked and uncounted. Its grounds were built on the truth of the matter. Not bent toward telling a better story.

And it was a story that came with names.

This was the place, too, that that young man who'd introduced himself when she'd gone to Lander's Bar-B-Q for lunch had mentioned. The first time she saw Julia.

Jeremy.

She remembered his first name easily. It took her a moment to recall his last—Houston.

And that was what she'd found at Melrose Estate. First and last names. Slave names. The names of their children. The names of their parents.

Their identities.

Who they were.

Records that had been preserved and that were available.

Like she'd been in Jackson, Nona was in awe. She had told the stories of the Old South and its peoples time and time again. This was the first time she was actually meeting them. For Nona, it was a rare, sweet moment.

In Jackson, she'd read the slave narratives and listened to oral histories. One had caught her attention: Evalina Wilson. Born in Natchez, the granddaughter of slaves, her family had moved to Tulsa when she was young, only to have lost most of her family, including her mother, in the massacre of 1921 in the Greenwood District of Tulsa.

The loss of a mother early in life affects people differently than it does when a child grows up with one. She'd learned that from Julia. From the stories she'd heard from both—in Julia's actions and emotions and in Eva's words—it seemed to have troubled them throughout their lives.

Nona hoped to help Julia rectify and turn around her loss by giving her their mother back.

After Julia had apologized in her call, Nona had added Cat to the line. There were so many tears that Nona didn't know how they'd made it through the conversation. But one thing had been clear: they wanted to see each other. So that had been arranged. Cat was coming to Natchez.

And that was when Nona knew she couldn't leave. Not yet. Not for a while. She wanted to stay with her sister a little longer.

And then after Cat hung up and Julia's crying had abated, the sisters decided they would find Benjamin, their brother.

"Not until after Cat Montgomery leaves, though," Julia had instructed, still sniffing back tears. "I don't want her to know we're going to see him."

"Are you going to call her Cat Montgomery when you see her?" Nona had asked.

Julia had stumbled over her answer. "Yeah . . . I guess . . . I don't know." She paused, thinking. "That is her name."

"Actually, it's not," Nona had said. "Her last name is Hawthorne."

"Is she married?"

"To Daddy. They never divorced. But she used a different name once she got to Chicago." Nona had let out half a chuckle. "But I'm sure she'll tell you about that once she's here."

"Yeah," Julia had said, the smile on her face evident in her voice. "Let her tell me."

And that had taken care of family. The start of the mending of it. The healing of all the hurt in it.

And then there were her friends.

She wasn't quite sure what to do about Marcus. She'd take her time and find out, though. Whenever she thought about him, feelings raged inside her about that man. Feelings that made her heart race and her head sense it was on the verge of exploding. But being in his presence, hearing his voice, brought her a sense of calm. And warmth. And contentment. She wasn't sure she could ever forgive him for not following her when she left Natchez. Or for marrying Julia. Or for confessing to her his still-unwavering love for her, even after all those years had passed.

And, she wondered. Did she feel the same? There was only one way to find out.

She'd need to untangle all of it to decide, but one decision seemed undeniable. She didn't want to not see him. She didn't want any more time to pass where he was left out of her life.

Eli was a different story. That decision for Nona was easy. From the day he'd come into her life, he hadn't made a difference. He wasn't good for her. He hadn't helped her grow. She hadn't become stronger. More independent. She hadn't gone back to being the strong, self-sufficient, self-reliant person she'd been growing up. The unorthodox thinker. The untrammeled girl who hadn't given a second thought to moving to a big city, all alone, if circumstances had warranted. It took her coming back to Natchez for her to discover how to blossom again. Like the blooms on the peach trees her father had always gifted her.

Eli was getting that ring back. She hoped he'd kept the receipt.

And Ruby. He had apologized, too, after the blow-up at Opal's house. Only he'd come to the hotel. Sorry for not ever telling her how he felt about her. Sorry for being a part of stopping Marcus from coming to the bus station to meet her that night. Sorry for his sister, Sanganette.

"But," he had said, his voice emboldened, "whether they are down there or not, you were once like those peach trees." He paused. "Not needing anyone to care for you and still flourishing. Strong."

"I'm not," Nona had said.

"You are when you're here, Peaches," he had said. "When you're here at home."

Nona didn't comment on that. It was true, she felt she had grown since she'd been back. Come to certain realizations about the things she wanted and the things she didn't.

Like Eli. She knew she didn't want him.

And Jayden. She knew she wanted to be a big part of his life.

And of course, Julia. She didn't ever want to be out of Julia's life again.

But Nona did say, "It's okay. No worries. You don't have to apologize for anything."

Nona had found she didn't want to reach back into her past and find whatever she'd need to work through all his sorries. She had been holding on to the past and all of its hurt for much too long. She wanted to move forward.

And because her friend Ruby had come to her with so much remorse, Nona didn't tell him how she hadn't thought about him over the years. And for that, she was sorry. He had always been there for her, and she hadn't seen what it meant. Not to him or to her. Or how she learned, over the years, not to blame Sanganette for that peach tree story, yet somehow she still seemed to be holding something against her. And now she was sorry for that, too.

In her time away, Nona had accomplished so much and done nothing. Coming home, she found that things rarely work out like they were supposed to, but it didn't mean things didn't turn out right. And coming home, it was easy to see the things she wanted to have and the things she'd wanted to do.

Over the years, she had attached moral and intellectual accomplishments in an effort not so much to burrow away from the cruelty of happenstance but to shield herself from the essence of herself.

But that was going to change.

Eva, as the woman who'd done the oral history had called herself, was the first person Nona asked about when she sat down to look at the records. For some reason, the woman reminded her of Julia. And she wanted to find out more.

"Oh yes, I know Eva well," the recordkeeper had said. "Her story starts here, but there is so much more to it. And it hasn't ended yet."

"She's still alive?" Nona had inquired.

"She is," he said. "A living, breathing witness to a significant event in our history."

"And a legacy to much more."

He nodded in agreement. A smile emerging on his face.

That, Nona knew, was how history was supposed to be told.

They had spoken for a long time. Exchanging views. Him showing her proof of their local history. He had been very knowledgeable, and Nona had enjoyed talking to him.

He'd introduced himself as Barney Schoby. Saying it had been "a pleasure" to meet her.

"I'm Nona Davenport," Nona had responded after returning the sentiment and promising to come back soon, maybe even bringing her nephew. "But you can call me Peaches."

ACKNOWLEDGMENTS

Writing is not a solitary endeavor, and there were so many people who helped me put this story to paper.

During the time the world was in quarantine, I had the company of my writing support group, #amwriting. It is a wonderful group of writers who support each other and help make what we do so much better. Thank you to Rose, Natassha, Cheryl, Molly, and Nicole. And a special shout-out and much thanks to LaBena Fleming and Brandi Larsen for being extra. *Peaches* wouldn't be in the world as it is without you. As always, I have to thank my writing partner, Kathryn Dionne, my consummate proofreader, Bernard, and the person who showed me the way when she knew I was a writer, Laurie Kincer.

And to my editors: Whew! I made it through. I was so nervous going into edits, but you made it easy and made my book shine. Thank you, Chris Werner and Tiffany Yates Martin, for all that you do.

And to my family—those with me now and those who watch over me from somewhere else—thank you.

ABOUT THE AUTHOR

Photo © 2019 Morse

Cade Bentley is a novelist and editor who is also published as *Wall Street Journal* and *USA Today* bestselling author Abby L. Vandiver, as well as Abby Colette. When she isn't writing, Cade enjoys spending time with her grandchildren. She resides in South Euclid, Ohio. For more information visit www.authorabby.com.